Praise for Billy Tapper – Zillionaire

"Billy's wild journey is both epic and intimate. Spurred by a desire to prove his worth to those he loves and protects, his coming of age takes him serendipitously through times and places he never expected to visit. This is a story that will inspire and delight readers."
    –*Lisa Fugard*, award winning author of *Skinners Drift*

"A colorful, funny and poignant story. Finnan conveys romance, angst, pain, and joy. He captures the humanity of simple relationships and the coming of age we all endure. A little gem of a book, tender and funny, that breaks your heart, yet inspires you."
    –*Debra Bassett*, Writer & Executive Television Producer

"The story is full, with many unexpected twists and turns to entertain and engage the reader. This is my book club pick. I envision an evening of lively conversation as we re-live the adventures of Billy Tapper"
    –*Julie Walker*, Writer, Sinclair Communications

"I was immediately taken by this book and impressed by the authentic representation of life in post-World War II working class North of England. I quickly became engrossed in the story. As I delved further into the book the plot got better, with the twists and turns of Billy's life and experiences. The attention to detail was exceptional and the unusual direction of Billy's life kept me turning the pages until the book was finished.
    –*Elizabeth Slater*, Writer and Marketing Savant

"The magic of this well written novel draws on secrets hidden inside a rail car that Billy Tapper uses to navigate his way through poverty and rigid class systems to an unusual perspective on power and wealth. Yet without losing his integrity and generosity. The story is placed in England after World War 11. It is wrenching in parts, yet Billy retains a Zen like compass to triumph. Well worth a read!"

—Dr. Ian Prattis, Professor Emeritus at Carleton University in Ottawa, award winning author

"It's not only Billy Tapper's size that sets him apart from his mates. Billy has a profound need for a life beyond Diggle's tiny pubs, grey muddy train yards, and low English expectations. Add a wee bit of luck, a fertile imagination and a quiet determination to defy generations of convention—and suddenly Billy found a way out. But his escape is problematic; his appetite for life is as deep as his Diggle roots. Balancing a great love of adventure with his passion for family and the women in his life leads to wonderful madness and mayhem—a tightrope act that's pure joy to behold. Billy is a raconteur after me own heart, and I'd gladly share a pint and a few tall tales with that lad!"

—John Springer, Raconteur – Fourwinds California

"Thank you for this glimpse into by-gone eras. I was immediately drawn into the eyes and mind of young Billy. Choices made in that thirteenth train car bought my ticket for a seat on this winding journey down the tracks of time, lives, loves, money and mystery that connected the characters of this poignant tale. You are a master storyteller!"

—Leslie Thompson – Writer USA

"This novel is adventurous and courageous in describing with keen details a world enhanced by strong personages. Here, I found a rich world filled with inspiration, humor, joy and celebration. Thank you, Gary for painting the story in this novel with such grace and acuity."

—Danielle Nistor, Speaker and International best-selling Author, Portugal

"Billy draws you in from the first page. Wonderful storytelling allows you to travel back in time and feel like you're part of the story as you easily and quickly move through each chapter. I thoroughly enjoyed this novel."

–Jennifer Henshaw – California USA

"Billy is like a British Forrest Gump of sorts, quirky and historic, touching, far-fetched and fun. I've fallen in love with Billy, Meg and Mam and this wonderful coming of age journey set in some of the most interesting decades of our time. All the wonderful characters in this story come from a rich and broken past, like most of us, which beautifully highlights love and family... the foundations of life. True to who Gary is as a person, he takes his readers on a unique and emotional journey. I can see the pages of Billy Tapper beneath the thumbs of many, with dog eared corners, oozing the signs of a good read. Well done! I'm so looking forward to the sequels!

–Julie Colvin, Best-selling author of *A Cure for Emma* – Wellness and Writing Retreats

"The journey through the life of Billy Tapper is one I enjoyed very much. I found myself wanting for Billy what he wanted, emotionally supporting him through his life experiences, and mentally defending him as he justified his questionable actions and bold choices. Like the director of a great movie, the author sets each scene by including colloquialisms of the time and descriptions that bring vivid images of the rural English countryside to life. A wonderful book I unequivocally recommend."

–Karen Andresen – Florida USA

"Following Billy as his life unfolds was a 'can't put this book down' experience. The fascinating peek into the ribald life of a tapper in 20th century England easily flowed into Billy's personal experiences outside the railroad yard. *Billy Tapper Zillionaire* is one of the best books I've read this year. It's full of excitement, poignancy, and fun. So, when's the next one coming out?"

—*Dawn Lauren Anderson*, Motivational speaker and writer

"Billy Tapper is a mesmerizingly well-told family saga. It shares the rapidly shifting times in post World War II Britain, then takes us on a journey as the McTaggarts leap across the pond to America where they connect with the turbulent political, social, and musical dynamic that made the 50s and 60s such an exciting time in which to live. I was captivated by how the family navigated life and a sea of change as the world sped up."

—*Priya Rana Kapoor* Executive Life Coach, Speaker & Author of *Give Yourself Permission*

"A delectable bouquet of Joycean melodic tone and phrasing. A Hemmingwayesque palate of deliciously detailed description. I so enjoyed Billy Tapper Zillionaire and the craftily created characters of Billy, Meg, Mam, and Lola. Their lives span ages and continents in a journey of serendipitous self-discovery with historical undertones. It is a page-turner of sweetness, romance, with a dab of debauchery, and the thread of humanity permeating each page! Thank you, Gary Finnan, for a super read!"

—*Karen O'Toole Dempsey*

Billy Tapper
ZILLIONAIRE

GARY FINNAN

Published by NorLite Books
762 State Road 458
Bedford IN 47421
www.norlitepress.com
Email: publisher@norlightspress.com

Printed in the United States of America
ISBN: 978-0-9906862-1-7

Book Design and Editing: Sammie and Vorris Dee Justesen

First printing: November, 2019

Dedication

For Maggie and Drew / Des and Renee – Thank you
for sharing your true love and true stories

The Tappers Art

Wheeltappers and shunters were railway workers commonly employed on British railways before the 1970s. Both worked in goods yards with the hundreds of thousands of goods wagons upon which railways depended for the majority of their income. A shunter was responsible for sorting wagons into trains bound for a variety of destinations and ensuring the empties were returned to their owners or points of loading.

Wheeltapper was a more skilled occupation; The West Somerset Railway remarks that: "a wheeltapper was employed at large railway stations to check that the wheels on the bogies were sound and the axle boxes were not hot. Using a long-handled wheel tapping hammer he would strike the wheels of the bogie and hear if it 'rang true' (a wheel with a crack in it would give off a dull sound), and with the back of his hand he would determine whether the axle box bearing was running hot."

Wheeltappers were vital to the smooth running of the railways, because a cracked wheel or overheated axle bearing would lead to delays and the loss of revenue. These were particularly common in the 19th century, where grease lubricated the axle bearings. During this period, metallurgy was a rather haphazard science and it was impossible to test steel wheels for cracks, making the wheeltapper's job one of crucial importance.

Table of Contents

Chapter 1

Tapper

God save the Queen thought Billy as he pulled an eight-inch crowbar from the poacher's pocket of his donkey jacket. He wedged the crowbar between the padlock and the door of the freight wagon. Pop!

The tunnel in which he stood cut as deeply into the Saddleworth Moor in the West Riding of Yorkshire as the gash from the dull edge of the padlock that now ran to the knucklebone of his right hand. The pain shot up his arm and out of his mouth in a hiss that threatened to become a scream of spit and profanity. Blood dripped down the cold steel of the crowbar into an oily puddle around his work boot on the dirty gravel that banked against the wooden sleeper of the rail track. He cast the yellow beam of his paraffin lamp across the ragged wound and thought again to curse out loud. He imagined the echo of his voice bouncing in the darkness on stone walls out toward the arched speck of light which framed the first of the freight wagons he'd counted on his way into the tunnel.

"Blimey! That's a bad un, I'll wager," he said with restraint, stoically pushing aside the throbbing pain.

"Another one for the yard." he mumbled, wiping a smear of blood up the side of his thin face and sharp nose as he pushed back a flop of dark, greasy hair. "Best get a move on, Billy boy, before you either freeze or bleed to death. They'll all be playing Tiddlywinks by the time you get back to the tea shed."

He slid his crowbar back into his work jacket and kicked the broken padlock against the tunnel wall, then turned his attention to ripping a strip of cloth from the bottom of his undershirt using his teeth and uninjured hand. His exposed skinny belly dimpled in goose flesh against the cold as he pulled the cloth loose and wrapped the wound. He looked at his hands and realized they had taken a fair beating in the past few years since becoming an apprentice tapper.

Other than playing football, going into the train yard where his Dad worked had been his favorite thing to do as a young boy. Billy loved the long early morning walks to the yard and the customary stop in at the warm, sweet-smelling bakery near the yard entrance. He fondly remembered Dad asking for a half a fresh loaf and two pasties as he flipped a shilling to the baker's wife with a wink.

Billy overheard the lads in the yard whisper of Big Jim Tapper's prowess. He was dapper with his smooth black Brilliantined hair and had a way with the women, they would say.

He owned the nickname of his craft, Big Jim Tapper, a rite of passage, an identity just like Jack the Horse who ran the draft horses or Harry Two Bellies famed for his obvious protrusion.

Dad had smelled of a combination of Woodbine cigarettes, hair cream, and Old Spice. Back then Billy was proud that he saved all year to afford a Christmas gift for Dad. Every payday at the paper shop was a step closer, another sixpence in the tin under his bed and, with the help of Mam for any shortfall, he could afford the gift of Old Spice. The aftershave was distinct in its white ceramic bottle with the red windjammer "Grand Turk" schooner emblazoned across the front of it. He knew Mam liked the smell of it on Dad too.

What he liked best was when they'd go into the large Victorian workshop with its high glass skylights, whirling vents, and metallic taste in the frigid air that sat heavy in the back of your throat. Upon entering the shed, Dad would lift him up to punch his time card for him, and the clock would give off a great "Thunk!" as Billy was swung down again in a single sweep.

Together they would navigate the shop with its rows of workbenches and well-placed tools and machines. There was always some large piece of machinery being repaired, parts of the great beasts that roamed the yard in darkness when the workers went home each night. Locomotives, cranes engines, boilers and giant rag tooth cogs, each looked like a fossil from a prehistoric animal waiting to be put back together just as he had seen in the basement of the glorious Manchester Museum, which they visited the year before he finished school.

Dad would direct him to the worker's tea shed where they made huge mugs of steaming, milky, sickly sweet tea with four spoons of sugar in each mug. Even at his young age, Billy knew this was a luxury Mam's food coupons could never afford outside of the government-run yard. He would eye the rim of the chipped porcelain mug with its dark brown veins running through the glaze like rings from an ancient tree, each ring telling a story, fixed in time amid the banter and humor of Dad's fellow workers. He would imagine the millions of cups of tea past and present like some stacked ancient forest where the great iron beasts lived and roamed.

Wheel tappers and shunters were types of railway workers commonly employed on British railways, Dad explained. Both worked in the rail yard with the hundreds of rusty steel and wood freight wagons upon which the railways depended for moving goods around the country. Dad said shunters were responsible for the sorting of wagons bound for a variety of destinations and ensuring empties were returned to their owners or points of loading, but he and Billy were of the noble clan of tappers, as he inferred his Scottish heritage as a right to the trade. Billy knew it was Mam's father who got his dad the job in the yard after the war.

Dad proudly said that tapper was a skilled job that required inspecting wheels on the train bogies, making sure they were sound, and the axle boxes weren't too hot when they arrived in the station. Using a long-handled wheel-tapping hammer, he would strike the wheels of the bogie and hear if it rang true. A wheel with a crack in it would give off a dull sound. Dad showed him with the back of his hand how they could determine whether the axle box bearing was running hot and had enough grease to lubricate the axle. Wheel tappers were vital to the smooth running of the railways as a cracked wheel or overheated axle bearing could lead to delays and loss of revenue, or even life, if there was the disaster of a crash when a wheel failed at high speed.

"We don't need anything like the great crash of 1923 when we lost four souls at Diggle Junction," Dad said solemnly.

Billy understood he was expected to follow in his dad's footsteps as a tapper. He had a fantasy of playing football for Manchester United, though he knew he was too small and probably not good enough. He'd thought of attending university as an engineer, but his headmaster told Mam he wasn't that clever.

With the bleeding staunched, Billy set about revealing the contents of the wagon he'd relieved of its lock. He had ignored the Do Not Break that was stamped in raised red letters next to the Royal Seal for the Bank of England on the aluminum tag running through the lock and the door handle.

"It's not like it's the first time I've broken a lock for the gaffer on a bloody door," Billy said aloud, anxiously in conversation with himself. "The gaffer did say to find out what's in it. No whiskey or nylons in this one I'll hazard a guess, judging by that tag." He leaned his slight frame against the heavy wooden door as it gave way and slid open enough for him to shine his lamp inside.

Earlier that day Billy had walked into the small tea shed that adjoined the workshop, where the air hung heavy with the stink of work and labor; a pleasant odor in the sense that it let him know where he belonged, among the sawdust, iron filings and good old sweat that lived in dirty overalls. Almost three years into his time and this was his final year as an apprentice tapper. For now, six-months away from becoming a Journeyman, he was still on the lowest rungs of the ladder every man in the room had climbed. The kettle was coming to boil on the potbellied stove that served to heat the room.

Billy had mastered the temperament of the hungry cast iron mouth in the last few years, and God help him if he let the fire go out in a train yard full of coal.

He grunted the usual, "'Alo," to his gaffer, Harry Two Bellies and the three workmen huddled in the room, each with a sandwich of coarse bread and thick cheese wedges shoved up against their faces. His mouth-watered for the ham and cheese buttie he knew Mam had packed in his lunch pail.

"I could murder a big cup of tea," Billy said to no one in particular as he slid out of his damp jacket.

"Billy boy," grunted Harry, "check the tunnel at the back of line six before you stop." Harry waved his hands in the general direction outside. "You know the one they bricked up in the back during the war when the Nazi bastards bombed the fuck out of us?"

"Now?" exclaimed Billy.

"Ay, now, and do a count on the cabs, there's a missing wagon the boss is looking for. Snarky Gibson thought he saw something up there last week when he moved the lines around. Count and mark them up for me, there's a good lad."

Billy pulled his workman's donkey jacket back over his shoulders and lurched toward the door. Outside the usual grey of the yard and sky engulfed him, broken only by the looming hulks of used freight cars all around. Line six was half a mile away in a sea of steel and mud. He pushed his collar up, head down, and fumbled with the chalk in his pocket as he stepped from muddy footprint to muddy footprint. The stride of the man who'd preceded him through the muck was longer, and the shoe print a good two inches bigger. He soon gave up the extended lope and reverted to his usual scuff and drag. A trickle of rain ran down the back of his collar, and he straightened with a shudder and pulled his woolen cap down against the wind.

He knew track six backed all the way into tunnel two, a remnant of the war Harry had mentioned, used to protect the engines as the bombers passed overhead. He pulled the chalk from his pocket, a big triangular wedge that resembled a block of cheese. He thought of his sandwich and hot tea as he began to mark the cars in the tunnel, 1-2-3 . . .13. He knew something was wrong—superstitious shunters would never put thirteen cars on a haul.

At the far end of the tunnel he worked virtually by touch as the light struggled to seep that far down into the damp darkness, but once again he counted thirteen cars, marking each one. He trudged back toward the tea shed, this time playing with his own distinct tracks in the mud that were easier to follow. Sliding back into the office, he tried to keep the crack in the door as narrow as possible, holding the wind at bay.

"Thirteen, Guv," Billy reported curtly to Harry,

"Thirteen? Are you sure? There is never thirteen to a haul, you know that, lad. You'd better double check again!"

Without thinking of his position in the hierarchy of the little tea shed Billy blurted out, "Now?"

Harry looked at him with such hard eyes that he flushed red in the face. He turned and fled, hearing the snickers of the other lads tumbling out the door behind him. Back out in the yard he made his way reluctantly through the mud to the tunnel and the train car a little faster this time and began counting, 1-2-3 . . . 13.

"Fuck!" Billy cursed aloud as he walked back into the work shed half an hour later. His rough woolen work trousers chaffed at his inner thigh.

"Thirteen, sir, yes I am sure, believe me." He began to take off his jacket, and pushed the cap back off his head, as he reached for the teapot.

"There can't be thirteen cars," Harry insisted. "What's in it, what's the registration number? Get back out there, Billy boy, and don't come back until you know every inch of that bloody car and where it came from... and, yes, now before you even think of asking."

"Bastard," Billy muttered under his breath as he pulled his cap forward and slid his jacket back on, again.

His mind wandered as he trudged back to line six, lugging a heavy paraffin lamp over his shoulder this time. The liquid inside slopped to the gait of his stride, taunting him to pee at the sound of it.

"Half a fucking mile," he said aloud as he passed the long line of trains before him. His rough woolen trousers rode up against his inner thigh and balls. He slid his hand into the deep pockets of his trousers and pulled the fabric of his underpants away from the sore patch which had become sweaty and raw in his exertions.

Last night, that's the reason for it, he thought with a grin on his face. Last night he'd taken Meg down to a local pub not far from her parent's tobacconist shop on the old Diggle Road. The Gate Inn had a snug that offered some privacy. The landlord was loose on the age requirements for the rail lads and their lasses—he turned a blind eye if they were near enough to seventeen and ordered something to eat, particularly on a Monday night when business was slow. Billy met Meg outside her parent's shop, and they walked hand-in-hand down to the pub.

"Did you tell your mother we were going to the pub?" Billy asked Meg.

"No, don't be silly, it's a school night. She thinks we're going into Oldham to the pictures, that way she'll expect me back a little later and I get to spend more time with you."

"Sneaky girl. I like it, by the way. Might I say you look lovely—I like your dress."

Meg smiled, and they stopped on the road outside the pub where she kissed him before putting on her lipstick. Billy led Meg through the dark, smoke-stained, wood-clad room with its drab carpet that had endured too many spilled pints, cigarette butts twisted underfoot, and blood stains from working-class brawls between overworked fathers venting years of frustration at having bent their backs to a pile of coal or a hungry engine furnace.

"A pint of black and tan and a Babysham, mate," Billy said to the barman. Oh, and two of your pickled eggs—not the ones up there on the shelf, the fresh ones in the kitchen—and a plate of chips, please." He stuck his lips to the creamy head on the pint placed before him, slurping back the first inch, enough to make it easy to carry without spilling. He made his way back to the snug in the ladies lounge by the fireplace which was separated from the men's saloon by a partition of decorative lead glass showing a hunting scene of men in red jackets on horses surrounded by a pack of dogs.

"Babysham for my baby," Billy said in his best James Cagney voice. "A pickled egg and a plate of chips as you like it. We must keep the law happy—spare no expense for my girl." He grinned as he winked.

He smiled at Meg as she sat on the hardwood bench of the snug—the straight high back of the seat was too far back for her to lean against, being only four-feet-six inches tall in her high heels. She sat perched like a small, lipsticked bird in a floral dress from Marks and Spencer's on the high street in Leeds. He slid in next to her feeling proud that he was a working man, almost a journeyman, out for an evening with his woman—just as it needs to be, Billy thought.

"You look seventeen to me," Billy whispered into Meg's ear as she slapped him on the shoulder and gave a darting glance toward the barman who just winked and turned away to clean some glasses.

"When do you think it will happen, pet, you becoming a journeyman?" Meg asked as she sipped at the edge of her glass, trying to avoid messing up her thick red lipstick.

"I don't know, love, another six months to a year at most is the plan if I make it as shift captain this summer. You know the gaffer, Harry? He's a bastard when it comes to doing your time and knowing the details. Wants me to learn just like him and my Dad did, and it was five years to qualify back then."

"I want you so badly, Billy. I want to be your wife, but not until you're out of your time and on a full wage," she whispered under her breath.

"You're almost sixteen and you'll finish grammar school soon, what about university? You could do that. Imagine, dead posh and refined," he said to her, fearful of losing her to the world beyond Diggle, but knowing she had a spirit and capabilities he could not deny.

"You said I looked seventeen," she said as she pouted. "Are you sure you love me?" Meg fluttered dark, mascara-caked lashes and squeezed Billy's leg under the table, digging her red nails into the thigh beneath his woolen trousers.

"Another drink," Billy coughed and stood abruptly, spilling the last of their drinks on the small table. He made his way to the bar using their empty glasses to hide his arousal. Two pints and as many Babyshams later, the two of them sat rosy-cheeked in front of the fire, like lovebirds wrapped in their courting dance. Emboldened by the drink, Billy spoke softly to Meg.

"My darling, I want to ask you to marry me, to be my wife, you know that. But there are so many bits to fit together to make it perfect, just like you want. I promise as soon as I get promoted, and we're approved for a flat on the new council estate, then we'll get married."

He would have to ask his Mam what she thought about that in the morning before going to work. He was sure she would want to move in with them but thought better not to bring it up with Meg at the moment. Meg had an urgency about her he hadn't seen before this evening; she was always demanding, but tonight she wanted resolution. They finished up their drinks at last call, and he invited Meg to step out into the chilly night rain. He liked it when she slid her arm under his as they walked home, stopping to buy a bag of scrapings from the fish fryer who sprinkled plenty of salt and vinegar on the greasy remnants. They took a slow, unsteady walk back to Meg's house.

Just inside the entry at the back of the shop, between the streetlight and the storeroom door, they kissed, bumping teeth in their rush to come together. She was flushed after one too many Babyshams, less cautious than usual after all the talk of marriage. He shoved his knee between her thighs, and she let them part as she pushed back against him, Billy, feeling emboldened himself by the beer, found it thrilling and the blood danced behind his closed eyes as he felt his hardness pushing against the buttons of his woolen trousers and the softness of Meg's thigh.

He felt her gather the folds of her dress and hitched up her skirt at the same time. She took his wrist as she slid his hand down over her skirt and guided it up over the lace-edged garter strap toward her lace panties.

"I bought these for you, with my babysitting money," she whispered. He opened his eyes in the dark. He could make out her open mouth, lipstick smeared around it in the dim light behind them on the street.

"Now," she said urgently. "I want you to do it."

"What?" He said, "I don't know how," Billy admitted sheepishly. "I thought we would be married." Her hand moved to his backside and pulled him against her.

"I'll be sixteen next week," she insisted. "And it's time, if you love me. We'll be married. I'm sure of that. I know you'll keep your promise, now! Put it inside me." He hesitated, and he tried awkwardly to French kiss her, pushing his tongue into her mouth. "Your cock, silly, not your tongue," she whispered urgently.

Fumbling, he pulled his cock through a gap of open buttons in his trouser fly. Unsure, he slid a hand under one of her thighs and lifted her effortlessly against the wall. He felt her pull her panties to one side as she guided him inside her with the help of some spit on the tips of her fingers.

Urgent and rough, they clawed at each other to stay upright against the wall. Meg bit into the lapel of his jacket as he cupped the back of her head, stopping it from banging against the stone wall. He worried that any noise might wake her parents upstairs. Billy could feel her nails digging into the small of his back as his cock chaffed somewhere between the rough wool of his trousers and her twisted panties, but nothing had ever felt like this. The smell of lavender in her hair, the warm wet that wrapped around him, the colors bouncing behind his eyes—he pushed away the questions that rubbed against his conscience as he gladly conceded to Meg's wishes, she knew what she wanted—

Suddenly he came.

"Fuck, fuck, fuck!" He tried to hold his breath while his legs shook, threatening to buckle. Meg gasped for breath between the crush of his chest and the wall, and their breaths steamed into the air around them.

He still stood with both hands above his head on the wall, legs slightly apart with his head down as Meg slid out from under his rigid body.

"I need to go in now. My Mum will be waiting up and something warm and wet just trickled down my thigh and ran into the top of my new stockings." She pushed away, straightened her dress, wiped her face with a small lace handkerchief and smoothed her hair.

"That was rare," he mumbled. "Now we need to get married." The words tumbled from his lips.

"I know," said Meg as she kissed his cheek and disappeared through the back door of the shop.

Chapter 2

Journeyman

Billy shone the lamplight, climbed onto the edge of the freight car, and pushed one of the sand-colored bags around to see its top.

"Postal bags by the looks of it, floor to ceiling," he said aloud into the musty wagon. "Bloody waste of time as usual."

He saw a small opening where the bag was crimped by a chain running through little brass eyelets and fastened by a small padlock with a wax seal. Billy peered into the three-inch hole and saw what looked like paper stacked tightly into bundles. He noticed a familiar smell—the scent money had to it after having been handled time and time again; sour and sweaty. He slid his small hand into the top of the bag. It chaffed at his wrist as he extracted a bundle of five-pound notes. He turned the bundle around under the lamplight and read the bright red wording on the band that held the notes together: Five Hundred Pounds – TO BE DESTROYED—TOP SECRET—COUNTERFEIT—OPERATION BERNHARD.

Billy let out a long, low whistle as he wiped his brow and leaned back against the tower of bags. "Fuck me!"

He sat staring at the growing pile of cash he'd extracted, in the dim light. White bundles contrasted starkly with the dark oily wood and the smooth, shiny steel edge of the door opening, polished by all that passed over it in years of service.

Turning back to the mountain of bags he tried to slide his hand into the top of another bag, but this one was drawn tighter and even his slight hand could only finger the top of the nearest bundle. Working with one hand made the task harder as he tried to favor his wounded hand that was still bleeding slightly. The next several bags he tried were more accessible. Billy began to work faster. He stopped mid-task and collected himself, realizing Mam would call what he was doing—what he was planning—theft. He sat quietly and considered his options. Meg flooded his mind, last night, his promise. Here was a solution, a wedding gift. He felt uneasy in this justification, as he had in making love to Meg up against the wall. It was more like fucking than making love, not the romantic ideal he imagined countless times as he had touched himself while thinking of Meg over the past few years of their relationship.

Her prompting had seemed justification enough for his weakness. He loved her, and here lay an opportunity to give her everything she could ever wish for. How long would it take, how long did he have, how much should he take, and where to hide it? His heart was pumping and sweat ran into his eyes as he kept glancing over his shoulder into the darkness of the tunnel, expecting at any moment to hear a voice call out or to see the flicker of a lamp searching the dark. Thankfully nothing interrupted him, so far.

He feverishly worked on. Knowing mathematics wasn't his strongest point, even after long afternoons being coached by Meg and compulsory rail classes, he did the calculations with his stubby pencil and notebook. Five hundred pounds per bundle, twenty bundles, ten thousand pounds. One hundred bundles, "Fuck me"—fifty thousand pounds!

"It's too much, I'd get caught, I'd get stupid," he whispered. But half would do fine for a journeyman tapper and his beautiful wife.

Working through the wall of bags, he meticulously searched for the bags he could slide his hand into. He needed to find twenty-five bags from which he would take two bundles each, and his work went quickly as more bags were loose than tight. He laid his work jacket on the floor at the door of the rail car and stacked the money on top of it. Within twenty minutes he had his pile waiting in the halo of light from his lamp. Resisting the temptation to take even one more bundle, he checked the wall of bags for consistency and felt sure it looked just as it had when he opened the door, random bags and millions and millions of pounds. He turned away to focus on the task at hand.

He knew the tunnels were built with little nooks or safety recesses every fifty feet or so along the walls, depending on the length of the tunnel, as a haven should someone be walking or working when a train approached. The recess allowed a worker to step safely away from the passing train. Ten feet from the bricked up back of the tunnel, on the opposite side of the rail car, his light found the black hole of a recess. A few kicks at the gravel around it revealed a sump at its base. This was one of the menial lessons he learned during his apprenticeship as he spent countless hours cleaning sumps that had blocked, usually with leaves and debris collected after a dry spell, or dead animals, cats, rats, and once a small newborn baby wrapped in tea towels with a big blue umbilical cord still attached around its neck. The water in the bottom of the sump had turned everything on the baby a bluish grey like a porcelain doll. He had gently closed its eyes and buried it in a patch of grass at the back of the rail yard after saying a little prayer to speed the soul on its way.

Billy worked the rusted grate with his crowbar. As he pried the metalwork loose a flurry of massive rats rushed out at him, eyes red in the lamplight. He fell back onto the gravel and kicked at them as they dispersed over his legs into the darkness. Pulling off the threadbare Manchester United jumper he wore beneath his heavy work jacket, he laid it in the bottom of the sump. It was dry, three feet square and stank of old oil and rat piss. He shifted and stacked the bundles of money neatly from his work jacket into the sump and wrapped the jumper around the stash best as would fit. The crest of Manchester United blazed in red and gold on the front left side of the jersey, stretched over the bundle like a puffed-out chest. Billy looked proudly at the crest with a red rose sported by both the lion and the antelope, which was the official symbol of Lancashire, the county. Embroidered at the bottom part of the crest was the motto of the city of Manchester, *Concilio et Labore,* which his dad had told him meant 'wisdom and effort' and that the stripes on the shield represented three rivers, Medlock, Irwell and the Irk.

"You'll be safe here my little sweethearts, with that badge looking after you, champions we all are now, season tickets and a member for life," he said as he replaced the grate. He started to kick gravel roughly back over it, sparking his boots as he kicked the stone, little stars of light in the darkness, like fireworks on Guy Fawkes Night. He closed the freight wagon and turned to head back to the workshop.

Billy stepped back into the tea shed and threw down a scrap of paper in front of Harry Two Bellies—Registration # Z3118UK, Wagon 13, line 6. Tunnel 2.

"I opened it and got this for my troubles," he held up his hand wrapped in bloodied cloth. "Looks like mailbags, no good shit like you have us keep an eye open for. There was a seal, government I think, Her Majesty, thank you very much."

"Bugger, are you sure lad? What took you so long?" Harry asked.

"I got stuck chasing a stray dog out of the yard. Fucker gave me the run around before squeezing out through the South end fence. I fixed the fence so he couldn't get back in, had me work up a sweat working with only one hand. I knew the train wasn't going anywhere soon, since it must have been in that tunnel for a couple of months by the look of it. What do you think they'll do with it now?" Billy felt uneasy lying to Harry; three sins in as many days he thought—fornication, theft, and lying. He picked up his lunch pail and found solace in the elusive cup of tea he'd wanted so desperately only a couple of hours earlier.

Within fifteen minutes of Harry placing the call to the Station-General, Billy saw the entire yard fill up with flashing lights and police cars, helmet-headed bobbies roping off areas, awaiting Special Branch detectives. Billy saw a big black jaguar saloon pull up outside the work shed, splashing mud on the growing crowd of onlookers as it passed. He thought it must look like someone had died; men were always getting hurt in the yard. Safety standards were not high on the list of priorities when a job was so hard to get or keep. A feeling of apprehension came over him as he realized the magnitude of his actions. This money was significant, and he'd stolen some of it.

He briefly considered confessing but thought better of it, rather than thinking of Mam and Meg seeing him taken away to jail.

The door opened into the tea shed where Billy, Harry, and the rest of their team had assembled in anticipation of the police arriving. Everyone fidgeted from foot to foot, being in such proximity to the law whom most of them tried to avoid at all costs.

"Call me DCI Williams," said the immaculately dressed policeman as he introduced himself. "Any biscuits, mate?" Detective Chief Inspector Williams tried to be familiar as he entered the small room and took a cup of tea from a young constable. Harry tossed a half-full box of Jammy Dodger biscuits over the desk behind which the detective took a seat.

"Well done, boys, you just found five million pounds of Her Majesty's lovely cash that was due for destruction because it was old and worn out. Provided none of you tinkered with the lovely seals on the bags as you did with the lock on the door, you just put my arse in the butter, thank you very much. I've been trying to find that bloody wagon for over three months now. You could have nicked the lot, and nobody would have known it. All usable around these parts I'm sure, what with Mammies keeping their money for years in tins up chimneys. If you hadn't told us where the rail car was, we'd still be chasing around Sussex two hundred and odd miles from here."

Everyone in the room stared at him in disbelief.

"May I speak, sir?" A young sergeant asked as he opened the door of the tea-room and leaned half in.

"Get on with it," replied the DCI.

"All bags accounted for sir, and all locks secure, that is except the lock to the cab door as you were aware. It was forced open by the young lad who found it, Billy somebody." He flipped his notebook open and read, "Billy McTaggart, an apprentice tapper, sir, the one with the hurt hand."

DCI stood quietly for a moment and looked slowly around the room. His eyes rested on Billy with his bloody hand that hadn't yet received medical attention.

"McTaggart you say, Sargent? Thank you, you can go now, get the clean-up started, son, there's a good copper. I do want to have a look at the wagon before they take it away." Slowly the DCI looked around the room again at the faces of the other men as they fidgeted nervously for no good reason in the presence of authority.

"Well, well, I guess you girls are in the clear then. So, you're the hero, Tiny Tim?" he asked, looking directly at Billy. "Did I hear that officer call you McTaggart?" It's a wonder you could get that car door open, judging by the size of you. I've seen more meat on a sparrow's kneecap. There must be more to you than meets the eye, Billy boy, pulling that plonker of yours too much in the outhouse I bet."

The men in the room laughed nervously, humoring the DCI.

Billy stared back at the detective and held his gaze, his face stoic as his hand started to pulse again in pain. He'd forgotten about the injury with all the adrenaline coursing through his veins. He refused to be intimidated by the clean shaven spiffy copper in his crisp beige Macintosh, striped navy-blue suit, and oxblood colored brogues spattered with mud from the yard.

Billy saw a small smile he couldn't understand spread over the DCI's face. The man put a finger to his lips and held back saying something. Then, turning away, he spoke loudly to the other men in the room.

"Okay, sweethearts, I am authorized to award our young hero McTaggart and your chubby Gaffer Harry here the fine reward of fifty pounds each from the Queen's own Royal Mint, so thank you, and by the way that was crap tea."

Billy watched the detective stride toward the door, then stop and turn.

"I may need to speak to you again, boy; you remind me of someone else I know called McTaggart. He was a little bastard as well, what a coincidence." The DCI pulled out a calfskin leather wallet and withdrew a business card. He ambled toward Billy and held out the card, his hand waving slightly like a cobra preparing to strike. "Billy, Billy McTaggart, would you happen to know a Jim McTaggart, Argyle and Southern Highlanders?" He held his card level with Billy's eyes, hovering.

"Aye, sir, that would be my dad, and you would be right in calling him a bastard if you have the right man." Billy took the card from the DCI.

"You've dropped some blood on the floor there, best get that hand seen to sharpish." Without another word, the DCI turned and went out of the tea shed, leaving as quickly as he'd arrived amid spinning wheels and spraying mud. Harry looked at Billy, then at the two small piles of five-pound notes on the table and grinned.

"I'll have a pint of Guinness, to celebrate your new promotion to journeyman, young man. Honest lads, that's what I like. You'll be Billy Tapper round here from now on, me old son, just like your dad, God bless that fucker too, wherever he is," said Harry. He tucked his fifty quid into his overall bib pocket that sat squeezed between his protruding belly and the large breasts pushing out against his sweat-stained singlet on each side. He handed the other fifty to Billy and said, "We coulda nicked the whole fucking lot, and they'd never have known it! Now he tells us, fucking snobby copper."

Harry lifted his leg and farted and everyone in the room groaned. "It would all be good until you bunch of stupid fuckers started spending it like drunken sailors and gypsies at the racetrack, then Mr. fucking DCI wanker would be back down here and on us like a ton of bricks. Let's get that hand of yours seen to young man, a warrior's wounds need to be treated after the battle between good and evil."

The motley crew of tappers converged on the Navigation Pub, and Billy got the first round in, as directed by Harry.

"A black and tan for me and a pint for each of the lads here. And a double whiskey for the Gaffer Harry," said Billy, with the biggest smile on his face. He wanted to run home and tell Meg straightway about their good fortune, but knew he had to buy a round or two first, no point raising any suspicion. *Keep being Billy* he thought to himself, no drunken sailor, thank you very much, and no DCI Mr. Wanker Williams. Unless they count every bag again, with no seals broken, there wouldn't be much to worry about, although he felt his conscience tweak. Mam had raised him to be honest, and forthright—but he was overwhelmed by his desire to please Meg at all costs.

He separated out forty-five pounds from his reward and tucked it into the inside pocket of his work trousers. This had been a wild couple of days, making love to the woman he loved, even if it was a knee trembler up against a wall. Cash for life hidden in a storm water sump, wedding money in his pocket, and promotion to tapper. *What could be better* he wondered as he looked out the window of the pub toward the tunnel where the train full of money was being pulled away. He felt a deep satisfaction knowing that in the dark at the back of the tunnel lay a whole new future wrapped in his Manchester United jumper.

Chapter 3

Butterflies

After the pints had been bought and all the backslapping done, Billy made his way back to his bicycle chained in the yard and headed home. His legs felt a little wobbly after the several pints of beer, but somewhere deep inside was a calm, a resolve. Riding his bike up the high street, Billy felt big for the first time in his life, even gigantic. His chest swelled to bursting with butterflies that needed to stay in the jar a while longer, maybe forever. Tonight, the butterflies carried him home. Billy wondered how Meg would take the news of the fifty-pound reward. Would it be enough for her wedding? Could he be enough for her?

The first time he remembered seeing Meg was in a classroom of the small village school he attended in Diggle. It was early winter of 1947. He was a year older than her, at six. The bright floral print on the dress she wore reminded him of the tablecloth his grandma used when setting the table for the grown-ups at Sunday lunch in the front parlor, where children were expected to be neither seen nor heard. They were sent to the kitchen to eat their baked Yorkshire pudding and suet gravy supped from tarnished spoons that scraped on small, chipped plates.

He hated the restraint expected of him amid the raucous childhood banter and petty taunting of his cousins, but he knew better than to test his parents. He would watch those diminutive relatives caught by aunts and uncles as they were dragged by the scruff of the neck and smacked unceremoniously up the backside all the way out the kitchen door to the outhouse in the backyard. Subdued, the children would return under heavy hands, dry sobbing and dealt with by flush-faced parents in wrinkled Sunday best wanting to get back to their pint of beer and social gossip on their one day off in the week.

At school, Billy was embarrassed as he sat in the classroom, having been sent to the junior class as a slow reader in hopes he would catch up with his peers. In truth, he preferred the younger group where he sat next to Miss Wallington's desk facing the class. She would correct his work periodically at arm's length with her jabbing finger when she caught him daydreaming.

He watched a particular girl whose whole world centered on a tin Mickey Mouse tea set. Miss Wallington told them it was one of many gifts given to the school by the Yanks to replace toys lost in the war. Carved wooden slingshots and handmade dolls dressed in remnant fabric with wool hair were a reminder that few luxuries existed in post-war Great Britain, including food and such. Billy had watched the Yanks drive around the village like they owned the place, saviors of the free world after a bloody world war. Everyone he knew in town was still recovering or emerging from under a dark cloud where scarcity was the norm.

He admired the bright, colorful tea set. It was a marvel; two cups with matching saucers and two side plates with Pluto and Mickey running around the edge.

The girl made bright painted slices of cardboard cutout cake for each plate and pretended to pour tea from the colorful teapot. Minnie Mouse smiled up at her as she shared it out into the tin cups with elaborate dashes of imaginary milk and spoons of sugar.

"Now that will do, young Megan," the teacher said. "I've told you enough times already, leave the tea set alone and focus on your reading."

Miss Wallington, with clenched teeth, abruptly pushed Billy aside as she stalked over to Megan and roughly hauled her back to her desk. He saw her give a little pinch to the girl's soft underarm. Megan screamed and kicked at the teacher while holding on for dear life to the teapot. He lowered his head to his desk and watched the chaos unfold through crisscrossed fingers just as the tea set took flight. The memory was vivid as he recollected the classroom erupting, some children laughing and others shouting, several little girls crying.

The teacher lost control when dark-haired Megan broke free and ran to the back of the class, where she climbed onto a bookshelf and tried to open a window through which to escape. The children cheered and ran around the classroom, glad for a break from monotonous learning. Billy picked up his reading book and satchel amid the chaos and slid out the classroom door, where he almost collided with the headmistress who strode toward him in her sensible shoes and tweed skirt, with a sizeable wooden ruler in hand.

He flattened himself to the wall, hoping his mottled grey jersey with its washed-out yellow V-neck and his oversized shorts would render him invisible against the asbestos-clad, prefabricated building.

"What's all this commotion about?" The headmistress bellowed as she entered the chaotic room. Stuck to the wall, he listened as the room fell silent with the teacher fumbling for words.

"She—I—this tea set—" And then he had heard a high-pitched scream from Megan.

"It's my tea set!" Meg screeched, followed by the dull slap of a ruler across bare legs. The class erupted again.

Billy hurried back to his own classroom. He knew he wasn't as brave or as defiant as the girl, Megan, with the blue eyes. He was small for his age and knew better than to run or fight back if attacked. He knew how to take his beatings from the bullies and had resolved that stealth was his ally; he knew how to hide in plain sight if need be.

But, if Megan had made an impression on him that morning, it was his second sighting of her that secured his affections and admiration of her forever.

The final bell had rung out just before four o'clock. He shouldered his satchel and crossed the room to pick up his duffle coat from the coat rack, and there came a shout of alarm from outside as he buttoned up the horn toggles on his jacket.

"Stop her, stop her, stop that child!"

Billy followed his classmates out the door. They crowded at the edge of the playground and he saw Meg run past, pursued by three adults. She ran like a hare pursued by a pack of blood-thirsty whippets at the races on a Thursday night in Oldham. He remembered the fury of the tracks as he'd watched from his father's shoulders; the smell of drunken old men waving losing tickets and flat caps as they looked feverishly on with bloodshot eyes, screaming and spitting globs of saliva on to the backs of the people in front of them. He felt the same tension hang electric in the air as he watched Megan's little white legs pumping up and down during her escape. He had thought it odd that she held her oversized blue knickers awkwardly high above her waist while she ran for her life and barely outpaced the lumbering, grimacing headmistress.

Something was wrong about the shape of Meg's protruding bottom, which extended unnaturally from beneath her floral dress as she ran. Then a teacup popped out from one leg of her expansive knickers, followed by a side plate. The smiling Mickey Mouse and Pluto cartoons never faltered as the teacup bounced and the plate rolled across the black tarmac playground, spinning and swerving over the hopscotch lines, flattening out face down with a "plunk" under the swing set. His heart quickened as Megan stopped for a second, eyes darting to and fro, to grope with on hand for the remnants of whatever she still had stashed in her fabulous blue knickers. She hiked up the broad elastic waistband with her other hand and set off again. He willed her to escape and hoped she would settle for freedom over the tea set as the school gate loomed beyond the playground with some promise of escaping with at least some of her treasures.

"That will be far enough, young lady. "I've had quite enough of you, Madam," the Headmistress raged as she caught Megan by the scruff of her neck and unceremoniously pulled down her knickers, exposing two tin saucers, a cup, and one Mini Mouse teapot, which Megan grasped, as well as a small white bottom with red imprints where the teapot, plates and tea cups had pressed.

The children around him giggled nervously at the scene and smarted when the ever-ready ruler cracked a sharp red line across the little white cheeks of Megan's bottom. Billy felt powerless to save her, but without thinking he threw himself at the Headmistress's legs, just as the she began to stumble backward. He got a sharp kick in the ribs as she tumbled over him and stepped on the teapot that had fallen to the ground, crushing it flat under her sensible lace up shoes. Billy lay winded on the ground where he noticed the deformed Mini staring back at him, her smile contorted and sporting one crumpled ear. Megan dropped abruptly to the ground, released from the unbalanced Headmistress's grip. She never faltered but crawled across the playground grasping for the squashed teapot.

"Mine," she whimpered, looking directly at him, as a wooden ruler came down over her knuckles. She wailed in pain and dropped the teapot again.

The crowd dispersed as quickly as it formed. He reached over, picked up the squashed discarded teapot, and slid it into the leather satchel that still hung over his shoulder.

A few days passed before he saw Megan back at school again. He was pleased that she now sat up front in the reading class, closer to his enforced purgatory at the teacher's side. He'd looked around the room for any vestige of the tea set, but it had been disposed of along with any other distractions in the classroom. He looked at the distinct thin blue lines on Megan's legs and hands that had now turned deep greenish yellow except where the skin had been broken. Eventually, over time, those wounds too would scab over.

At playtime Megan sat alone at the edge of the playground in self-imposed exile and guarded solitude. She didn't raise her head when Billy walked over and sat down opposite her on the curb. He offered her one of the shortcake biscuits Mam had packed for him in his satchel. Without really knowing why, he felt compelled to talk to Megan, to admire her.

"I think you're brave and daft all at the same time," he said as Megan looked up and stared him full in the eye, her blue eyes shining with tears. Feeling awkward, he lowered his extended hand that held the biscuit. "I have something else for you," Billy stammered. From his satchel he pulled the teapot. "It's not perfect," he said to her sheepishly, "I put back together. The paint is scratched. My Dad helped me fix it for you."

"Mine!" Megan took the teapot and pulled the treasure to her chest, her eyes darting around the playground.

"You are pretty," Billy stammered, hoping they might be friends.

Megan held his gaze and spoke in a soft, confident voice. "Bugger off."

Confused at the abrupt dismissal, Billy felt a little tickle in his tummy as he reluctantly stood up and walked away. It felt like butterflies, millions, and millions of them trying to escape.

Chapter 4

Man O' War

The hour was late when Billy pushed his bike into the walled backyard and parked it up against the outhouse. He had a quick pee, made his way toward the back door of the kitchen, and crept inside. On the table he found a note written by Mam's shaky hand, saying his dinner was in the oven. Pulling out the warm plate he sat down at the table to eat the cottage pie. After washing his plate, he slid quietly into the hallway toward the stairs leading up to his bedroom. As he took the first riser, he noticed the light still on in the front room. He crossed to the door and pushed it open. Mam was asleep sitting by the unlit fire with a travel rug pulled over her chest. He shook her gently and asked her to wake up.

She roused, groggy, and smiled at him. "You're home. I expected you sooner." She gave him a kiss on the cheek. "I can smell the beer on you. It's a work night, son," she said as she stood up, pulling her housecoat around her, and shuffled stiffly to the stairs.

"Sleep tight, Mam, and I love you. I have some news for you in the morning. Its good and I'm excited to share it with you and Meg."

Mam nodded sleepily and disappeared around the top of the stairs with a wave of her hand. Billy stood for a moment looking back into the front living room. He seldom went in there because the room held too many memories for him.

Dad would talk to him of the war only on a rare occasion. Mam had told him most soldiers shared little or nothing of their experiences so not to expect too much from his Dad regarding the war. He'd seen the dark clouds form quickly when the subject arose, but once in a while the door opened ever so slightly, and Billy would creep in.

"What did you do in the war, Dad?" he remembered asking his father as they sat in that same front room. He watched his dad draw on his pipe, deep blue eyes penetrating in the glow of the fire burning in the hearth, his black hair combed back with one thick wisp hanging lazily over his left eye. Mam was at the social club for bingo night, and Dad, for once, was awake after his dinner rather than being slumped, exhausted, in the kitchen after a long day at the yard.

Billy had watched his Dad with a quiet reverence and more than a little curiosity. He knew it was a rare moment to catch him like this, just the two of them in the front room. Over the years their walks to the rail yard were often more instructional than conversational, and Billy craved a conversation, an opportunity to banter with Dad, but he was content to listen if his father would speak to him.

"I was lucky, my boy," Dad had said softly to the fireplace as he leaned forward from his chair and struck a match on the mantle. "I had a grand time of it, me and the lads." His Scottish brogue came through as his tone shifted. He straightened in his seat, ready to tell his story, and Billy held his breath.

"I was a young cock sparrow, all jaunty in my uniform, full of beans, in the Argyle and Southern Highlanders, straight out from out under my mother's apron and about as wet behind the ears as a new baby. I would have done anything to get out of Lesmahagow in Lanarkshire, no coal mining for me, boy. I was going to see the world. Scotland held no prizes I wanted to win.

"I spent a month in Manchester, including my posting to Diggle, before we were shipped out. I eventually volunteered for special training in the Libyan and Egyptian desert in North Africa, the Long-Range Desert Group under Lieutenant General Bernard Montgomery, 'Monty' or the 'Spartan General' as the lads would call him. It was The Desert Campaign, in Morocco, and Operation Torch, in Algeria and Tunisia." His Dad had paused, and Billy had sat silently, waiting, watching his fathers knitted brow, a million questions on his lips.

"A grand adventure, me and my mates, Harry and Monty. Not the general, Monty Banks, just a good solid lad who taught me how to fire two machine guns at once and navigate by the stars."

Dad fell silent again, paging through his memories. Billy wished he could somehow see them play out on the big screen at the Sunday matinee in the Odeon cinema in town. It would be fantastic he thought, his imagination running away-Cinemascope, bold title, My Dad's Adventures in the War, ten feet high, machine guns blazing, special forces trucks driving through the desert chasing Rommel back to El Alamein in full flight. He noticed his Dad's hands, muscular and veined from manual work. The long slender fingers now wrapped around his tea mug had held a gun, pulled a trigger. His dad was a man who'd killed and lived to tell the tale. Billy felt a surge of awe.

"I was lucky. I was singled out, probably more stupid than brave, and sent to the Commandos, the brainchild of David Stirling and a bunch of soldiers who would probably have been in jail if it weren't for the war. A Nazi SS Major had managed to get a hundred and forty-two Jewish counterfeiters together in one concentration camp in Germany. They were making forgeries of the British pound and the US dollar among other stuff, and our job was to stop them.

"The mission was what we came to know as Operation Bernhard, after Major Bernhard Kruger who lead the program. The plan was to destabilize the British economy during the war by dropping forged notes from aircraft into public areas. That was 1943, and the Germans were expecting the Brits would collect the notes, spend the money, and trigger inflation."

Billy recollected feeling ignorant, having no idea what *destabilize*, or *inflation* meant, but he nodded that he understood the plan. He acknowledged the need for the Commandos to prevent the inflation of Britain, which must be code for 'blow up', like inflating a tire on your bicycle until it burst.

Dad took a long deep drink of tea and went on.

"Britain learned of the plot as early as 1939, and by 1943 the sequestered Jewish counterfeiters of Operation Bernhard were printing more than one million Pounds a month. We managed to get to Sachsenhausen just the day after the Germans shipped the forgers to Redl-Zipf in Austria, a subsidiary camp of Mauthausen-Gusen Camp. Then, in May of 1945, they moved the prisoners to Ebinsee where they were going to be killed by the SS. Lucky for some of the forgers the truck broke down on the third trip, and they were marched to the camp, where they refused to go into the rocket tunnels where the Germans planned to kill them. In the chaos, the forgers dispersed among the general body of prisoners and saved themselves from certain death."

Billy leaned in, fascinated with the details of secret missions, forged money, and the dreaded concentration camps.

Dad continued. "The Yanks got there on May sixth, 1945, the day before your fourth birthday. We followed the money trail to Lake Toplitz near Ebensee, and that was it, almost all of the money had disappeared."

"Tell me more Dad," Billy pleaded, his excitement creeping around the ridged facade of his fathers' somber mood. This moment could evaporate as quickly as it had appeared and he grasped at the wisps of story much as if they were smoke rising from the fire they had sat before, the precious embers holding deep secrets that, if untold just this once, would in the morning be nothing but cold, grey ash.

"We found a couple of boxes of the money," Dad said. "I have two or three of the notes in my war tin upstairs, big white five-pound notes. The notes were made so well the cheeky buggers even sent some of them to Switzerland to be verified for authenticity. The Swiss sent them to the Royal Bank of England, who verified them as real. Bloody ridiculous! But brilliant at the same time. They even added pin holes in the corners where people pined the notes together instead of using a wallet because they were so big."

Billy desperately wanted to ask to see the notes, but he chose not to break the mood in the sanctuary of the living room.

"I always wondered what happened to all that money, a hundred and thirty-four million pounds they told me. Where did it go?" Dad sighed.

"They never made many dollars, mainly pounds. The war ended before they got the dollar going, thanks to a couple of brave forgers who stalled the process." Dad said this as he kicked off his slippers and curled his toes to the hearth to draw the last of the heat out of the fire. "I was lucky," he said again, "I got to come back to all this, Billy Boy, to you and your Mam, to Tapping and Diggle, lucky me!"

Billy noted the sarcasm in his voice. Even at his young age he'd recognized disappointment, he recognized the defeat in the slump of his father's shoulders and the glisten of remorse in a wet eye. But no tear had fallen. Dad would not cry; he knew that much about him.

The fire died just as Mam came through the front door at the stroke of ten. "What are you two doing in here?" Mam asked, but didn't wait for an answer. She had won three pounds and a picnic basket full of treats at an event sponsored by the local American base.

"We could never get all this with our ration book," she said in triumph, taking off her coat and headscarf. "The two top prizes," she enthused, trying to get Dad's attention. Dad's melancholy was palpable, and Billy had realized Mam was avoiding the apparent awkwardness of finding Billy and his Dad sitting in the front room together with a dying fire.

"We could take the bike up onto the moors, or out to the beach and have a picnic feast." She tussled Dad and Billy's hair at the same time and shouted, "Bingo!" Dad stood and gave her a peck on the cheek.

"Now that will do, lass, don't get too far beyond yourself. Working folks don't picnic these days, and the money will do well to go to the rent, with ten percent to the church, and perhaps a new headscarf for yourself, pet." As he spoke, he punched Billy on the shoulder in a way Billy thought comrades might do, a familiarity of restrained proportions in the heat of battle or warfare.

"Time for your bed, big man, and me for mine," Dad loped off without looking back. Mam threw an arm around Billy and pulled him to her. He felt her chest heave, but no sound had come out of her tightly clenched lips. It was his last memory of that night.

Billy closed the door to the front room and hoped the ghosts of the past would stay where they were. He made his way upstairs to his bedroom, pulled on his pajamas, and slid into bed. The cold sheets made it hard to sleep. He could hear Mam snoring in the next room and found comfort in the rhythm—just knowing she was there. She was the one thing in his life that had always been there for as long as he could remember. He found himself wishing he could tell Mam his news, even of the money taken, but he knew she wouldn't approve and would probably march him down to the police station, holding him by the ear like a five-year-old, to confess his sins. The thrill of the day washed over him, again and again, every time he almost fell asleep his life suddenly appeared to expand before him. It had seemed impossible before today that he might live the dreams he and Meg had shared.

Not more than a week after their fireside chat, Billy had helped his dad get ready for his ritual Friday night outing by polishing his father's shoes for sixpence. He noticed as he finished up that Dad—dressed all spiffy and ready for a night with the lads, not a hair out of place and shoulders set—with his clean-shaven jaw showed a little tension as he stared out the bedroom window.

Billy's tenth birthday came that Friday, and Mam had arranged a small party with four of his cousins, her sisters, and Meg, with whom he spent most of his time. Mam wanted to invite boys from his school, but he managed to distract her from that embarrassing effort. He had no friends except Meg.

Billy and his cousins eyed the big trifle made by Aunt Kath, and Meg took a scoop of cream on to the end of her finger and dotted it on to Billy's nose.

"Happy Birthday, silly boy!" She danced around the room, laughing.

Aunt Kath had locked Billy in an embrace and kissed the cream from the end of his nose. "I put a drop of sherry over the sponge," she said with a wink, "and that's pure Devon cream on top, with sprinkles. Just how you like it."

Billy saw Mam nudge Dad when the singing started, bringing him back from his thoughts. Dad glanced out the front parlor window, distracted as he joined the singing of Happy Birthday in his deep baritone voice. Then he left after kissing Mam on the forehead and tussling Billy's hair, telling him to be a good boy for his Mam.

Even back then, Billy knew his dad wasn't a drinking man as many of the local men were. Drink was their respite from daily manual labor and the memories of war held deep inside a shadow of themselves. The need for camaraderie drew them to the pub.

Beer was the working-class pleasure and curse of most families in the village, with Catholic families seeming to take the brunt of the scourge—frustrated men agitated by menial labor and the guilt of war too recent in their minds; too many children hung on the aprons of milksop wives standing in doorways on Friday paydays, praying their husbands made it past the pub. A right that was believed to be given by God. According to Harry Two Bellies, a man's Friday night beer was divine.

Mam had a different opinion of what a man's rights and responsibilities should be, and she voiced them freely around the dinner table. She sympathized with the wives of the men who dragged their hobnail boots up the cobbled road on drunken legs. The unlucky ones with too many children, cold, and hungry in soiled beds who would sit waiting for a drunk singer with hands of steel to push down the door, yelling for his supper. Inebriated men would often unleash the wrath of hell when there were no vittles found in the cold kitchen where fearful children huddled together trying to keep warm at the grate of a meager hearth.

Mam only had Billy, and she said she was lucky if you looked at the lack of a large family a certain way. The circumstances of Billy's birth had been hard on her, according to Aunt Lil, though little more was said of the situation, and it was rather common knowledge that Dad would have loved a wee girl to fill his eyes.

"Our boy is our blessing," Billy often heard Mam say in defense of her situation. Her inadequacy was evident in her sorrow, as Billy would see her sit by the window of the front room watching children play in the street, envious of their mother's bounty, but he knew she was honestly thankful that she and Dad only had one mouth to feed.

"That lot need to have sixpence stuck between their knees and saltpeter put in their Guinness. Little Popes will overrun the world if that lot keep at it. It's a blessing half of them die sooner rather than later," Dad would rant whenever Mam lent the O'Shaughnessy's next door another cup of sugar or pint of milk.

Whatever happened, Billy knew Dad always came home first before the Friday night outing to wash, put on a clean shirt, jacket, and tie, and add as splash of cologne. He used pomade for his thick black hair that he would brush with his tortoiseshell brushes with fine badger hair bristles. He had a matching shaving set inherited from Grandfather McTaggart.

Every week Billy watched Dad hand his pay package to Mam, who would then go to the kitchen and open the cupboard, move some crockery, and reveal a small hole in the wall where Dad had removed a brick to create a hidey-hole for her housekeeping tin. Then she would stand in the kitchen pressing Dad's shirt, using a sprinkle of starch infused lavender water as she pulled the iron from the range and spat on its surface to ensure it held the heat. She took great care to press the seams on the shirt to a knife-edge. She would then offer Dad his freshly pressed shirt, holding it up for him to slide into, warm and crisp.

"You look nice," she would say, buttoning up his shirt and straightening his tie. Dad would get his allowance in silence and, after pulling his jacket on, he kissed Mam on the cheek while she picked non-existent dust off his lapel, a rare sign of affection between them in front of Billy.

Billy knew Dad would always be home precisely fifteen minutes after the pub closed, never later, and then he would relish the cup of tea and the pork pie supper and slice of cake Mam would have waiting for him as he shared the stories from the pub that night. Billy would sit on the landing at the top of the stairs and listen.

"Mickey 'Three Fingers' Turner is getting better, but said he's going back to Scotland to work his father's farm. Bob 'Pony' Robson lost all his wages on the horses last week and the lads had to pass the hat for him."

Billy would run off the landing when he heard the kitchen chair scrape back and, as the sound of Dad's boots hit the stairs, he'd jump into bed. Dad would come into his room to kiss him and wish him goodnight.

"I hope you liked the stories, Billy boy, now off to sleep with you, you rascal."

That was how it once was.

On the night of his birthday and an hour after the pub closed, Mam asked Billy to go with her to look for Dad.

"It's not like him. You know he's always prompt, never more than three pints with his whiskey chaser. I'm worried, Billy. Get dressed, just put your trousers over your pajamas, we won't be long, he's probably helping one of the lads get home."

They walked down the street toward the Navigation pub together, against the flow of men walking home, reduced now to the drunkards incapable of walking a straight line so they hung on pillars and posts, sliding down walls into pools of puke and pee. He stayed close to Mam as they passed the fish and chips shop when Harry 'Pony' Robertson stood at the door with his hand in a newspaper poke full of steaming chips. He shouted over to them.

"What are you pair doing out at this time of night, and what the hell happened to your man? The flaky bastard owes me two quid I laid on for his horses tonight!"

Mam stopped dead in her tracks, and Billy felt her hand tighten. As twisted as her arthritic hands were, they were working hands, and strong. He held his breath, too scared to tell her she was hurting him. She was unpredictable when she was out of the little control she had over her life. The streetlight made Mam seem formidable as she took off across the street with Billy in tow, dragging him stumbling through the pools of lamplight right up to Harry. The smell of beer and fried food filled the air. Billy felt nauseous.

"Want a chip lad, they're grand?" Harry asked before Mam showered Harry with a barrage of questions. Billy could barely hang on to every second word.

"Pub— After the party— Seven o'clock— Always in— Seeing him? Help me Harry!" Mam ended her tirade in a scream, and Billy's knees buckled as she crushed his hand.

Once Mam calmed down a little, they learned Dad hadn't been at the pub as usual. No one missed him until the horses were drawn for the Saturday races but, even so, it wasn't unusual for someone to miss a Friday night now and then, even Jim.

Mam rushed off, still gripping Billy, to the nearest phone box to call the police. He felt relieved when the police finally came to the house at two in the morning. After several cups of tea and a million questions, they reluctantly agreed to list a missing person's report.

Weeks of useless leads brought no resolution, and after a while everyone stopped asking Billy and Mam where Jim was. They just gave a sympathetic smile to Mam, asked how she was doing, and told her to keep her chin up.

Over the next few months Billy and Mam adjusted from blind panic to a sort of forced acceptance of their new circumstances. The police had not uncovered one clue to the disappearance of Dad. Life slowly moved on. Sometimes Billy would go to the dresser in Mam's room and bury his nose in the freshly pressed shirts that still smelled of his Dad. No matter how often Mam washed and pressed them, her routine was unbroken, and it gave her a fragile purpose and hope.

He noticed Dad had taken absolutely nothing with him other than the clothes on his back. Billy would look but never touch the hairbrushes that sat next to the black-and-white photo of Dad in his uniform. It was like a shrine, he thought, Mam's altar where she sacrificed her tears in silence, hiding her grief from him under a thick stoic blanket that threatened to suffocate her most days.

Then almost a year to the day and a week before his eleventh birthday a letter arrived. He didn't consider the letter a gift, but more a coincidence, and that cut deeper.

Tel Aviv, Israel was the postmark on the Air-Mail envelope that hung limply through the letterbox in the hallway door. Mam wouldn't touch it, but she watched as Billy slid a butter knife along its spine, tentatively drawing out the contents like some form of autopsy to find the cause of death.

The single sheet of thin blue airmail paper held only six lines and his name in the firm slanting hand both knew as Dad's, words written in the globby lines of a fountain pen—the pen, Billy supposed, Mam had saved up to buy him. "Tortoiseshell to match your granddad's brushes, real posh, the band is real gold," she'd gushed when she gave it to him. "I used all my green shield stamps and some of the washing money I made." Billy wondered if Dad thought of Mam when he used it, but Mam interrupted his reverie, asking him to read what the letter said. In one breath Billy conveyed the stacked brevity upon the page, words that couldn't fill a wasteland of blue paper.

It's me.

I'm sorry.

No words will answer your questions.

I had to leave.

I won't be back.

I thought you should know.

Jim.

Mam's shoulders heaved when Billy fell silent again, and she bit her lip. The envelope also held forty pounds in big white five-pound notes. Billy knew this was the last they would hear from him.

Later that night as Billy tried to fall asleep, all the old dreams of Dad flooded back, but now the details of his face were gone and he could sense him only as an elusive, fallen hero spirited away on some secret mission. By the time he woke up the next morning, his ability to remember what his father looked like was so vague he let it slip away, knowing now for sure they'd been abandoned. Mam packed up the shrine on the dresser and called the police so that they wouldn't waste any more time looking for someone who did not want to be found. Billy stood outside the big red phone box and listened through the hole of broken glass to his Mam.

"It's just us now Billy. It's just us," Mam said as she took his hand and they began the walk back home.

In his dark bedroom Billy shuddered at the remembrance and pressed his head into the pillow, caught between the memory of his father's disappearance and the exciting news he would share with Mam and Meg in the morning. What rang true he wondered, the clear ring of his future with Meg or the dull noise that sat deep in his chest as proof that his family was indeed broken?

Chapter 5

The Yard

Billy's last day of high school was uneventful in the usual grey of life that was Diggle. As a Tapper, at least he knew he'd progress from plimsolls gutties to hobnail boots he could spark on the street as he walked to work. His first day as an apprentice tapper had started with a wake-up call from Mam.

"Get up, lad, you'll be late. It won't do to be late on your first day as a working man. I've laid your clothes out and there's a hot breakfast for you, and I also made up your lunch pail."

He watched Mam spoon oatmeal porridge onto a tin plate and sprinkle it with sugar before adding a dash of milk. "You'll make a good Tapper, like your dad, son." Mam added as she held him to her chest. "I'm proud of you, and I'm trying not to cry, I promise."

At the yard, Billy scraped off sticky mud that clung to his boots from his walk, using the rail by the door of the enormous steel work shed. He felt uneasy being there without his Dad even after all those years, but he pulled back the heavy door and walked into the brisk welcome of the shift manager.

"So, you're gonna be a Tapper, son?" The yard manager said, as Billy noticed remnants of breakfast egg on his beard and vest.

"Ay, Sir, like my Dad." Billy answered boldly, eager to get off on the right foot into his future.

"I knew your dad, so I'll sign you on for your mam's sake. She's a grand housekeeper, but you're the man of the house now, okay? One pound and six shillings a week, and no screwing around or I'll kick your arse so hard you'll have a double set of shoulders. Now get down to the work sheds and speak to Harry Two Bellies, he'll set you straight, and none of that Houdini shit like your old man. The fucker landed me in a bunch of trouble, even if he was a good lad and a great tapper."

Billy understood this was as much sympathy as one might expect in a rail yard.

He already knew his way around the yard from his days there with Dad, helping shunt cars and check loads, tapping alongside the lads as would now be his lot. He walked across the yard towards the work shed with a quiet sense of being at home in some way.

The shed was huge, the hub of the busy workday, a massive corrugated iron Quonset hut sixty feet tall. He glanced up at the rows of dusty skylight windows and ventilation fans monotonously humming above the constant grind of iron wheels from the rail cars outside. He listened to the clack and bang that made a dull vibration underfoot and formed undulating rings in cups of tea that sat on workbenches as shunters moved different cars into place, ready for their next journey out there into the world beyond the gray.

Harry Two Bellies farted and laughed as he entered through the work shed door, his large belly bobbing up and down as he hung onto the end of the workbench. He'd been one of

Dad's mates and had taken it hard when he had disappeared. Harry's long mop of greasy hair hung limply down onto his pockmarked shoulders, and his grease- and sweat-stained singlet gathered under his arms beneath his flopping skin that the lads called Bingo Wings—his claim to fame was his grand proportions and the ability to fart on demand.

"Loved your dad," he said when Billy entered the shed on his first day of work. "He was salt of the earth, even if he was a sweaty sock, Jock, like me, tough as nails he was, and my best mate. You'll be as good a tapper as he ever was if I have my way. Start by making some tea, lad, and I'll be back shortly. Until then you can get to know the other lads on the shift."

Harry stepped out to the yard and Billy had made his way around to the far end of the workshop where he encountered the two lads standing at a workbench. He knew them from around the village and, as fourth-year apprentices, they were almost out of their time. The taller of the two boys slouched over toward Billy with a long-handled tapper's hammer in his hand, twirling it just in front of Billy's face.

"I'm Eddy. You must be the shrimp. And that's George. Just so you know, you're ours, sweetie, so hurry up and make the tea." They circled him like wolves sniffing the kill.

"Stop the chit chat, you lot, and get back to work," shouted Harry as he walked back in the door, lifted one leg and let out another long slow fart punctuated by hearty laughter and much belly wobbling. "Billy, where's the fucking tea, lad?"

Billy appreciated the reprieve but knew he needed to keep his wits about him now that he'd landed at the wrong end of another food chain.

Those early days were filled with the usual menial tasks of an apprentice and figuring out how to avoid Eddy and George

He found that pissing in their tea helped avenge any attempts they made to intimidate him, but keeping close to Harry or the other journeymen who used the work shed was the real protection. He quickly learned the ropes and knew how to get out of the way fast, utilizing any distraction, even Harry's farting, if need be.

The worst of the pranks, courtesy of Eddy and George, ended in a split head for Billy after he was hung upside down by the legs from a winch high above the floor of the shed. His skinny ankles slipped their bonds, and the lads just managed to catch him as his head bounced off the edge of the old anvil next to the forge. His revenge was to put a couple of dog shits in their work boots—a few weeks apart with one of the shunter's time slips and work cap left nearby as a decoy. He knew they couldn't retaliate on a journeyman, being apprentices themselves and recipients of the same pranks from their elders that they dispensed on him. A good laugh always came at someone else's expense, it was the way of the yard. You lived or died by your wits as part of an unruly brotherhood. The new lads always got fucked around with; for generations this was considered the making of a man.

The first six months he worked directly for Harry, hands on. As they built a respectful rapport between Apprentice and Master Craftsman, he felt for the first time as close as he could remember to something that resembled a father.

"It's all in the wrist and in the ears, Billy boy, treat each wheel like a lover, touch her gently with your hammer and listen to her sing or weep back to you, like this." Billy watched Harry touch the hammer to the large cast iron wheel as it rang out with a clear metallic *ping*. "Tha's n'goodun," Harry said as he placed his hand on the axle box. "Make sure her juices are full and don't let her get too hot, grease her up, nice and slippery."

He slopped a large paddle into a bucket of axle grease and flicked it playfully. "I'll need two left-handed screwdrivers and a pint of tartan paint for the Flying Scotsman, due in today for repair, Billy boy."

"What clan colors would you like sir?" Billy quipped back.

"Get the fuck out of here, you're just a smart arse," Harry offered with a playful kick to Billy's backside. Grinning, Billy moved quickly out of Harry's reach.

At breakfast the day after finding the money, Billy had told his Mam a simplified version of the previous day's events. She was particularly happy about his promotion and told him how proud she was. She agreed the reward would come in handy after he also told her he wanted to marry Meg.

"We will have Meg over for dinner tonight and you can share the news." She cupped his face and gave him a big kiss on the forehead. "We can also think about you both being ready for marriage."

At work that day, Billy thought the day couldn't go fast enough as he worked on a train boogie with Taffy Smith, a big Welsh tapper. As he worked, he caught a flash of color from the corner of his eye, something tucked up in between the wheel casing and the carriage; a postcard. He twisted it loose under the watchful eye of Taffy. Palm trees stared back at him from the card in his dirty hand. His greasy thumb slid across the once shiny surface of the card.

Greetings from Florida, USA.

"What's thou got there, lad?" Smith asked between lips that held the stub of a hand-rolled fag butt.

Billy stared at the card, transfixed. "A postcard with a beach on it, must have blown up from the tracks."

"That's grand," Smith said of the image on the card and ran his battered finger over the blue sea and white sands. "Another planet," he whispered.

"You ever been somewhere like that Taffy?" Billy asked.

"Me! Bloody hell no, lad. I did go to Blackpool once after the war, on leave. Woke up on the beach in a pile of puke. Grand it was, although I can't remember much else about it."

Billy slapped Smith on the back, slid the postcard into the inside jacket pocket of his overalls, and got on with the work at hand.

That evening when Billy came home, he hung his heavy work jacket to dry near the kitchen and pulled the postcard from the pocket. He took it upstairs to his room. Alone, he lay on his bed, turning the card over and over as he tried to decipher faded writing that had run in streaks down the back. The words held just enough ink in the scratches of the fountain pen that must have been used to write it. He traced the elegant writing with his dirty fingernail.

My Dearest Eugene,

The journey by ship was indeed fantastic and most stimulating.

We dined at the Captain's table twice and danced each night until Mama sent us to bed at midnight. Mama and I are to buy bathing costumes tomorrow, as we will be going to the beach you see on the front of this card, we will bring you home some sand.

Love, Stephanie

He sniffed at the card, almost hoping to catch the sea air, expecting sand to brush his face. Never had anything in his life looked so good, so clean, blue and warm even on a grubby postcard.

"Eugene, Stephanie," he whispered. Such posh names, sophisticated, it felt exciting and unusual even to say them. Absentmindedly he'd been biting at the grime beneath his fingernails. *One day*, he promised himself, *one Day, my Meg and I will go somewhere just like this postcard.*

"Billy, Billy, Meg is here, are you washed up?" he heard Mam shout up the stairs. "She's come to hear your news, and dinner's ready."

"Fifty pounds!" Meg raged, as she pushed her dinner plate of stewed sausage away from her across the table. Mam sat quietly.

"Fifty pounds for finding five million bloody pounds? We could've been rich!" She scraped her chair back, stood up, and paced the room back and forth.

"And in jail," Billy added.

"I would have waited for you as long as needed if we could've kept more than just fifty bloody pounds."

He watched Meg spending the money in her mind as she waltzed around the room in imaginary furs and silk stockings, forgiving her instantly as he imagined her bejeweled and beautiful.

"We could have been married in style." She sat back down; eyes filled with tears.

"It'll be all right—they gave me a promotion and four pounds a week after finding the money, for excellent service, they said. Harry said he was proud of me. Fifty pounds is almost a quarter of a year's wages if you look at it like that."

Meg slumped in the chair. "Let's do the dishes. Then you can walk me home."

They stopped at a playground behind the Catholic school at the end of the terrace block. They sat on the swings and Billy sparked his boots on the tarmac as he swung.

"Have you ever fancied going to America, Meg?"

"America? That's awfully far away Billy. Why bother anyway? It takes ages to get there, costs a fortune, and you would never get that much time off work anyway. Besides, what would we do there?"

He knew the answer without thinking,

"Go to the beach. A beach with white sand and blue oceans, and big green palm trees. We'd lie in the sun and bake like berries." He gazed at the ground, his hands on the cold iron chains of the swing. "We could go out West and see the Grand Canyon."

"Oh, I don't know. We could go to Brighton if it's the beach you want, Stobs Quarry in Uppermill is a big hole in the ground if you need to see one. We would need to get a house first and be settled, you know, just in case," Meg said.

"In case of what?"

"Now that we're to be married, I'd either have a job or just look after the baby, although the thought of that scares me. I'm not sure I'm ready to just stay at home, but I'll not live in some hole in the wall. You will get promoted and work in the office as a clerk, and maybe you'll be a yard foreman one day. I mean, don't you want to be more than just a tapper and have nice things like I told you?" Meg grew quiet, then added, "I'm sorry about being ungrateful for the reward and your promotion. I'm very proud of you my love—will you forgive me; will you still marry me like you promised?"

Billy laughed and took her in his arms. "As if that were ever a question, although you might have to be a little gentler with me."

They linked arms and walked home. Meg kissed him at the back door to her parent's shop just before her mother shouted from an upper window that it was too late for a school night and nice girls don't linger in dark doorways with young men.

"Too late," she whispered into Billy's ear and giggled. He left her reluctantly, relishing the smell of her on his jacket and the taste of her on his lips as he made his way home. He so wanted to see the world beyond the streets of Diggle, and he wanted to share that journey with Meg, but for the first time he felt a little unsure about Meg—about what *she* wanted. He was glad he hadn't told her about the other money. For now.

He trusted it was right to approach money matters with no rush, no changes, keep it all the same; little men seldom made it big around here and certainly not without someone feeling that you might need a lesson if you stuck your head out of the bucket too far. He knew this better than anyone and resolved to keep everything just the same for now. Funny how a bit of luck could change so much, he thought; how money could be a catalyst for emotions one never imagined existed.

Doubt was a sneaky bugger that skulked just around the corner of contentment. On his walk home, he imagined his own Meg dancing on a beach in a new pink bathing suit with tiny lime colored flowers on it and a plastic bathing cap to match. He imagined her dancing through the waves, salty water splashing up her legs, with little droplets reflecting in the sunshine on her thighs.

Chapter 6

Stealth

Almost a month after hiding the money in the sump at the end of the tunnel, and once the excitement of the incident died down, Billy brought a small knapsack to work. The knapsack had been part of his father's army webbing, and he began using it to bring his sandwiches and soup flask to work so people would get used to seeing him walking with it. Day after day when he worked near the tunnel, he used it to take home a few bundles of the money at a time.

The money he'd stolen was slated for destruction, but still usable according to the DCI. Still, Billy wanted to test it. He went to see Jacky the Hound, the local dog racing bookie. As Jacky took the bet, Billy said he was using a fiver his dad left him, and that it might be a bit dodgy as Dad had socked it away after the war.

"Money is money," said Jacky. "You can lay a bet with me any time," he added, fingering the note. "The Bank of England withdrew all notes ten pounds and up in 1945 and the White-Fiver was the largest currency available, but I was still a little sprog back then. The release of the new Blue Pound came later that year and, even so, they say the White-Fiver will probably stay in circulation until 1961."

Billy couldn't take that chance. He realized he probably had only six months or so to launder the money before the new currency became prevalent.

The tunnel stood empty now, and the presence of the rail car was a ghost in Billy's mind. He wished it was still there, pressing against his back, hiding him as he scraped back the gravel and pried opened the grate to the sump.

The rats had returned, and Billy was dismayed to see that the one side of his jumper was eaten through, leaving little-chewed remnants of money strewn on the floor of the sump. Thankfully the damage was minimal, and the rats only feasted on a couple of hundred pounds. The nibbled and urine-stained edges would pass even better in the pub as everyone knew about the reward and weren't shy about helping him spend it.

"A bloody rich feed you hairy buggers," Billy cursed as he spun the beam of his torch down the tunnel, picking out the red dots of a hundred eyeballs staring back.

He planned to speed up the 'transfer of funds,' as he now liked to call it.

"Would you like to transfer five thousand pounds, sir?" Billy mocked in his best posh English banker's accent.

"Why of course my good man," he answered in his thick northern brogue.

"Bank of England, sir?" his English teller asked.

"Bloody no, lad, the Bank of Mam's house, under the stairs for now, and make it snappy."

His safe haven was Mam's coal cellar, the place he used to go when the bullying got too much. The cellar was his sanctuary to dream, and with the little money Mam and Dad made between them, there was never much coal in there anyway. He had fashioned a small room for himself as a boy, digging in behind the cellar wall. His original intent was a tunnel to Australia to find his dad, but after the letter arrived it became a mission center, like Winston Churchill's War Room under the city of London where they strategized the defeat of the Germans. This was where Billy planned his adventures. He posted a map of the world on a wall, surrounded by pictures of exotic lands torn from National Geographic pages, and from the local newspaper whenever they posted an advertisement for many of the emerging "Rock and Roll" bands—Chuck Berry, Bill Haley, and the Comets, but mainly the new, fresh face of Elvis Presley. Billy heard "Heartbreak Hotel" by Elvis on the radio just once and was mesmerized by this white man who sounded like a black man and who by all accounts wriggled when he sang. He would do anything to see Elvis live. In America.

"Der Bunker" was what Billy liked to call the coal room and it had every comfort—an old car seat that filled the small room with the smell of damp leather, a Tilley lamp he saved for and bought at the Gypsy market, and two old biscuit tins. One was his father's old tin where he kept his most precious possessions, and the second tin held emergency supplies—a tin of Lion's syrup, a small paper bag of digestive biscuits, a jar of Bovril, and a can of tomato soup.

He never told Meg about Der Bunker; Mam knew, but was sworn to secrecy, even if the Germans tortured her should they ever end up in another war. Mam understood that boys build secret forts and dens, and she also understood he didn't have typical friends to share secret hideouts or tree houses in the woods. She said whatever he was doing in the bunker was just where she'd rather have him. Now that he was grown, she took some interest that he seemed to be spending more time down there than usual.

"Billy, love, you're a workingman and no longer a boy. You can use the front room if you need space to yourself," she offered.

"It's okay, Mam. Der bunker is best for the reading and studying I need to do if I'm ever to advance from a Tapper to a clerk in the front office. Big Harry suggested it after giving me the promotion, and even said he was willing to recommend me if I studied."

Billy formed a small recess at the back of the bunker, digging deeper into the earth where he fashioned a rat-proof, watertight box to hold his money from scraps of steel he took from the yard. He covered the door to the hidey-hole with a mixture of earth and wallpaper paste so it blended perfectly with the dirt around it. He had the idea from watching a wartime escape film where prisoners of war had dug tunnels below the camp barracks and built such panels to hide the entry hole. If the tunnel were exposed, then the escape hatch dug by the POW's would look like soil under the stove in the camp mess hut.

Once he had a safe hiding place for all the money, he took time to look at it more closely—and figure out what to do with it. First, he recounted it, then separated out the five-pound bundles from the few ten- and twenty-pound bundles he'd taken in haste; as Jacky had said, they were out of circulation. He shredded them and burned them in a coffee can. There was an opulence in burning something he and Mam had had so little of for so long.

He pulled out the big white note Dad had given him. from his treasure tin. Every aspect of that note was perfect and comparable to the notes in the bundles he looked at. All the stolen cash looked and felt used, and each note had a different serial number on it yet looked identical in every other way—the large, black sweeping writing and font that promised to pay the bearer the sum of five pounds.

He now understood that DCI Williams hadn't told the lads the whole truth for obvious *top-secret* reasons—this was Bernhard counterfeit money that had made it back to England.

He pulled an old notebook from a shelf that held his *National Geographic* magazines and other adventure books and studied the plans he'd drafted out.

1. Go to America and see Elvis.
2. Marry Meg and have babies.
3. Buy a new coat for Mam with a fur collar and take her on holiday to the Grand Canyon.
4. Become a clerk and run the yard wearing a jacket and a clean shirt.
5. Buy a fleet of holiday busses.

On second thought, he moved marrying Meg to the top of the list, knowing it would have to happen now that he'd made a promise—and because he assumed her to be pregnant after their encounter. Still, he wanted her to be there when he saw the King in real life.

As part of this new plan, Billy decided he needed a name, a stage name, like the Big Bopper or like the young upstart messenger from Liverpool he'd met in a British Rail training class who called himself Ringo Starr and was a member of the Eddy Clayton skiffle group. He needed an American alter ego who could be all the things Billy McTaggart, Tapper from Diggle, was not.

A few days later, after Sunday lunch, he sat on the toilet in the outhouse at the back door of the kitchen staring at his sinewy, white, hairless thighs. He needed some cool name, something befitting an international man of mystery. He imagined shaking hands with Elvis.

"Nice to meet you, Mr. McTaggart, Uh, Uh, very nice man," he said curling his lip. It didn't roll out well in his attempt at a southern drawl "Misa Motaget" the last thing he wanted the King thinking was that he was a character from Kipling's *Jungle Book*. The label on his jeans crumpled between his feet and caught his eye—Levi Strauss. His mother bought them from a church fair, used clothes sent over from America by the Red Cross. She'd fought with another woman who also wanted to buy them, because she knew Billy loved all things American and she had to have the jeans for him.

"Levi," he said, thinking aloud, "kinda Jewish and rich." He did have, after all, dark hair and pale skin like the orthodox lads down at the synagogue next to the pub. Staring at the triangular stitching of the gusset below the zipper he expanded his thought looking for a surname. "Levi Gusset!" he said, trying it out in his best American accent, "No! Zipper! No! Blue! No! Indigo! Levi Indigo!" That sounded classy and international.

He wiped his backside and pulled up his underpants and jeans, kicked the outhouse door open and stepped out boldly.

"Levi Indigo has arrived," he shouted in his best Elvis impersonation as he swung his hips and flopped his hair with one hand.

He noticed the old woman next door turning away from her laundry to see what all the noise was about, and Billy hunched his shoulders and loped off, red-faced.

"Nosy old bat" he mumbled, just out of earshot, as he entered the coal bunker chute that went down to the cellar and his stash.

He slid out eight five-pound notes, each from a different stack of money—never more than two notes from the same batch was his rule. It was his day off, though he told Meg he'd be working overtime to make up the difference needed to afford the wedding reception, and the engagement ring and wedding band they'd picked out together a few weeks earlier in the Uppermill jewelry store.

"One ticket, please, return to Manchester, third class, Marge," he asked at the ticket window, recognizing Marge Piper whose son Ralph had just started as a clerk in the front office. "How's young Ralph doing?" he asked, knowing he might be working with Ralph soon if his exams went well.

"Ooo, he's doing grand, he's a wonder to us, that boy," Marge said. "Grand, I say, in his pressed white shirt, dark suit and polished shoes, no shunting for him like his dad, thank God."

Billy nodded and didn't hold Marge's pride against her. His own Mam would do the same, given half a chance to be proud of him.

The rhythmic click-clack of the train wheels on the track soothed his apprehension for the first stage of his plans. Dress like the man you want to be, his Granddad had said, and he intended to do just so. "A man's a man for a that and 'a that Billy, remember yourself and you'll not forget yourself. Not like that bastard of a father you had in my son, and dress like the man you want to be, for the world will recognize you for what you make of yourself."

Billy watched the countryside change from green fields to grey stone buildings and work yards teeming with workers in dull clothing going about their menial work, blending into the scenery like spilled paint as the train sped by. The train slowed as it approached the Manchester Victoria Station and suddenly came to a stop, Billy watched the first-class passengers disembark and noticed the men in their suits with polished shoes and beautiful leather briefcases. They all looked like DCI Williams.

This shopping trip was the first real step he would take outside the insular world of Diggle, where he thought it best not to spend any of the money. He had to be cautious in Diggle, even after receiving his reward—people knew money didn't grow on trees around the village.

In the first shop he came to, not far from the station, a young assistant appeared through the curtain behind the counter at the ring of the doorbell, which a spring released as the door opened. Billy looked around the paneled store that smelled of heavy tweeds and refined leather.

"Good morning...sir," the assistant said as he eyed Billy up and down, "how may I help you?"

"I need something special," he said in his best American accent. "A sports coat, reversible, dark gray with a pinstripe on the one side, four buttons, and on the reverse, the inside, I want something Western. Fishtail cuffs, velvet collar, double darts in the back and fabric with a little shimmer to it. Do you have a red silk handkerchief as well?"

Billy caught his breath and stood there nervously. He'd thought this through; he had a plan to dress himself and Levi Indigo literally at the flip of his jacket. It had seemed a brilliant plot while seated in the outhouse, but now he felt unsure. Judging by the look on the shop assistant's face, he may have just made a fool of himself.

"Yes, most unusual, two for one it sounds like." The young assistant looked at Billy and tightened his lips. "Unfortunately, we can tailor to any requirement a *gentleman*, may have." He drew out his words in mockery of his customer. "Where are you from, sir?" He pointedly stared at Billy's working man's boots and coarse trousers.

"Sparkle. Sparkle, California, near Walnut Creek. We call it a mobile home park but, funny, it never moves," Levi said, trying to sound funny. "I'm here on my working vacation for the next few weeks."

"Of course, you are, Sir. Will you need a shirt and tie to go with your reversible jacket, Kemosabe?"

Billy ordered three shirts and a slim Jim black tie with a tie stud that kept the tie attached to his shirt with a thin gold chain.

Billy never considered the assistant could spot a working lad from the countryside a mile away, and the American accent was straight out of the *Lone Ranger*.

The assistant leaned forward and beckoned to Billy with a fleshy, clean-nailed finger to step a little closer. Billy thought the young man must have had a hard time understanding an American accent. In the lowest of whispers, which Billy had to lean in even closer to hear, the assistant quietly said, "Bugger off, you little twat. Get out of this shop and don't come back in here again stinking of grime and grit. We are a gentleman's prerogative here."

Billy stumbled from the shop with the help of a hard push on his back and the door slammed shut behind him. He walked swiftly away before he caught his breath, finding himself outside another shop window where he saw his reflection. Flat cap, ill-fitting, jacket and coarse trousers hemmed with work boots—the only shoes he possessed. Beneath his flat cap, his hair was tightly cropped up the sides with a heavy flop of hair on top, greasy and unkempt. He laughed out loud and startled a passerby. *Of course, of course,* he thought, *dress like the man everyone thinks you are!*

At the next tailor shop, he set about his request a little differently. He first looked through the window, breathing steamy patches on the glass as he spied a small older man, grey-haired and well-dressed, behind the counter.

He slid into the shop and introduced himself as a bridegroom in need of help. The gent introduced himself as Levi Goldberg and offered to shake Billy's hand, blessedly before Billy could blurt out his chosen name.

"Of course, my boy," Mr. Goldberg said after Billy repeated his unusual selection of clothing.

"Can you also please give me two pairs of black stovepipe trousers, a pair of winkle-picker boots, slip on, none of that lace up like these old boots?" They both laughed, and Mr. Goldberg asked Billy to step into the fitting room.

After fitting for the jacket, Mr. Goldberg rang up his bill. "That will be twenty-six pounds. How will you be paying, sir?" Billy handed over fifteen pounds.

"Take thirteen pounds off this, and I'll take the change. I'll pay the balance when I come and pick up my order, if that's okay.

"Of course, it is, my boy. I see a young man coming up in the world, and he will need a tailor to accompany him on his journey. Cash is always the currency of kings for me. Your order will be ready in two weeks."

Billy walked down the street feeling rather proud of himself. Mr. Goldberg was more than helpful, and Billy couldn't wait to come back and pick up his order in time for the new year's party at the Diggle Rail Yard Social Club. No one would question his new clothes after his recent windfall.

Ring shopping was next on his list. The main road had many jewelry stores to choose from. He spent half an hour window shopping, using the same technique of gazing through shop fronts to assess the right shop to visit. Meg agreed that he should choose the rings and surprise her, although she was quite clear on her expectations when they saw rings she liked in the Diggle jeweler's shop. She emphasized the importance of being able to show her ring to the girls at the New Year's party, if he could have it by then, of course after a formal proposal declared from one knee.

Billy liked the matched sets he saw in one of the shop windows, and upon inquiring with a well put-together and helpful shop girl, he found a lovely set that included an engagement ring and a wedding band, with a groom's band for himself. The engagement ring was a cluster of real diamonds atop a ruby band set in white gold, very posh and undoubtedly substantial enough he thought; an upgrade to Meg's expectations.

He handed over another fifteen pounds, leaving twelve pounds as a deposit, and slipped the change of three pounds back into his pocket. He would do the same when the balance was due once the rings were sized. He had brought along a twist of electrical wire he'd used to measure Meg's finger the night before. He noticed his hand as he offered it to the assistant, grubby and beaten when he placed it on the counter for measurement.

He walked briskly to the station feeling rather proud of himself, exuding an air of confidence he had seldom felt. Laundry done, he thought as the real money no one could question lay in his pocket.

For the next few weeks leading up to Christmas his newfound confidence was evident in everything he did. He managed every penny to the total of his fifty-pound reward, the wedding deposit money to Mam, the Christmas presents, his new clothes and jackets, and the booking of the reception. No one could wonder where the money had come from, least of all Meg. She kept her own journal of expenses, just to make sure Billy watched their cash. In every transaction he always paid enough to get change, and every real pound went in a separate cocoa tin in the bunker hidey-hole.

The last thing he did was confront Meg's parents and ask for their daughter's hand. He knew they disapproved and were set against the union, but he was bound to ask. They told him they disapproved but had no say as to how their daughter's mind was set. All they could do was refuse to contribute to the wedding. Billy thanked them and hoped they might come to see him as a part of their family in time.

Two weeks later, the last day of the year, he picked up the three rings as promised, followed by a visit to the tailor. As he slipped into his new jacket and stood looking at himself in the mirror of the dressing room, he knew it was going to be one hell of a year ahead.

"You come back and see me when you're ready for a new suit, tailored one hundred percent. That is the mark of a fine man, a well-tailored suit, and I can see you're such a man, my boy, you look fine. I asked my wife for a little of her special soap, for your hands. Polished shoes and clean hands are a sign of your beginnings, if you will excuse my manners."

Mr. Goldberg slid the soap wrapped in wax paper into the bag. "A journey, as I said, and we are on it together. Good luck, my boy."

Billy felt overcome for a moment. He awkwardly reached out to shake Mr. Goldberg by the hand, and the old man stepped forward and hugged him instead. "I never had a son, so you go and make me feel proud when you marry your girl."

Billy thanked the tailor again and left the store with a lump in his throat. He'd never realized a man could be capable of sharing affection, or admiration for that matter. The hug stayed with him all the way home as the train slid from the grey city back to the green countryside.

At the party later that night, Billy sat next to Meg in the corner of the room, chairs against the wall, leaving space for the dancers in the center of the room. He noticed the single boys who sat on the left side of the room and the group of single girls hovering around the drinks table with little glasses and napkins in their hands, making small talk and eyeing the boys in sideward glances. A few of the younger girls sat near the door, wishing they'd be asked to dance before the stroke of midnight—then there would be someone to kiss. The band played rock and roll, Little Richard or Chubby Checker, and occasionally something sweet, like Max Bygraves singing "Heart of my Heart," or Nat King Cole, one of Mam's favorite singers. Relatives and grandparents milled between the kitchen and the food table, drinking and occasionally venturing onto the dance floor during something slower and familiar. Mam served tea and cake behind the safety of the counter, even as many of the men asked her to dance. Billy knew by the look on her face that she could never imagine someone taking her hand or holding her, especially at New Years as the prospect of another year without Dad loomed.

"You look quite dapper in that jacket and tie, my love," Meg smiled and kissed him, "I might be the luckiest girl in the place. Why do you look a little glum?"

Billy shifted awkwardly on his seat, looking for some excuse to delay his proposal. His nerves were shot.

"I miss my Scottish grannie's New Year's parties," Billy mumbled to Meg, with a mouth full of egg sandwich. "We would dance, but we always sang first and last. We started with highland reels, the classics, everyone knew the words. The road and the miles to Dundee, the Sky Song, then the dancing would start an hour before midnight."

He closed his eyes and let a small smile cross his face. "Auld Lang Syne would take us at least half an hour past midnight after all the kissing and well wishing, and the first foot, of course. First foot was the first visitor after midnight to enter the house with a fish, a dram or two of whiskey, and a lump of coal for prosperity the next year through. A drunk relative in a kilt if you were lucky, or even better a visiting piper. Uncle Tam normally fitted the bill as he was tall, dark, and handsome and had played the pipes until he lost three fingers between two colliding coal trucks just after the war. He always joked at not needing his trigger finger anymore. 'Just the one would do for Aunt Lil and her itch,' he would bellow aloud in his excellent tenor voice, warming up for his song."

Billy gazed at the dancers now filling the floor of the hall, wishing the crowd would open up and Aunt Lil would step out into the glitter of a million reflecting lights swirling around the wall and floor from the mirrored ball that hung in the middle of the ceiling.

"Aunt Lil would get the singing going once uncle Tam made the rounds, and Granny would stand at the window resting on the heater, keeping time with her tapping feet and Parkinson hands."

"Did everyone sing?"

"Of course, they did. That was the beauty of it. Everyone had a particular song, and they'd find their place in the sequence of it all and start-up solo with the first verse and chorus, then everyone joined in the next verse followed by a raucous chorus. It was mad, brilliant, and everyone knew who sang which song and never upstaged each other even if they were crap!" They both laughed.

"What was your song, Billy?" Meg asked.

"I was too young. We played spin the bottle in the hallway with the cousins and stole shots of some yellow Dutch liquor from Grannie's cupboard in her bedroom. We would watch from the door or peek in through the frosty window over my Granny's shoulder, depending on how cold it was outside or how deep the snow was." He smiled and took Meg's hand as he reminisced of a time when all was as it should be, mummies, daddies, and families creating memories that should last a lifetime.

"What happened, love? When was the last time you went there?"

"We never went back after Dad left. I never got to sing. I never had a song."

Meg pulled her chair closer to him. "What would your song have been?"

He didn't hesitate. "*A Red Red Rose* by Robert Burns for my traditional song. *When I Fall in Love* by Nat King Cole for the contemporary, you know the one they played earlier tonight, the one I would want at our wedding."

Meg smiled and cuddled into the boy who tapped the wheels of big iron trains for a living and touched her heart in revealing moments like this. He looked at Meg and knew she was perfect for him; she would nurture him, protect him, fight for him, and guide him. In this way, they would break free of the working-class life into which they'd been born. Her little flurry over the fifty pounds was just the side of her that came through when her wants were more than her needs. In a way he liked that it pushed him to try a little harder and work a little smarter. He knew she had their best interests at heart.

She had told him honestly that she thought he was an over-looked soul, and he surprised people most days with his good nature and the words of curiosity that fell from his mouth, placing him in harm's way. He needed to be cautious. He might be small, but he was brilliant, and nobody around Diggle liked a smart arse in their face.

"Dance with me, my love," Meg asked. "It's almost mid-night. Sing me your song as we move around this room, sing to me. I am your family, and I will join in after the first verse if you want me to. Mind you it needs to be a song we both know, even if we are crap!"

He smiled, "You're a smasher. Let's sweep the floor clean, cut a rug." He pulled her to an open space on the floor, and they wrapped themselves tightly together. Billy whispered, a little off key, "When I fall in love, it will be forever." Meg smiled and nuzzled into his neck when the clock struck midnight.

"Happy New Year, my love," she shouted above the din of celebration as the two stood amid the revelry, their own family singing their own song of past, present, and future together.

He pulled Meg to the side of the dance floor and sat her down at one of the small cocktail tables around the edge of the room. He pulled a little burgundy leather box from the pocket of his new jacket and opened it as he knelt in front of her.

"Marry me," he said.

Meg squealed and shouted, "Of course, you're such a silly boy. I knew tonight was the night. My nerves are on edge I thought you'd forgotten about it and I was about to ask you." She squealed again, "Who can I show my ring to?"

He watched Meg run first to his Mam, who smiled and looked over at him as she put her hand on her heart and blew him a kiss across the room. He could see the tears well in her eyes and a lump caught in his throat. Meg stood radiant in a circle of girls with her hand extended, proud as could be.

While walking home in the early morning, he told Meg he was on a shortlist for promotion to clerk. Harry Two Bellies had put his name forward for a position in the front office, as promised. As a journeyman, he also passed the qualifying exams and could start off part-time in the station ticket office. The rest of the time he would work as a wages clerk and support payroll and procurement for the Station Master. He would wear a suit, a white shirt and a tie; no more boots to spark, and he was fine with that.

Meg stopped him dead in his tracks, she stood in front of him and, as short as he was, she needed to go up on her tiptoes to kiss him.

"I'm so proud of you, Billy McTaggart. Our baby will have everything it needs, including you, the best husband and daddy in the world." Meg looked at her engagement ring and kissed him again. "One month to go and I will be Mrs. Billy McTaggart, with my own home and a baby on the way. Perfect!"

Chapter 7

Sons

DCI Williams sat at his large, walnut desk, and looked at the binders before him. Billy McTaggart, the son, and James McTaggart, the father—the coincidence was absurd beyond belief. Emotions surfaced from a grave he thought well dug and covered half a lifetime ago.

He poured a sizeable brandy into a snifter and closed his eyes. Memories still raw in their vividness played over the back of his eyelids as the heat of the brandy burned down his throat.

He remembered with fond delight the flashes of strong thighs and knitted socks sullied by weeks on the road campaigning—a rowdy bunch of soldiers dancing in a crowded room, wild-skirted men now sodden, in and out with beer and cheap whiskey, a ragtag array of fiery lads testing themselves and everyone around them in this slum bar in the center of Cairo.

He'd been there in that dank, piss-sodden Egyptian bar, but not by choice. His attendance was a form of reconnaissance, a fascination with human nature and a direct order from the Home Office. "What they do, why they do it and how they do it is the key, man. Leverage whatever makes the bloody savages work and double the ration of booze for the night. It gets them stirred up and ready for the fight," his Brigadier said as he handed him the beige folio stamped in bold red letters as classified.

There were whoops and yelps of delight as the Highland Dervishes twirled, clinging trancelike to the music of the straining bagpipes and a battered fiddle that had accompanied the regiment over land and sea, the only remnants of a home they carried wherever they went, save some photographs of sullen wives and hungry children. Sensibility aside, Captain Williams admired their passion and bravery. The folio contained no shortage of heroics and displays of camaraderie among its reports, and these men spared nothing or no one in the name of the regiment. It was not his first encounter with the motley crew. The first time he learned of them he'd laughed at the thought of grown men traversing through the desert wearing skirts.

As a minister's son, he'd lived a somewhat sheltered life in a small Welsh village of Brecon where he attended the school where is father taught, Christ College Boarding School for Boys. The school was founded by royal charter in 1541 by Henry VIII and had a dining hall that dated from the 13th century when a Dominican Priory had occupied the grounds. To this place the better families of England sent their troublesome sons for education and straightening out, far from the gentrified society where the rigors of a brisk education and an active life would allow for a release of their boisterous and entitled nature. Christ College coupled adequate training with physical exertion to curb their ardor, and a sound beating if need be. He'd schooled with better boys whose parents owned coal mines and farms and had found a fragile acceptance as the schoolmaster's son; like his betters, he would never have to go down the coal pits, plow fields, or weave a loom. He was guided by a thin but common thread woven between and above the working classes who were never expected to aspire to the school motto, "Possunt Quia Posse Videntur"—*"They achieve because they think they can achieve."*

DCI Williams was a Special Branch police officer now, but he had been Captain Williams, Intelligence Officer in his army days and, back in his youth, was called Timothy Williams or Timid Will by his peers. He hated the name, but in truth he was quiet and studious by comparison to the rambunctious privileged classmates with whom he shared school and a dormitory. He read history voraciously and had discovered, much to his displeasure, that the Scotts couldn't have done more to antagonize the English for hundreds of years. Even through officer training Will had never seen a real Scotsman other than pictures in the Encyclopedia Britannica collection that had lined the walls of his father's library or the regimental gallery of the training school. He had relished the joy of pulling each substantial volume from its slot amid consecutive, identical, leather-bound books, differentiated only by the deeply embossed gold leaf letters and ridged roman numerals that identified their contents. The regimented fashion of their order and selection appealed to him, lined like soldiers on parade, gateways to the world outside the walls of the school, a controlled dispensing of knowledge accessible should his father permit him to enter the library. The books were an inspiration for an administrative military career, a natural progression to cautious adventure against the wishes of his father, who wanted him to join the priesthood as a servant of the Lord.

"If it's officer training he wants, then that's what he'll get," his father had bellowed to his frail wife. "I've schooled him, fed him and now, by God, I will dispose of him. The church is too good for the likes of him. He can burn in hell for all I care."

Timid Will had listened as he stood disgraced, his father becoming purple-faced and unhinged as he ranted his regret for his son. He understood his father's disappointment at finding him naked and entwined with several other pink, squirming adolescent boys in the small Spartan bedroom above the vicarage adjacent to his school dorm.

Timid Will said nothing as his father begged that the Lord might steel his son against his desires and, if not, then his advice was to keep the perversity hidden and under control. Timid Will was dispatched to the Royal Military Academy and a life under a new motto, "Vires Aquirit Eundo"—"It gains strength as it goes."

Upon first hearing the bagpipes of the regiment emanating from the encampment, Captain Williams held his ears and shouted through the noise to his sergeant, "What in God's name is that noise?"

"The pipes, sir, the bagpipes and the Long-Range Desert Group, or LRDG as we call them here, heading out on a night mission. Three hundred and fifty misfits from New Zealand, Southern Rhodesian, and British forces. A lot of wild Scots, Black Watch and Argyle and Southern Highlanders, formed as volunteers to carry out deep penetration, covert reconnaissance patrols and intelligence missions from behind Italian lines. They're experts in desert navigation, sir, and that man leading them is Jim McTaggart, previously of the 1st Battalion of the Argyle and Southern Highlanders who came here for the Western Desert Campaign with the rest of us. Although they're not all in the Black Watch, they still call him and his lads the 'ladies from hell' on account of him and a few of the other lads wearing their kilts in combat, sir."

Captain Williams watched the stone-faced troop march stoically through the camp and out into the desert where their custom, lightweight Canadian Chevrolet WB 30 CWT 4x2 truck, mounted with .50 caliber Browning AN/M2 heavy machine guns among other salvaged or acquired armaments, were lined up. Their voices carried a song of war that made the hair stand on the back of his neck. He imagined them stealthy in the barren Libyan desert, taking no prisoners, guns blazing, glowing cherry red at the tip of the muzzle changing to deep orange and then gunmetal blue as it cooled. Jim was evident as a leader by the set of his Tam O'Shanter hat with its blacked-out insignia and his effortless direction as the pack of renegade soldiers maneuvered comfortably around him in quiet respect where each man was capable of leadership. These were men of few words, hardened by action and forged in war and the Highland slums from which they came. Men like Timid Will aspired to be, but never would.

"Best you come back into the officer's mess, Sir. Best not to mingle unnecessarily. They are heathens and no ladies, I assure you." The sergeant brought over a large gin and tonic, and Williams stepped back into the shade of the tent and watched the sun slowly begin to set.

The next morning, Captain Williams requested that Sergeant McTaggart present himself. He wanted to evaluate him for Special Operations. As the desert campaign drew to an end, they had other issues to deal with in the ongoing theater of war. Fingering the folio before him, he flipped the pages until he saw an image that bore the insignia of the Long-Range Desert Group, a scorpion within a wheel with the motto *Non Vi Sed Arte (Not by Strength by Guile)*. This moto was indeed a qualification for the job at hand. On the opposite page was a crisp new letter from the ministry of the war office and David Stirling informing him of the new group he'd be part of as L Detachment, Special Air Services, and the mission to be undertaken in total secrecy. The SAS had a newly minted insignia, simply a shield with a winged dagger, and the motto of *Who Dares Wins*. The lack of Latin showed a turning of the tide toward the common man, of which Captain Williams still felt unsure. The SAS had been conceived as a commando force to operate behind enemy lines in the North African war and would initially consist of five officers and sixty other ranks. He knew their mission would take them further afield.

"Big Jim," he thought as he watched the man approach the officer's tent in a direct line across the dusty parade ground. Jim strolled through a small herd of goats that frequented the sparse green square of grass surrounding the flagpole. Dark eyes and a mop of jet-black hair that hung over his left eye, a freshly shaven jawline glinted a blue shadow—Sargent McTaggart was much smaller than Captain Williams expected when he stood up to receive him and they exchange salutes. Desiring a rapport with this man, Williams broke protocol, extended his hand, and stared into the Sergeant's ice-cold blue eyes.

"Sergeant McTaggart, sir, reporting as requested, sir!"

Williams invited the Sergeant to sit and give an account of the previous night's raid, taking every opportunity to capture the nuances and attention to detail the Sergeant conveyed. He admired the rare and unexpected intelligence behind those eyes, and the physical presence that spoke to a quiet propensity for violence as needed, as a means to an end.

"I need a man who can move fast, act if need be. A man who is trustworthy where greed and temptation may be an issue," Williams offered as the debriefing ended and he flipped through the folio in front of him. Captain Williams anticipated that McTaggart, if he was worth his salt, could make out his photograph and some of his men next to a top-secret stamp in blood red, and the bold heading to the page that read 'Operation Bernhard' next to a seal for the Bank of England and a big white five-pound note.

"That would be no problem for me or any of my lads, Sir. We've all been around the mill a time or two in the past couple of years. As you know, we've seen action in Europe and North Africa, and most of us volunteered for this operation looking for the fight. We can get in and out of most situations, particularly where the Krauts or Italians are concerned—" Sargent McTaggart paused and then added cautiously, "You've seen how we handle ourselves after a few pints in the local from that chair in the corner you like."

The Captain took his observations into account and replied a little more formally now that they both knew where they stood. "If you would allow me to treat your lads to an evening at my expense. I'm sure a few thirsty men would drink to your leaving."

The evening, as usual, ended in melancholy, and the singing of Grannies Highland Home and Danny Boy, followed with a final punch-up as some Australian troopers preparing to ship out to Gallipoli broke in and tried to drown the throng out with Waltzing Matilda. Captain Williams slid quietly out the back of the bar, avoiding the fight, but was enthralled by a glimpse of Jim knocking one of the Aussi troopers out cold with one punch. The thrill of it set a buzzing off in the pit of his belly, and he felt a little giddy as he made his way back to the solitude of his tent.

"The Germans are making money. They are forging it, to be precise. Lots of it, we believe, and we need to get to it before they flood the world with it and devalue not only the British pound, but the US dollar too. Even worse, they're using the bloody stuff to fund their war effort."

He spoke as Sargent McTaggart stood, immaculate, in front of him the next morning and listened attentively. He was composed, clear-eyed with slick pomade holding his glistening hair. A slight smell of Woodbine cigarettes clung to him and resonated a masculine earthiness that Captain Williams found appealing, in a common way.

"That sounds like a big problem, sir. How are we to help?" Sargent McTaggart asked.

"We've known for some time that Bernhard's division assembled the best of the best Jewish forgers in camps around Europe and are using the money to fund war efforts with an ultimate plan to airdrop millions of pounds into Britain. We'd like to get to the source of the problem before the advancing Russians do. The Russians would make that money disappear to the four winds, and they'll make more if they get their hands on the presses and plates." He paused before handing the Sargent the large white five-pound note from the file. "Lots of these are good enough to fool our own Bank of England and a bunch of Swiss bankers. I need surveillance and intelligence collection from people who may be less than willing to part with their knowledge. I believe you're the man for the job. We depart first thing in the morning for basic commando training, then on to the front as soon as possible. Your men will go for advanced commando training and we'll call on them as, and when, they're needed."

Over the next several months of covert operations, Captain Williams found Jim McTaggart essential in extracting critical information as well as essential personnel who'd been captured into POW's camps. He was also skilled at convincing civilians who had some form of intelligence around the various counterfeiting operations of the Third Reich to share their knowledge. The war was drawing to a close and a sense of urgency overtook their mission as concentration camps became liberated and swathes of dazed Jewish prisoners of war spewed out. In their bleak camouflage of despair, they blended back into a ravaged world. The various places of production to which he and Sergeant McTaggart tracked the counterfeited money gave up little evidence, and any trace of actual money evaporated into pockets and trucks overnight. The remnants of the German war machine crumbled, making survivors and criminals of men, with little distinction between them.

Captain Williams received information that the hub of operations for Operation Bernhard was a camp called Sachsenhausen and that it was being moved to Redl-Zipf, an Austrian village about sixty miles South of Mauthausen. Intelligence told Captain Williams this camp was so secret it was identified only by the code name of Schlier. It had been a production line for the V2 rockets that plagued London in a bombing blitz. Now, with the Germans in full retreat, no further production of money was occurring—indeed, the Germans were trying frantically to burn or destroy millions of pounds.

Captain Williams shared his intelligence with Sargent McTaggart, including reports of trucks loaded with machines and currency leaving Redl-Zipf for Ebensee along refugee swamped roads across the mountain passes. On the early morning of May 22nd, 1945, the two men stood looking at an overturned truck that had plummeted down a ravine. In the truck were two dead German officers wearing civilian clothes over their uniforms and several skeletal prisoners in the now familiar striped pajamas. The back of the truck also held twenty-three coffin-shaped boxes of counterfeit five, ten, and twenty-pound notes, four crates of forged credentials, and associated stamps and dies.

"This is the tip of the iceberg," Captain Williams said to Sargent McTaggart as he stretched a map on the hood of their truck. "It's on to Redl-Zipf, though I think we missed our chance to catch the buggers after all."

Within a week, they managed to make their way back to Frankfurt and report to Brigadier Babington-Smith, head of the British currency section, and Mr. Phillip Reeves of the Bank of England, who then accompanied them to Freishing. In Freishing, all the found counterfeited notes and paraphernalia would be sent under armed guard to a nearby base and then on to London for safekeeping and eventual destruction. With increasing futility, they followed leads from one village to the next amid stories of crates of pound notes, suitcases of gold, and paintings and jewels amid the wealth stolen, hoarded, and killed for in the frantic chaos of emerging post-war Europe.

Over dinner one evening in a ramshackle boarding house on the outskirts of the village of Toplitz, the landlady spoke in her broken English about the Toplitzee lakes and the fact that the SS was known to have dumped their secrets, including stolen gold, into a mile-long lake flanked by perilous sheer cliffs. The lake was a safe harbor for their riches, all at the bottom of a lakebed as deep as Big Ben in London was tall. She got her information from high ranking SS officers she'd hosted in her boarding house until they had fled a week before the arrival of the Captain and Sergeant.

She also heard the SS officers discussing plans to return and recover the loot once the war had settled, at some time in the future.

"The world has ended, and we'll never be the same again," the landlady lamented. "Our innocence has been lost forever. You, our so-called liberators, you are but our new dictators. I am a survivor and have no choice but to share with you a bottle of my best brandy, but now used in solace, knowing the SS never did anything for me or my Fatherland."

She asked Captain Williams to help her pry open a floorboard where she had a bottle hidden. "I have nothing left; no sons, daughters, or husband, all used in some form of cannon fodder for Hitler and his dreams, my nightmare." She opened the dusty bottle with her teeth and placed it between them after pouring three full glasses. "May I ask you to join me? Good conversation and handsome men have been as scarce as bread these past few years." Her British guests knew her complements were a necessary yet futile tactic for survival, and so they drank.

The warmth of the brandy slid smoothly down the Captain's throat and put him at ease. He and Sargent McTaggart had executed their duty and pursued the Bernhard myth relentlessly, if to little avail. Captain Williams had counted bodies and the cost to nations and men alike in witness to the arrogance of the Bank of England, who wished to hide their folly at authenticating the forged money years earlier rather than admit to the depth of their incompetence and embarrassment. This endeavor had been unleashed around the world, effectively with their name all over it.

Captain Williams let the fire warm him as he bantered in a mixture of English, German, and French with the landlady. She had become amorous now, in a stupor of the strong drink, imagining his rank gave her an undeniable benefit she might leverage if she curried his favor. In truth, thought Captain Williams, Sargent McTaggart was the beauty in the room and, after several more glasses of brandy he felt emboldened to approach the quiet Scotsman. Their camaraderie and proximity over the past months had forged an easy if still guarded informality unusual among the ranks. With limited accountability to senior officers or a designated company, they maintained casual respect and an unspoken recognition of their obvious class distinction. They shared stories of their youth and families, and of their aspirations once the war was over and they were back home. Covert operations, necessary killing, and long hours driving and camping in close quarters allowed a physicality that was normal to men in war.

When the landlady eventually passed out, Captain Williams walked over to the Sargent who'd fallen asleep in a window seat near the fire and thought to cover him with a blanket taken from the knees of the landlady. Watching Jim sleep was delicious—the opportunity to watch him unguarded was rare. He traced the line of his jaw with his eyes and was tempted to push away the hair that hung over his white ear and sinewy neck. He watched the Sargent breathe in a restless sleep, eyes dancing in battle behind closed eyelids in fits and starts of remembrance. He could smell the musty uniform on clean skin scrubbed raw with carbolic soap—skin that had been bare as the man had bent over a bucket of ice water, stripped to the waist earlier that morning. Captain Williams had watched him in the courtyard of the inn, scraping his face clean-shaven with a dull razor. How he would love to bathe this man, lower him into hot, lavender-infused water, scented steam rising in a mist, he alone with the right to feast upon the ghost white, battle-hardened body of the Highlander.

Captain Williams found himself aroused and, in an instant of temptation, he reached out and placed the blanket on the Sargent, his hand resting wistfully for an instant on the sleeping man's chest. The captain's motion erupted in a twist of bodies and flashing steel. The specialized double-edged commando knife rose quickly to Captain Williams throat, and a glancing blow knocked him to the ground as the sergeant instinctively straddled him and pushed him into submission, a single breath between life or death.

He saw the sergeant's eyes adjust as the soldier held himself in check for the instant it took to realize the situation. He let out a long slow breath, stood up and stepped away from Captain Williams.

"I'm sorry, sir, I thought…" he said as he avoided eye contact, re-sheathing his blade and dipping his head. He reached down and offered his hand to Captain Williams, who accepted. He was pulled to his feet as the sergeant asked for permission to be dismissed, turning abruptly and walked from the room.

"Believe me," Captain Williams mumbled feebly as he watched him go. "You looked cold. I thought you needed a blanket. Please, believe me."

The request for transfer was not unexpected and came as no surprise. It was only disappointing. Captain Williams received it respectfully. He'd learned a long time ago that a stiff upper lip was the backbone of the British Empire and could help one endure the most trying circumstances. He told Sargent McTaggart they would have one last interview to complete together before returning to London where they were sched-uled to be disbanded, though Captain Williams was asked to join the Special Branch Financial Division for Fraud and Counterfeited Currency upon returning to England. His mis-sion would be to continue to chase down the money which the Bank of England knew would circulate indefinitely, if not found and destroyed.

"Oskar Stein, the bookkeeper," he told Sargent McTaggart, "is the one man we can rely upon knowing what happened in block 19 in Sachsenhausen." The sergeant acknowledged Captain Williams with a nod. "Oskar has made it home to Prague," he continued as they drove east. "He lives there with his sister, another survivor of the camps. We will make it in about eight hours, depending on what we run into on the road. No need to stay anywhere until we get there," he said cautiously, still trying to dismiss any further discomfort the Sargent may have formed around his intent.

He knew however, that Sargent McTaggart, was not stupid. Williams had dropped his guard with him foolishly, showing affection and touching a man trained to kill. "Your old regi-ment has a billet there, and there's an officers mess in Prague, I believe. Good to be back with the lads."

Sargent McTaggart said nothing in return, sitting rigidly, no longer allowing for the incidental touching of shoulders and legs as a matter of the rough roads jostling them around in the truck.

Captain Williams perceived Oskar Stein as a man in a cor-ner, having to choose how to tell his story—how much truth to reveal, leverage, and trade for the survival of both himself and his sister.

"She didn't have the talent of a forger and needed to rely on other assets to maintain a job as a maid in the home of the camp commander," the bookkeeper told them when the sister, Rebecca, left the men alone in Oscar's room. "A different counterfeit was stamped out day after day, night after night on her body. A currency exchange worth the price of her life.

They all dropped their eyes as Rebecca returned, bringing coffee and sweet biscuits into the room.

Captain Williams listened intently as Rebecca served coffee and Oskar shared his story of forced recruitment and ill-treatment at the hand of Bernhard Kruger, and of his escape in the last days of the war. Oskar told how he tried to conceal the ledger in which he kept a record of every document and piece of currency they had counterfeited. In truth, this information did little more than help Captain Williams realize the enormity of the venture. The Royal Bank of England would not be pleased; the game of cat and mouse had just begun, based on the paltry amount of money they recovered.

Captain Williams noticed Rebecca dipped her head as she passed Sergeant McTaggart after handing him a coffee cup, a sign of respect—or coyness; he saw the slightest smile rise to her lips when she picked up the tray and left the room once more. At the end of the interview, their cups empty, Sergeant McTaggart excused himself and asked for the bathroom. Oskar directed the sergeant to the kitchen, and the outhouse in the garden. Shortly thereafter, Captain Williams stood up and stepped out into the hallway. He caught an awkward shuffle in the kitchen and his eyes met with Sergeant McTaggart's, who seemed to be embracing the girl. She turned, flush-faced, and walked out the back door to the garden.

"Sergeant!" Captain Williams shouted.

"Sir!" Sergeant McTaggart snapped in reply as redness crept up his neck and over his cheeks.

"I believe we've finished our work here. Get the truck started and make sure you keep the keys in your pocket, man!" Sergeant McTaggart left through the front door, but not before Captain Williams saw him reach out and give something to the girl that made her dark eyes welled with tears.

"Fucking Jews," Captain Williams shouted as the sergeant slid behind the steering wheel of their truck. He spat the words into the windscreen, feeling the pain of raw jealousy in his inability to be little more than a puppet to his own desires. "Drive man," he yelled at Sergeant McTaggart, "drive and get me out of this shit hole." Clinging to a small leather ledger taken from Osker Stein, he covered his face with a handkerchief, hoping the Sargent would ignore the sobs and focus on the muddy road ahead. Soon he would be free of looking for invisible money with the blood of countless men and nations upon it in this cesspit of war-torn Europe. But at that moment he realized his heart would never be free of Sergeant McTaggart.

DCI Williams stood from his chair, wiped his eyes with a hanky, reached to the desk, and closed the files. His past was closed and safe with Jim McTaggart missing. He would retire in the next few years and put all the years of chasing this money behind him. He'd been a career man and succeeded in hiding his need for a love still punishable as a crime. By all outward appearances he was the consummate policeman with promotions attesting to the diligence of his work. This business with Sergeant McTaggart's son puts the matter of the Bernhard Money to rest, and the Blue Pound would eventually take the last of it out of circulation. One thing, however, did bother him.

When they'd pulled the wagon into the yard from the rail tunnel, he took a good look around—after all, he was responsible for the disposition of this crime scene. He saw nothing out of the ordinary, although he was frustrated at the audacity of Billy McTaggart to break an official seal on the door. He'd seen enough petty pilfering during the war and knew how the common man worked under pressure to survive, yet not a bag was broken open and, as hard as he tried, he couldn't get his own hand into the top of the bags even as his fingertips brushed against the money.

But then, just as he had told the police officer to close up and reseal the door to the freight wagon, he noticed a dark smudge high up on the pile of bags that sat neatly stacked in the wagon. He climbed up and scrambled over the collection of bags to the smudge. In the sea of stark, clean mailbags stuffed with money, there was a smudge of blood. Upon a more thorough look, he found several more drops of blood and smudges around the neck of other bags. He remembered Billy's hand was bandaged with a rough cloth, still bleeding when they met in the tea shed. Every sense in his gut told him the little rat had made off with something. But how?

He'd seen that the money was destroyed—he couldn't have justified a recount with none of the bags having been opened, and any publicity would've compounded government embarrassment about the whole affair of the Bernhard Millions. Still, his pangs of frustration and remorse were fueled anew as he thought of Billy, a replica of his beautiful father Jim. He blamed Billy in some way for the loss of the young sergeant who'd gone back to a family at the end of the war. He imagined he'd been jilted, though he knew well enough now that Jim had ended up jilting his own family as well.

If Billy had taken a single pound, he would find out.

Chapter 8

A Girl

Suzie McTaggart swore the war was, without a doubt, the most defining experience in her life—other than the birth of Billy and the disappearance of her husband. The Second World War dominated everything and affected everyone. In the blitz of August 1940, the Greater Manchester region was one of the hardest hit. Diggle sat on the far edge of the impact, just rural enough to receive some of the first children evacuated as part of the Pied Piper program, yet close enough to receive the occasional stray bomb falling through the darkness to shake everyone's spirits.

"You can't imagine it if you didn't live through it," she said to Billy when he asked her to tell him her stories again. As a mother she felt the need to guard him against all the details; that was what Mams did. His own life would give him enough to worry about without burdening him with more questions about her own, though now as he grew older, she was less reluctant to provide answers.

That evening, as they sat around the kitchen table drinking hot Bovril, the age difference between the Mam and her son diminished. Meg would be part of the tiny nucleus of their family now, and Suzie loved the prospect of grandchildren. She loved that her own son would soon be a father.

"I was a young girl of thirteen when the war started, and I remember being at my Granny's house and hearing the talk of men being called up. I remember my Uncle George, my father's youngest brother. I loved his laughter, and his racing whippets which he let me feed after school each day. Uncle George went into the army months before the formal call up, just rumors of war. Later, the family told stories of his exploits, but no one knew for sure, as he never came home." She paused, and a tear came to her eye, "I was heartbroken at Uncle George going away, and terrified my dad would also have to go. We were a close-knit, working family, and I'd never been anywhere outside of Diggle other than into Manchester for shopping. Luckily for us, my father suffered from thrombosis, so he wasn't A-1 as they would say. Also, he was a supporting train driver and lead tapper, which was a reserved occupation that classified him as exempt for service. Same as you as you go through your apprenticeship, Billy. No National Service for now, and I like that. I know you'd go off in a moment, but best not for now, son." She put her hand on his knee and patted it protectively.

"Mam, it's only National Service, weekend warriors, and bridge building." He kissed the top of her head as he stood to top up their hot drinks with the last of the Bovril in the pot that simmered on the stove.

"My family scraped a life together and I loved going out in the early morning with my Dad poaching or collecting coal that fell off trains in the night." It felt good to share the stories with Billy she thought, so many memories were shrouded in pain. She cautiously separated out the good and bad.

"I've told you a million times before, son, that I lived with my sisters and my parents over a butcher's shop my mother managed after leaving the mill. There are your aunties, Peggy, Katherine, and Lillian who was six years older than me, all of them with little prospects other than working at the mill like our parents and grandparents before them. My mother was known as a 'restless beauty' and she had asthma brought on by the fine dust and general bad work conditions at the mill."

She never, of course, told Billy of whispered rumors that her sister Lillian resembled the mill's Italian foreman, with her olive skin and blue eyes. "We had no idea what the war was to be in the beginning. We were still close enough to The Great war of 1914, the War to End all Wars as everyone called it, including my own father, who was in it."

She watched Billy as he listened intently. She knew he wanted to glimpse his father in the stories, and she would get to that.

"We were all together the morning war broke out—the third of September 1939 at eleven AM. I didn't hear the Prime Minister, Neville Chamberlain's famous broadcast because our family didn't have a radio, but the buzz ran down the street quick enough over cups of tea, garden fences, and washing lines in back gardens." She told Billy she didn't know what she expected now that the nation was at war—perhaps soldiers parading up and down the street, or German aircraft dropping bombs. The nuns at school warned them that the bombing would happen soon enough, and God would protect them all from the evil of the Hun. She thought it funny when one of the boys in her class asked who would look after the German Catholics who'd been to visit their school that summer past—did God pick sides? She watched the Nun give the boy a sharp crack across the back of the head with a cane as the only reply when he followed up by asking if "Square Heads" was another name for Germans, as his dad liked to call them.

"I remember the first impact of the war came when all the family stood outside the butcher shop and watched long lines of children streaming along the street traveling from the railway station to the Diggle Hotel, which had been converted into a makeshift reception center."

She knew Billy was listening to every word, so she chose her words carefully.

"I never had any idea why no evacuees came to our house. Perhaps it was too small with all of us living there already. I remember being appalled by the sight of those children. All of them carried little bundles and gas masks, many of them looked dirty and dressed in rags. My own family wasn't rich—we wore patched jerseys, and hand-me-down dresses and shoes like most of the townsfolk—but that was my first glimpse of real poverty. Even the Upper Mill tinkers or gypsies were much cleaner and better dressed than those evacuees. They came from some of the worst slums of Manchester where conditions were beyond imagination."

When he was a child, so he could appreciate what they had, Mam showed Billy photos of rotten toothed, bedraggled children, little boxes of belongings wrapped in twine, a barely legible hand-written name scrawled on a piece of brown paper hung about their necks. She now knew that many of the children never went home, but were shipped off to Canada or Australia, falsely believing their parents were dead. She understood some of that hardship happened right in her own village.

"When the other children and I went to school, we had to take our newly-issued gas masks. I never went anywhere without it. At school we practiced air raid drills where we would all put on our gas masks and lay down on the floor under the desks. The celluloid visor of the gas mask soon misted up and before long all you could see were blurred outlines of each other stumbling around laughing as the teacher shouted this wasn't a laughing matter."

She often wondered how many people had been injured by running into things when trying to get to an air raid shelter under that particular "fog of war," a term misused often enough around town.

Apart from carrying gas masks and hearing the air raid sirens sounding for practice at set times, she told Billy nothing else seemed much different—at first. Gradually food and sweets started to be more challenging to get, although for some time she was still able to buy a penny dumbbell, a double-ended lollipop, or a buttermilk dainty and a licorice strap on a Saturday afternoon on their way to the Odeon Picture House in Upper Mill.

"Everyone got pocket money of sixpence per week and usually spent 1d on sweets, 3d on the pictures, or 'flicks' as the Yanks called them when they came to town. That would leave me 2d for the rest of the week, where I usually bought a half pound poke of puff candy from Meg's granddad's shop.

"Rationing came in slowly but surely, and soon everyone had ration cards for all essential food—bacon, eggs, sugar, butter, margarine, milk and tea amongst others."

The talk of food made her hungry. "Time for a little supper when Meg gets here," she said and took a moment to go and put the kettle on and place some crumpets on the edge of the open flame of the stove. She had brought some fresh butter and a little wild honey home from the farm where she cleaned, and it would be a treat as she continued her story. She set a tray and brought it back to the table, placing it next to Billy so he could do the honors just as Meg arrived.

"Mam, can you tell Meg how you and Dad met?" Billy asked.

"I don't know why you want to hear this again, Billy, and Meg's heard it too I'm sure. You know it makes me wonder where your Dad is now, all handsome in the Middle East or somewhere, anywhere more exotic than here, with someone more exotic than me." She cupped her tea with her twisted hands and stared into the beige liquid as though divining the worn story before she could see the tea leaves. "I suppose it will do me good to get it off my chest now rather than thinking about it all the time." She breathed deeply and started in on the story.

Meg clapped her hands excitedly and curled up next to Billy on the couch.

"It was just before Christmas 1940, your Dad's first introduction to Diggle. The Germans had begun to blitz Manchester in August or September, and they dropped tons of explosives and incendiary bombs, killing several hundred people and injuring thousands. Diggle wasn't a high priority in the war effort, and the police sent a token force of trainees to manage and support the home guard. At eighteen, your dad was drafted in as a soldier to the Argyll and Sutherland Highlanders. He was brought into Diggle on Christmas Eve, at the height of the bombing, before being shipped out to the Western Desert Campaign. As part of his duties, he was sent to our street where a landmine, a large bomb that came down by parachute, had dropped in a nearby field. We didn't get flying V-1 rockets until 1944 and Manchester was beyond the range of the V-2."

Billy and Meg listened attentively, barely breathing as Suzie told her story.

"The nearby residents who lived within a mile of the bomb had to be evacuated and taken to the Labor Club. Your dad was ordered to stay at the T-junction with a small detachment of soldiers and to stop people from returning to their homes for any reason. The residents outside of the cordon saw that he and the other soldiers had plenty to eat and drink, with a few hot toddies of whiskey to keep them warm.

"I remember seeing him standing there in his full army kit, all serious and important." She blushed and gave Meg a tap on the knee as a language between women. "I'd grown bored of the cramped quarters of the Labor Club, and after telling my Mum I needed to pee, I snuck outside."

Suzie looked at Billy and Meg sitting, slack-jawed, and listening. She held back the fact that as a curious fourteen-year-old with three mature sisters she was bold and looked older than her age, and that the girls in her family were all blessed with ample bosoms.

"He stood stone-faced, guarding the road, and I took it as a challenge to make him laugh. He had the bluest eyes I'd ever seen, like sapphires set in a pale skin with the black of his hair peeking out from under his helmet. I remember the little bristles of hair running up his neck, a boyish, skinny neck that looked too thin to hold up his head with that big tin helmet. It was love at first sight. Yes, I was fourteen, but when these things happen, we know it, don't we, Meg?" she asked, tapping Meg's knee again.

"He was there for a week, young Jim, while they cleared the bomb away. Every day I would say hello. Once, after he came off-duty, he played a game of football with some of the younger boys. I brought out cups of orange squash and touched his hand when I gave him a cup. I felt all tingly and hovered around the street for hours afterward.

"'How old are you anyway?' he asked after the game was over, while he was pulling his shirt back on over his string vest.

"'Are those your ID tags?' I had said in reply. 'What do they say?'

"'Private James McTaggart and I'll have to kill you if you ask any more questions.' He grinned at me and I thought his teeth were too perfect for a Scotsman as I heard his accent.

Meg raised her head from Billy's shoulder and asked, "Did he fall in love with you?"

"I like to think so, or so he told me, but I suppose eventually," Mam said. "That was a few years later, after he'd seen the war and he came back to me." She set her empty cup back on the tray. Her mind took her someplace else for what seemed like minutes. "I'll keep the next part of that story for another time," she concluded. Too much for one night perhaps, I need another cup of tea just for me."

She shooed Billy and Meg out of the house "Walk young Meg home now, son." and she started to clean up the cups and saucers.

She heard the door close behind them in the hall as the whistle of the kettle escalated to a high-pitched whine, causing her heart to flutter. She shuffled from the front room back into the kitchen, the cups and saucers on the tray clinking as she walked, worn slippers hanging off her heels, scraping the linoleum floor with little swooshes amid the crescendo of the wailing kettle.

Suzie turned the gas off, and the noise slid back down the spout as steam danced around the kitchen ceiling, condensing on the windows like muted tears. She picked up a threadbare tea towel, using it to take the kettle off the stove, wincing with the pain of her arthritis as it shot up through her wrist and into her thin arm. *We had our moment,* she thought, the memory not the hardest part. It was the consequences that burdened her for years afterward.

She'd been out walking the bridle path that followed the canal when she met Jim walking alone. He was off duty. They fell into a comfortable conversation and quickly kissed as they sat on a bench alongside the path stretching from lock gate to lock gate along the multiple shifts of elevation that would lift and drop barges along the way. He was gentle with her even in their haste and, in their escalating passion, they navigated into a nearby field among a thick bed of fresh grass near a low rock wall. They were both virgins and even in their clumsy fumbling she would never forget the moment.

They would write to each other wherever he might be sent, they said, and he promised to come back after the war, no matter how long it took. In the days after their encounter they met twice more, their passion a distraction, and then suddenly he was shipped out on short order without time to see her before leaving. They never took time to give each other their addresses. She tried to get his information from the stoic captain of the home guard, but he apparently considered it a national secret. She had waited for a letter to come.

I once had such beautiful hands, she thought, pouring the water into the teapot, adding three spoons of tea, swirling it as it darkened and sank into the rust colored water. The light caught her wedding band as she stirred the spoon around and around. She realized she'd never thought to take the ring off, and she doubted she could get it off now anyway. Thoughts sprung to life against her wishes, like some pouncing cat hiding under the table, lunging at her from every corner of the room, moments from the dark recesses of her memory, better times of his return and her wedding day.

She never thought of marriage, especially not to him. Washing was all she knew, hardship, raw hands. Washing laundry, only washing. She'd been devastated when she had discovered herself pregnant. Her sisters hadn't conveyed all the mysteries of life to her, assuming she wasn't likely to fall off the cart at so young an age. She told her mother, who in turn took her to confession before even considering telling her father. The priest was plain-spoken, a soft-faced man with hard eyes.

"The sisters of the church will take care of this. Wayward girls can do nowt but pay penance for the sin of fornication outside of marriage. We will take her in and put her to work, serving the poor, saving her from eternal damnation in the service of the church." The priest said all this with foul breath, as he slid his arm around her waist smiling a toothless grin.

She resented that her father was able to do so little for her. By the time he heard the news, he barely managed to get the priest to agree to let his own sister take the baby when it was born, an unusual arrangement she knew in hindsight, considering the value of a child unofficially adopted to good American families who made generous charitable contributions to the church.

Her Billy had come in early morning. By midday she was back at the sink washing her own bloody sheets, tears running down her cheeks into the grooves of the washing board and down the drain with her life.

She despised the four years she had spent in penance—hot water, cold water, wringing and twisting sheets, rough hands, and wrists aching at days end. Only Sunday was a day of rest, with a full Catholic mass twice during the day and a chance to do her own laundry of milk-soaked blouses, which lasted until she had eventually dried up, body and soul.

She poured the tea into her cup using two hands to lift the teapot, straining the tea leaves through a small silver sieve, careful not to chip the last remaining cup of the original wedding gift from her grandmother. It had been a set of excellent Royal Dolton China with blue willow trees cascading around the sides, delicate details fractured by fine stained lines of use, and time.

As she stood holding the teacup to her chest, looking out the window into the small backyard with her pots of daffodils and string peas, she remembered how she felt the day Jim came back. She never believed it would happen. The visit had been his first chance to return to Britain in almost five years. He shared no more than the fact that he was a commando and had no desire to tell her where and what he'd done in his time away. It was best like that in their new start. When he found her in the workhouse, he'd told her with tears in his eyes that she was so much more than a knee trembler, a quick fuck in a field. He was sorry, but he had no idea there was a baby. He thought about her every day that he was gone. Would she marry him, make a family?

She had her wedding at last. Her dad had been so proud as he gave her away, enamored with the handsome young Jim in his uniform standing at the altar. He would have kissed the groom himself given half a chance, such was his relief. Her mother sat sheepishly as the resentful, bloated priest performed the nuptials. Her mother gave her a pair of silk gloves that once had belonged to her grandmother, something old to cover the redness of her scalded hands. There was something borrowed, a dress, not white, and the gold band, something new, for a new life.

As Suzie looked at the teacup, the memory of pouring his tea on Sunday mornings came flooding back. Her hands healed on the outside in the weeks after her release, her skin soft enough now to run over his chest and back as they lay in bed listening to the low breathing of four-year-old Billy in the bed across the room. These were the days she lived for, her wee family, as she and Jim would call themselves, content in their love. Billy had taken to Jim instantly, being more cautious in his acceptance of his mother, reluctantly leaving his auntie as the only mother he'd known but believing both his parents had been away winning the war in their own way.

In the small dark kitchen, Suzie spooned two small scoops of sugar into her cup. She looked down at her ring worn thin and tarnished, fingers twisted and gnarled, beauty gone. The milk swirled as she poured it slowly into the teacup, around and around, marking the inevitable cycle of time like dirty water down a plug hole, running away to the sea forever.

Chapter 9

Meg

Meg knew that, whenever he could, Billy watched her as she went about her day. Whether she was chatting with people in her parents' shop as she worked the counter or as she drank tea when visiting with his Mam, he was always watching her. Meg loved that his eyes followed her around, shadowed her every move, relishing that he needed to be close enough to smell her on the air as they passed each other. His intense stare made her conscious of every move. She found it endearing when she'd look at him with a tilt of her head, allowing a smile to rise to her lips and her eyes to inquire after his fascination. It was a game.

At times he would turn and walk away as if he had his own independent thought or reasoning beyond her presence, creating busy work somewhere else. The truth was, she knew how to mesmerize him to incompetence. In many ways, it was the game she relished most, but she sometimes wished he could tell her how he felt in romantic words, Mills and Boons like, rather than being the stoic working man surrounded by smelly rail men.

She longed for him to comment on the intentional sway of her slim hips under her ankle-length dress, or the tiny slip of skin she allowed to show as she reached for something high on the shop shelf. She longed for him to admire the elegance of her neckline as she leaned over the counter to put groceries in old Mrs. Aldington's string shopping bag, or the grace in the way she pushed back a stray hair from her face with a finger. She desperately wanted to have him remember the scent of her, a mixture of perfume and that deep essence she knew he had tasted on her neck when leaning hard into her lithe body, her long dark hair tickling his face, wrapping him in the cocoon of her. She believed her purpose was to awaken him to passion, no matter how many books she needed to read.

Meg saw Billy from the top of the stairs as she came down into the living room where he stood making idle conversation with her father. She took his hand and rescued him. "Let's go, we'll be late for the Red Cross Social at the club," she said, her lips to his ear and her fingers tugging at his coat sleeve. She expected the night ahead would be the usual bevy of her parent's friends mixed with randy old lads pinching her on the bottom and slapping Billy on the back as they smirked and winked.

"Are you going to wear those shoes to walk? It might rain," was what the romantic Billy said to her. She dismissed him with a wave of her hand and pulled him to the door.

The evening was uneventful. They listened to Steve Whitelaw read the meeting notes, report the results of the White Elephant sale, and finally announce the proposed Art Fair for local artists in the city hall. All this was followed by a light supper of ham sandwiches and strong dark tea served by women with blue hair who smelled of a deadly concoction of mothballs and tainted lavender Eau de toilet. At the end of the evening, they walked out of the meeting hall into the street where a light rain fell, leaving a fresh crispness to the air and a clean sheen to the streets and terrace houses

"They asked if I would be a docent, for the art show," Meg shared excitedly with Billy as she wiped a raindrop from the end of his nose.

"What the hell is a docent?" Billy asked, and she realized he didn't even consider that she might find him ignorant.

"I'll be a guide, or instructor for the various works of art, informing visitors to the show as to their meaning or materials used. Stuff like that. Do you understand?" Meg asked.

He huffed in mock indignation. "It sounds very posh and smart, love. You'll be just the lass for it, I'm sure," he answered, putting his hand on her hand where it rested on his sleeve, looped under his arm. "Of course, I understand you're my lass, aren't you? Mam always said you were a good un, a keeper. She also said I'd do well to put on a good suit, shut up, and learn something from you once in a while."

The dark, starless sky hung heavy above them as Meg playfully jumped over a large puddle in the road, pulling him behind her, his boots breaking the water and distorting their reflection under the streetlight.

"Watch your shoes, pet," he said, "your feet will be stained red for a week if the dye runs. I told you not to wear those ones."

"Shall I take them off and walk all the way home in my stocking feet?" She stood, hands on hips, defying him, a broad black belt squeezing her waist to an almost impossibly tiny proportion. She knew he'd be able to make out the shape of her legs as a streetlight illuminated her dress from behind. She was proud of her petite shape. Rather than being like most of the buxom and thick-thighed women around town, she thought of her thin ankles as a sign of good breeding, although she couldn't figure out which side of her family they might have come from, based on her parents' physiques.

"I don't want to go home yet," she said, the shadow of a smile teasing at the edge of her ruby red mouth. "I realize I may have been a little grumpy after all your good news recently, and I'm sorry." She knew he couldn't argue with her, that he'd walk all night to make things right if there were any issue between them, and in anticipation of a kiss or more if she desired to forgive him. "Take me to my old house, the one over by the yard," she demanded with a flutter of her mascara-laden eyelids.

"It's through the yard, pet, all muck, and grime, mud that will get on your lovely dress and shoes. Why do you want to go there?"

"I'll walk to the yard gates and down the tracks to the turntable. After that, you will need to carry me, piggyback—oink!" She poked him and skipped up the street ahead of him.

She waited until he gave in to her; it was not even a consideration that he wouldn't. No use him raising even the concern that the night watchman may be lurking around—he knew as well as she did that Fat Bob would more than likely be curled up behind his stove with a good cuppa in his hand. She sprang lightly onto the shiny steel of the track and disappeared into the darkness of the yard.

She convinced him to let her climb onto his back as they started to crisscross the rail tracks, avoiding puddles and mud, weaving between the great silent hulks of the engines. By day the engines were alive, lords of the yard, but without steam, they were just steel. Still, amid the machines, Meg found herself aroused by their rustic masculinity.

Billy stopped and steadied himself against a piston, casing as Meg shifted on his back, her firm legs holding him fast in their grip. She shimmied up a little and tightened her grip on his shoulders with her slender fingers as she leaned forward and bit his ear.

"My, that is a rather large piston you have in your hand young man," she said and broke into a fit of laughter. Billy shushed her, warning her again of the night watchman. He wrapped his arms back around her thighs and hiked her up. She could feel every muscle twitch in his back against the inside of her legs. Meg loved the push and pull of their bodies as Billy walked. She found herself moving her hips to the rhythm of Billy's gait as they crossed silver polished rail tops.

"Let's cut back over the river, you know where the little footbridge is just below the old house." With a nudge of her knees in his side, he changed direction. "Okay, donkey, giddy-ap, giddyap!"

They paused on the bridge upon a chance encounter with the yard foreman's cat that sat unmoving, waiting for affection as the price of toll. The dark grey feline moved on once she tired of Meg and Billy petting her, seeking night quarry of rats and mice who fed on remnants from the day's passengers in coaches around the rail yard.

"Look Meg, the moon," Billy said as the clouds broke for a moment. "Look at the moon in the water, it's beautiful now that the sky has started to clear." He paused. "Like you, beautiful."

She wanted him to kiss her right there on the bridge, romantic, like a Hollywood moment with the river, the moonlight, and gray muted colors as close to black and white as the light would allow. She wanted nothing more than a moment at first, but what she truly longed for was a carefree afternoon to get to know him as a man, away from Diggle, rail yards, and his Mam. She wanted to be more to him than a lass he discovered hidden beneath a skirt against a wall. She wanted him to taste her passion unencumbered by a ticking clock and parent's watchful eyes at a back door. Fresh and alive with the vitality of bright eyes in broad daylight rather than hidden in dark corners fumbling. A day out in the country with nothing to do but wrestle each other to the ground, soft grass in a meadow, entwined and delirious with love, spurred on by pure passion and romance. She imagined *From Here to Eternity*, when Burt Lancaster kissed Deborah Kerr amid the waves on the beach in Honolulu, just days before the attack on Pearl Harbor.

"Beautiful, am I? Then catch me if you can Billy boy."

She topped the embankment and disappeared into the small, green-painted house that once belonged to her parents. The row of little box houses had been used as temporary homes for displaced families after the war, but they were now disheveled by time and suffering the harsh English weather from their original shoddy construction.

The church bell struck ten as she slid into the doorway of her old house. He followed her inside and she instructed him to light a match from the box of Swan Matches he carried along with his Woodbine cigarettes. He preferred the unfiltered "gaspers" which anyone new to smoking found hard to inhale, and she laughed when he told her they were for the working man and people like James Dean as Jim Stark in *Rebel Without a Cause*. If James could smoke them, then so could he. She watched Billy lay a cigarette lazily on the edge of his lip and walk through the old house ahead of her, his match light held above his eyes, its heat nipping at his fingers until he dropped it and lit another.

She followed him as he led her to the back bedroom that overlooked the rail yard. Meg stood looking out of the window, broken glass and shredded curtains matched to the floral remnants of wallpaper which rolled back and separated from the wall like banana skins, dusty linoleum on the floor and little else as a testament to those who had lived there before.

"I don't like that you've taken up smoking. I mean, it looks good on you, but it smells and tastes bad for me as your woman." She turned from the window as he lit another cigarette. She watched his last match be consumed by the darkness, leaving his face imprinted on the back of her eyes for a moment longer. "You never saw my room back then, did you? I would watch the trains every day, asking my mother where they were going, and if we might go there too." Meg voice was soft, almost as if she were talking to herself. She walked around the room, the place where she's spent so much time as a child. Dusty outlines of furniture long gone imprinted a ghostly silhouette on the wallpaper.

"I used to think of you all the time when I was alone in this room, though it was different then. You were a friend to me, my only friend."

"You know I'd watch you from the yard when I came to work with my Dad," Billy replied. "He always gave me little jobs to do over by the fence, just below the embankment. I think he knew I liked you before we truly became friends, the early days just after the Mickey Mouse tea set incident."

Meg stretched out on the windowsill, the slight moonlight silhouetting her porcelain skin against the darkness of the night. "I don't want to waste any more time. I want to explore great passion, and our great love." She closed her eyes and gave off a low murmur.

"I love you," Billy whispered, as he gently kissed her after dropping his cigarette to the floor and putting it out with the thick leather sole of his steel capped boots.

Meg had been reading French novellas procured through Cynthia at the hairdresser—she knew where to find the good parts that would make Father O'Connor's head turn around three times—especially if the priest knew the girls from his communion classes were reading this stuff behind Bibles held in snow white gloves, pressed against satin stretched across hungry thighs as they made promises of chastity. "I always knew you'd be the one for me, after that first kiss in the storeroom of my Mum and Dads shop, do you remember it?"

"I do, it was kind of an accident. We were lying in the stockroom at the back of the shop, reading the Sunday funnies and eating chocolate mice that sported white string tails. I remember every word."

"I bet you can't eat the tail before I eat the chocolate," Meg had taunted,

"Want a bet, you silly cow?" Billy had shot back.

"Okay, I'll hold the mouse in my mouth, and you take the tail in yours, see if you can get to the chocolate before I eat it."

Silly, thought Billy. I'm too fast for her.

Getting to his knees in front of her, he placed the tip of the string tail between his teeth and stared Meg in the eyes.

Eye to eye, gunslingers with a mouse between them.

"Go," grunted Meg and Billy sucked in the string tail as hard as he could without falling forward.

Meg had pulled the chocolate into her mouth and Billy's lips pushed up against hers, both refusing to let go, chocolate and saliva running down their chins. Each grabbed the other and they wrestled to the ground, entwined, lips fixed together. Realization slammed into their red flustered faces and they pushed apart, each wiping chocolate smudges from their lips onto the back of their hands, an instant of quiet embarrassment, a transition old as time and inevitable. Breaking the silence Meg had burst out laughing. Billy took a second to collect himself, and then they both laughed and went back to reading without disputing the winner.

"I never told you, but that was the second time the butterflies appeared in my tummy. I wanted to go home and ask Mam if I was sick or something. The taste of chocolate on my lips was so sweet as I ran my tongue around the edge of my mouth while I walked home up the terrace from your shop, still unsure of what happened."

They left the house and started to make their way home. As they walked he told her that, before her, he never really understood girls or desired to be more than friends with them, or friends with anyone for that matter. He remembered the Duncan twins, two girls he had included in his adventures only once. Things had not gone well.

"Tell me naughty boy, tell me," Meg squealed as they crossed the road arm in arm.

"You know I've never been a rebel or troublemaker, never played truant. It was all innocent," he said.

"The Duncan twins, a great misunderstanding." He shouted into the empty street. He jumped off the curb into a puddle that shone iridescent in snaking rainbows of streetlight, engine grease film on its black surface splashing his boots. Billy reminisced about the fated team selection in the playground, a brutal process of elimination by the strongest of the weakest. Everyone lined up and the two captains selected from the line, the best players going first with yip's and shouts of established alliances. He recalled the humiliation of being selected last, scorned, and reluctantly added to a team that didn't want him—relegated to some obscure fullback position where you would do the least damage should the ball mistakenly arrive at your feet.

Billy had quickly learned to avoid humiliation by going to the bathroom as they were released out into the playground. He told Meg he'd find a sunny refuge near the school gate until the bell rang again for class. On that fateful day Billy had pulled the hood of his duffle coat up over his head and proceeded to take his comic out of his pocket. Seemingly out of nowhere the twins appeared from in front of him. He looked up from the inside of his hood at two redheaded stick insects in grey sweaters and shorts from which hung white legs with even whiter knee socks.

In unison, they asked, "What are you doing here alone? Can we play with you?" They stared at Billy. "Do you know where the park is, the one with the swings and the roundabout?"

Billy confessed to being no older than them at five years and hadn't the benefit of learning all the school rules. He was happy they talked to him without calling him names or demanding he give them his comic in order to spare is life. They seemed friendly enough, even as girls.

"The park itself wasn't anything special, the usual council estate structures of chains, poles, and wooden slats constructed into a variety of mechanisms where children could, swing, rotate, and seesaw until they fell to the hard tarmac ground or crashed into sharp iron edges, drawing blood and ending play for the day. Everything was painted dark green and lubricated with a thick black sludge that stained school clothes, resulting in a slap on the head if I ruined another precious school jersey," He told Meg as he recounted the story.

"I do know where the park is. Do you want to go there?" Billy had replied with a little bravado, feeling some level of elevation from the bottom of the pile.

"Will you take us?" The twins said in unison again.

"I will," said Billy boldly as he stepped between them and took each of their hands, "This way, but watch out for the road. Mam told me to look left, look right, and look left again."

The park perched on the side of a small valley through which the canal ran south from the Stanstead Tunnel. The challenge in visiting the park when walking from the school was crossing of the main road which carried busses and lorries running in and out of town. Crossing this road was a nightmare even for most adults with their wits about then. Billy's Mam and Dad assumed he feared the road but had never said not to go near it on his own. Billy led the girls without consideration of the danger.

"Okay, look, left, look right, and look right again," he said, and they scampered quickly across the road as soon as several cars passed and there was a slight lull in the traffic. The girls held his hand so tightly and ran so fast he was almost swept along by them. Once there, Billy led them to the swing sets and all three climbed onto their own swing. Wriggling up on to the wooden seat and grabbing the chains with both hands, they started pumping their legs to get the motion going, back and forth.

"We can't do it" both the girls said in unison as they went nowhere.

Billy had started to build up speed and was pumping his legs. Faster and higher he flew, back and forth, shouting, "I'm Flash Gordon, Master of the Universe, faster, higher I will go." He'd watched the bigger boys swing in graceful arcs high above the playground, and then they'd jump from the swing at the top of its arc and land like cats on the ground as they reached out and caught the returning swing before it hit them.

"Watch this, watch me!" Billy shouted to the redheads who dismounted from their perches and stood watching him in full flight, his first audience. Never had anyone paid this much attention to him. He let go and launched himself into the air, soaring, spinning, landing like a cat on his toes, impressive. He turned to look at the girls faces, their obvious admiration... Thunk!

The returning swing waits for no man and it hit him edge on in the nuts. All the grace of that fine dancer was lost as he crumpled to the ground, eyes squeezed shut, hands cupping a new pain, knowing instantly his willy was connected to every nerve in his body. I screamed, and the twins came running.

"Are you okay boy, are you dead?" The girls prodded at him as he tried to compose himself, breathing deeply amid dry sobs.

"I think I've broken it, broken my, my, wi...willy," he stammered between breaths. Desperate to look and see what damage he'd inflicted to result in such pain, he hobbled over to the hedgerow and lodged himself into a break in the foliage. Chaperoned immediately by his twin companions who flanked him, curious to see the willy that had been hit. Billy undid his shorts and exposed himself. The small head of his willy and foreskin was red and angry with the first tinges of dark blue. One of the girls reached to touch it just as the all-consuming hand of the headmistress wrapped around Billy's neck, dragging Billy and his cohorts from their sanctuary in the hedge.

"What are you doing Boy! She shrieked at the top of her voice, spinning Billy around to the full view of her red exploding face that resembled the damaged goods protruding from

Billy's open shorts. The two stared at each other for an instant while the world fell into a blur, "Back to school at once! We shall have parents to deal with, perversion and sin, naked boys and scarlet women," the Headmistress shrieked as she dragged Billy up the hill by the scruff of his shirt, one hand holding his shorts and the other holding onto one of the twins who was attached to the other by skinny hands and tiny wrists, gangly legs, red hair, and red eyes.

Meg burst out laughing and tried to cover her mouth with her hand as the tears rolled down her face, "You poor thing, you poor thing... what happened?"

"Back in school we had to sit on hard wooden chairs outside the headmistress' office, with mocking eyes of the office staff branding us as deviants who should've been monitored by our parents. We stared straight ahead, hands on our laps, confused amid tuts and sighs from the plump receptionist who'd already called our parents from work. Nobody asked us what really happened. We were victims of the reality adults put on simple adventures of children." Billy said as he finished the story.

Meg linked her arm back into his and said, "Okay two timer, now take me home. You have an early shift in the morning and I'm feeling quite romantic, I'll keep a few surprises and stories of my own for you on our wedding night."

Chapter 10

Courting

Billy had borrowed the Morris Minor Panel van from Sid the Pig, owner of the butcher shop on the high street. As he climbed into the van, he breathed the sweet smell of dried blood and sawdust, oddly familiar and comforting. After cleaning out the sawdust, he built seats from a pile of blankets for Meg and Mam to sit on. Mam had worked for Sid when his wife was pregnant and needed time off from working in the shop; he trusted Mam and was more than pleased to lend them the van. Sid even kicked in the petrol and some bacon sandwiches for the trip to buy Meg's wedding dress from Aunt Kath, who had a second-hand bridal shop in Preston.

Billy set off first thing in the morning with Mam and Meg bundled into the van on a trip almost guaranteed to be un-eventful—until they stopped for a cup of tea at a trucker's café near Bambers Bridge.

"Can we go to Blackpool, Billy love?" Mam asked quietly and unexpectedly, as she sipped at her cup of tea. "I'd really like to do that if we have time. Aunt Kath won't mind if we run a little late—we might even sleep over if we can get all her bloody cats out of the way. I want to have a little adventure since we're out of town. You know I don't leave the village that often."

Mam was nothing but smiles as he and Meg agreed to the diversion. They finished their fried breakfast, got back into the van, and headed toward the seaside town of Blackpool. Upon arriving, Billy parked on the promenade where they walked toward the pier and the famous Blackpool tower, though they'd agreed to leave well before dark and that left no opportunity to see the famous Illuminations. Meg noticed a sweet vendor and asked Billy to buy her a stick of rock." Mam schooled them in the art of how to eat the sweet.

"When we were children, we'd see who could suck the hard stick shaped sweet into a needle-sharp point. Then all the writing that ran around the inside telling you the seaside town of origin would be distorted and stretched in strands of pink and white peppermint."

Billy looked over every shade and color of the sweet candy—pink, red, lime green, yellow—in the small, green stall. The clapperboard structure was strapped to the rusty Victorian cast iron railings that lined the seawall, or "front" as Mam liked to call it. He could see that in severe weather waves had crashed against the back of the little building, leaving sandy, salty swirls that had dried on the weathered wood on rare sunny days like today.

He ran his hand over the bright sweets that lay stacked and wrapped in clear cellophane, twisted tightly at each end where you could read the pink Blackpool in irregular block lettering. "Don't touch it, lad, if you're not buying it," said the large woman with a hairy chin who sat behind the counter. He wondered how she managed to get into the little shed.

"I think they must have built her into it, and she probably gets up and walks home at night, stall and all," he whispered to Mam and Meg. The woman glared at him as she took his money with pudgy fingers that poked out from fingerless woolen gloves.

Billy pushed between Mam and Meg and linked arms with them as they walked off arm-in-arm, laughing, toward the fish and chip shop. Hot fresh fried fish and chips wrapped in newsprint and soaked in salt and vinegar smelled tantalizing, and they each broke into their wrapped bundles and pulled out steaming hot chips as they walked back down to the beach.

"I love the fresh sea air, the salty smell of the water, the rumbling waves, and even the bloody seagulls trying to steal my chips." Meg laughed.

"Me too," said Mam softly. "This is the beach me and your dad came to the day we had our honeymoon. You stayed home and cried with your grandad, so upset you weren't allowed to come along. Do you remember, the week after your Dad came home to us?" she asked, looking vacantly out to sea.

"Let's sit on the beach and get some sun," Meg said.

"Ay," Billy agreed and took her and Mam's hand as they walked down the boat ramp on to the pebbly beach.

"I remember Whitley Bay for our summer holidays," Billy said, not mentioning his dad lest he upset Mam. "That water was bloody freezing, dark green and scary, nothing like that postcard I found from Florida. How old was I Mam, four or five?"

Mam looked thoughtful and put her hand on her chin. "You were five and so proud of your new leopard print swim trunks, and the sailors' cap with the anchor on the front that your Dad bought for you. There you were, bucket and spade in hand, lifting rocks and yelling like Tarzan of the apes." Mam started to laugh. It was good to hear her laugh out loud, Billy thought as he watched her buttoned-up coat jiggle around her.

"Ho me, ho my!" Mam jiggled, tears running down her cheeks, "Billy"—she caught her breath— "I remember you looking like a string bean in that bathing suit, more meat on a soup bone than filled those trunks." She had to stop talking as the memory shook her to the point where she dropped her fish and chips. "Ho…Hee, my gosh, and then you went in swimming, wading more like because you didn't know how to swim back then. My goodness, the bravado as you belly flopped into the first big wave that came toward you in the ice-cold North Sea of the English Channel. Dark blue is the only color that comes to mind as you stood up instantly with the perfect look of shock on your face."

Mam was overcome now and chortled between snorts as her head flopped back. "Your Tarzan trunks were gone out into the surf, and your wee willy had disappeared too. All you could do was cup your frozen bits in one hand and run up the beach crying into my big warm towel."

The three of them sat laughing on the rough, pebbly beach, sun fighting with a brisk wind, fingers greasy from the fish and chips, salty air and salty tears of joy, simple pleasures. The moment made Billy realize it was sometimes right to take the scenic route, to divert from the straight line of getting somewhere. To trust the experiences waiting out there in the world and know who you love. He couldn't imagine being happier as he looked at his Mam and Meg together.

It was tea-time when they arrived at Aunt Kath's shop in Preston. Meg had her fitting and they decided to stay the night after calling Sid the Pig who let them know there was no rush as he had no deliveries on Sunday.

In the morning they left to return to Diggle, stopping for a quick breakfast at the same roadside café where they'd decided to divert to Blackpool. With the dress bought, the wedding plans were starting to come together, and Billy turned his thoughts to the tradition of a stag party for himself.

Harry Two Bellies took on the task of organizing Billy's party, an honor reserved for the best man. Harry had started to cry when Billy had pulled him aside after work one afternoon and asked him.

"Of course, you need to be my best man, you blubbering idiot. You're the closest thing to a father I have, and a good friend to the father I don't have, and you've known Meg and me since we were sprogs."

Harry took to the task with gusto. Billy had never before been inside a Gentleman's Club, one of the illegal casinos in the bowels of the docks in Manchester. The Diggle Shunters and Tappers Social Club offered the occasional backroom poker night and a sing-song. This would be different. Girls in fishnet tights carried little silver trays while gliding through the cigarette smoke with drinks and friendly smiles that grew in proportion to the tip left on the tray.

"Alcohol may be man's worst enemy, but the Bible says love your enemy," Harry shouted, trying to live up to the velvet jacket and tartan waistcoat he was wearing. He gave a winked to the waitress.

"Fuck off," the leggy waitress said in a thick Liverpudlian accent, "we only do champagne, Babysham, wine, and lager here, darling, so don't get too uppity in that waistcoat." She winked at him and blew him a kiss from full red lips, then she ran her hands over her slim waist and set about taking drink orders.

"I suppose it will be the bubbles, my dear, and you may need a glass yourself to put some pop into that routine of yours."

The group of lads cheered at his bluff, then cheered again as the waitress melted at the lure of a five-pound note Harry waved as he teased her down on to his lap and ordered the round of drinks for the lads.

Billy could barely make out human shapes around the gaming tables through the cigarette smoke. Harry Two Bellies grabbed him by the scruff of the neck. "Let's start with Black Jack and another pint of lager, Billy boy. This is going to be one hell of a stag night. Get your cash out, lad, I'm only paying for the first round.

At the tables, Billy found he had a natural aptitude for gambling and soon moved from blackjack to the roulette table in a private area of the club. He followed a few of the winners in placing bets and once he figured out how the game of chance worked, he bet a little more aggressively and won, much to his surprise.

The night wound steadily into an inevitable slump of drunken men on a semi-circular couch in the corner of the casino. Only slightly drunk compared to the rest of the lads, he sat side by side with Harry.

"I've dug holes and tapped wheels most my life, other than a little bit of fighting for lost causes, Billy boy, and I've shagged at least a couple of hundred lovelies along the way. This is why we need to have the talk." Harry slurred as he lifted his leg and farted and then dispensed what amounted to the best father-to-son advice he could through a flurry of spittle and sour breath.

"I was eighteen years old, full of piss and vinegar and living in a shithole town called Dundee in Scotland, one week before your dad and I were due to ship out for basic training."

Billy knew Harry was genuinely drunk now and, like all good Scotsmen, he became melancholy when full of the drink. As he talked, Harry continued drinking an Irish coffee. He slurped between licking his lips free of the heavy cream topping the drink.

"Our mates were hell-bent on arranging for your dad and me to lose our virginity before leaving Scotland for the war. I can't remember your dad's story right at the minute, but my first mistake was listening to the advice of fools telling me where to find the 'man in the boat'. They said that when you find it, rub it, rub it bloody hard. I had no idea what the hell they were talking about, and several young girls had the misfortune of being victim to my ignorance, none of them willing or inspired enough to follow up with the deed."

He demonstrated hand motions that were useless in context to the act of meaningful foreplay. "So down to the night before I'm due to leave with your dad," he continued, "we end up at a party in a rather shitty tenement home of a woman whose husband was working in the service—India, Burma or something exotic. She liked young servicemen, lads really, as we were coming of age. She was fortyish, an old tart to us young lads who were being sent off to war by mothers the same age. Although I'd love to meet her again, that would make her almost seventy, so I suppose not, but she was a real ride and a half, believe me."

Billy listened, intrigued to cross-reference any of the recent methods Meg had imparted through their mutual education, hoping for more clarity on the "man in the boat" Harry had referenced. Harry tugged urgently at Billy's sleeve to get his attention, the urgency in anticipation of passing out.

Harry slurred on, "I sat drinking a beer in the living room, waiting, some other lads who were ahead of me, as they came and went from the room and then sent me in with several more boys waiting expectantly. I was waiting for some trick, some of the lads to bust into the room and stand laughing at me as I tried to do it. I stripped down to my underpants, skinny white legs, spotty pubescent face and back, and stood there shaking. I noticed a large chest of drawers and decided to push it in front of the door. It must have been funny seeing this half-naked strip of skin trying to shove a large piece of furniture across the floor as she lay there watching me. I was scared shitless. However, the mind was willing, and my little hard-on pushing against my y-fronts drove me on. I'm sure it was the one pushing the chest of drawers."

Harry paused again and took a long drink of his Irish coffee and waved to a waitress to bring another before he went on. "The woman in the bed, I never knew her name, told me to hurry up, that others wanted to have a go. My first endeavor into romance was to be one of speed!" He laughed and scratched his nuts. "I slipped both legs out of my underpants in one fluid movement and left them on the cold linoleum floor as she pulled back the bedspread and invited me in. I kneeled between her parted thighs and had no idea what the hell to do. I could smell her perfume, overpowering and cheap, and the air was stale and sweaty in the cold room. I could see condensation running down the window above her head. I could smell her in a way I'd never experienced, mixed human smells of desire and lust, juices, damp sheets and primal sweat. You know what I mean?"

Billy nodded as if he knew what Harry meant.

"She put her hand on my hip and said that I needed to get inside her. I lay down on her fat white tummy and slid inside her. It was so warm and wet, so deliciously natural.

She slapped my bottom and told me to push in and out, and to hurry up. I don't think I thrust more than twice before I came, but it was fucking brilliant. I became a disciple to the hairy clam in that instant."

Harry slid closer to Billy on the velvet couch and pushed one big arm over his shoulders. His breath was thick with the smell of coffee, and a slight sweetness of the whiskey, and Billy could feel the sweat of Harry's underarms press against his shoulder and dampen his own clothing. He smiled and leaned in, waiting for wisdom from the only man who, unfortunately, might ever impart such knowledge.

"The banging on the door brought me back to reality, Billy boy," Harry said. "I had done it! It was over before I even knew what I'd done, but it was done! I asked her if I could try again and she told me to fuck off and send in the next lad. I pulled my undies up after retrieving them with a sock-covered toe, feeling the cold air rushing around the wetness that covered my cock, and hobbled back to the door as I pulled my trousers on. I was begging for one more go, feeling my damp crotch radiating in the dank room, it was brilliant, *brilliant*! Now powerful enough to conquer the world, I push the chest of drawers back from the door as I did a strut out into the hallway. No longer a virgin, a man!"

Harry lay back on the couch and let out a long slow fart as he relived the moment. He rubbed his crotch without thinking, reaching around the sumptuous belly Billy was sure had not been there for his first conquest.

Harry paused, then pulled Billy even closer and whispered. "Never replace your passion with reason, always trust what makes your heart sing, lad." With that, he passed out, and Billy realized as he looked at the fat man snoring beside him, that you should never judge a book by its copious cover. Billy ordered another drink; the night was still young.

He awoke the next morning chained to the railings in front of his Mam's terrace house. He realized through the fog of a hangover that the lads took it as a rite of passage to defile the groom with as much abuse as possible, preparing him to go into battle with his new wife. One shoe was missing, and he had a head full of train grease. One knee showed through a rip in his trousers. He reached to it with his free hand and brushed the gravel from the small red welts. He remembered nothing after they started drinking from a bottle of Tequila the waitress had mysteriously produced after her private dance for the group.

As Billy hung there, DCI Williams pulled up in his black Jaguar. He rolled the window down slowly. "You look a little indisposed young man," he said. Billy grunted and tried to compose himself, and DCI Williams continued. "I just found out you've come up in the world and are about to be married. That fifty pounds seems to have gone to good use—you and the lads frequented that little place down on the docks last night—"

Billy froze.

"Word does get around. I had a couple of questions for you, but I suppose today isn't the time to chat. DCI Williams rolled his window back up and pulled off slowly just as Mam came outside and shrieked at the sight of her son.

Mam pried the handcuffs free and brought Billy into a bath in front of the kitchen fire. As he lay in the warm water, nursing his aching head and sore wrists, he thought of the conversation he'd had with Meg the night before.

Meg hoped for a hotel in Leeds or Manchester for the wedding, but in reality, the Diggle Hotel was the best his Mam could arrange at such short notice. Meg's mother and father were resentful their daughter was marrying below herself, to a boy they thought was just a friend all these years, not husband or—God forbid—father material. They still refused to put a penny toward the wedding or lift a finger to make the event happen, even as Meg chose to telegraph the pending birth.

"They said they'd save their money and their effort for the next wedding I have," Meg told him.

Still, even through the fog of his pounding headache, Billy felt a sense of contentment. Meg was his and always had been. Several cups of sweet black tea and a brisk scrub to remove the grease and paint and he was pressed and dressed before Harry Two Bellies arrived, fantastically fresh and perky to continue his duties as best man.

Chapter 11

The Wedding

Meg looked beautiful in her off-white dress when she walked down the aisle with her father. Billy, still recovering from his stag night and wedding day nerves, thought he might be sick as he stood at the altar waiting for her. Harry placed a hand on his shoulder.

"Steady, lad."

Meg's Dad cried as he lifted her veil and handed her to Billy.

"She's all I have, take care of her," he said through clenched teeth and a forced smile. Billy grimaced and knew their fragile resistance to this marriage was a testament to Meg's power of persuasion—and their inability to control her own sense of destiny. Meg faced him and made a declaration.

"I am here, and you are my family now, Billy McTaggart."

After the brief wedding ceremony in the church, Billy and Meg arrived at the reception on his dad's old motorbike. Meg's broad smile shone out from a face speckled with oil as he helped her out of the sidecar, but a large dust coat protected her dress.

The reception, as he and Meg had planned with Mam, was a simple affair of pork pies and finger foods such as the fashionable cheddar cheese cube with a cocktail onion on a toothpick, and dainty cocktail sausages on more toothpicks, and lashings of good bitter and sweet sparkling wine to wash it all down. The highlight of the reception was Harry Two Bellies' speech as best man. It was out of character, but reminiscent of his brief moment of sensitivity at the stag night, when Harry lapsed into a state of eloquence never before seen or heard from him. His usual crass humor was replaced by gentle storytelling of Billy and Meg's lives, their courtship, and their strengths as a couple. He indeed became the father Billy never had in that moment.

Billy walked across the dance floor with a plate full of wedding cake and a big grin. He placed the cake on the table next to Meg and pulled up a chair across the corner where she sat. Deftly, he proceeded to scoop a thick lump of lemon vanilla icing up on to his thumb as he stared Meg squarely in the eyes, she sat tight-lipped with a smirk on her face. He scooted his chair forward and pushed his knee between her knees and brought his iced thumb to her mouth. She didn't flinch a jot. Defiant, he felt her knees grip his leg and saw her jaw lock. A little grin escaped the edge of her mouth and danced in her eyes; she egged him on with a squeeze of her knees, opening them to allow his knee to slide beyond and between her thighs. He slowly panned his thumb over her mouth, leaving a thin smear of creamy butter icing that teased her senses. Her eyes darted around the room as he knew she expected to catch onlookers talking behind hands at this rare public intimacy. There was still gossip about the impending baby, but only from die-hard fatalists who hated the success he and Meg represented and who wished them ill. That was the working-class way, but he never doubted they would rise above their station, having a right to find happiness.

He looked around the room; not one person noticed them in the dim light speckled by the luminous hot spots from the mirrored ball swirling around the room. Everyone was busy consuming free beer and food.

"Taste the icing Meg," he whispered in her ear. "It's sweet and sticky, just like you."

She refused to take his thumb into her mouth and suck the icing off even in the relative shrouded seclusion of the dim lighting in a room full of people she knew. They were in the Diggle Hotel of all places, festooned with paper streamer's in an endless chain link from one end of the room to the other. He could sense a fair shindig coming on; it would be a long one and the best night of their life thus far, perhaps the best night ever.

He slid his other hand onto Meg's thigh, emboldened by her waning resistance and squeezed. A little noise escaped her lips, and he took the advantage by slipping the tip of his thumb into the edge of her mouth. She bit down on his thumb as it slipped past her lips, but only enough to hold him there. He felt her swallow eagerly, sucking at his thumb in tiny motions, trying to avoid detection of her pleasure. He knew that from afar in the dimness, it would look only to be a husband cupping his wife's face in gentle affection.

She held him there as she took his other hand on her thigh and slid it upward beneath her skirt, over her stockings and brides garter belt to soft flesh. She parted her knees and he pushed forward on his chair. Ensnared by her invitation he was oblivious to the rest of the room. He let her guide his fingers to the edge of her knickers he knew would already be wet and stained in a delicious line he desperately wanted to cross.

He ran his thumb around the edge of her panties, then effortlessly and swiftly slid his thumb inside her wet lips before she had time to resist in the flurry of it all. He moved both his thumbs in small rotating movements and felt her grip her legs tighter the more she salivated and ground herself into the chair. She squeezed her lips above and below, and he could feel the pulsing strength of both simultaneously.

Meg straightened her back, wide-eyed as though she thought to stand up abruptly and push the chair away in some statement of defiance, but as he felt the warmness engulf his hand her mouth let go of his thumb. He licked his thumb clean of the icing and picked up a napkin and gently wiped Meg's mouth. Their eyes fixed on each other in the play of things. He raised his other hand and slowly licked his fingers and thumb.

"You make a fine icing yourself," he said to her, Meg flushed, and he asked if she cared to dance now that she had a fire about her.

Meg took Billy's hand and squeezed it. She was beautiful, Billy thought. He held her hand and led her to the dancefloor as Mam put on a record, Nat King Cole—"When I Fall in Love." After the first verse and chorus, Harry led Mam to the dance floor and everyone joined in singing and dancing.

Three hours later, after the cutting of the cake and the tossing of the garter—which Harry's girlfriend caught amid screeches of disbelief—Billy and Meg bade their guests goodnight amid further hoots and hollers as they retreated up the stairwell of the Diggle Hotel, Pub, and Lounge. Meg had hoped for a grander exit but was content in the claiming of her man.

The stairs creaked and they giggled under the influence of bubbly white wine and in anticipation of what was to come. The knee trembler at the back door to Meg's house three months ago may have sealed the deal in his mind, but this night would be the culmination of their exploration and learning of each other. Tonight, they would share the marriage bed as husband and wife. Billy stopped outside the door to the room. Meg hadn't seen the place yet, and he was apprehensive, knowing her expectations. He remenbered the day he and Mam had paid the deposit.

"The Honeymoon Suite, all satin sheets, Mr. McTaggart," the landlady had said, "and a full breakfast whenever you wake up, my little love doves. Wink! Wink!" She had nudged his Mam as she took the twenty pounds deposit and tucked it into her ample bosom.

Billy stopped Meg as she fumbled with the door lock and key. "I want to carry you over the threshold."

"Shouldn't that be to our own home?" Meg asked.

"We don't have our own home yet, and with staying at Mam's we can save some money for our travels. This will have to do, pet."

He took her by the hand; he didn't want to get into an argument, not tonight of all nights. Meg could fight with the best of them for what she believed she deserved.

"Okay," she said with a hint of dismay in her voice. She'd fought the decision to move into Mam's, but there was a waiting list for the new multi-story homes under construction on nearby council estates. "Pick me up before I fall—besides, I feel a tad frisky." She flashed a naughty grin and released a little snort of laughter.

Her dress rode up as he placed a hand on the small of her back and the other mid-thigh. He felt her sweaty skin against his forearm, clammy, but sensual, skin on intimate skin. Aroused, he pulled her to him, savoring the damp sweat of dancing and the perfume he'd bought for her as one of several small wedding gifts. He fumbled with the doorknob, kicked at the door, and they entered the dark room. A damp smell of mold and old cigarettes and fried food wafting up from the kitchen caught in their throats.

He made out the shape of their overnight bags as he crossed the room toward the bed with Meg in his arms. Gently he laid her down on the salmon-colored candlewick bedspread and moved slowly to kiss her.

"Hold up cowboy," Meg whispered as she wriggled out from underneath him. "I need to go fix myself for you." She moved toward the bathroom.

"Don't worry, I like you just as you are," he tried as she slipped into the small bathroom, a private bath being a luxury she'd insisted upon when he and Mam came to look at the hotel.

It wasn't as if he couldn't afford it. At the final rehearsal for the wedding, when Meg's father still refused to contribute, Billy had slipped his Mum fifty pounds all packed up in an old wage packet.

"This is for the wedding," he'd told her.

"Where did you get all this?" Mam asked.

"I've been saving it for a while. I knew this day would come. I knew one day I'd marry my Meg. Let me know if it is enough, and get your hair done as well."

Now he kicked off his rental shoes, the rented frilly shirt, and the rented tuxedo. With his socks, singlet, and y-fronts still on, he lay on the bed waiting with his hands behind his head, three pillows propping him up. "Are you done yet? I need to pee." He pulled himself from the bed and moved to the door where he pressed his head against it. "Please honey, hurry up."

"Just a minute more," Meg called. He lay back down on the bed, sliding effortlessly into dozing under the weight of the several pints of beers and glasses of sparkling wine he had consumed during toasts of the evening. Somewhere deep in his slumber, the memory of that first time with Meg surfaced in his dream, the warm wetness engulfing him and the cold night air nipping at any exposed flesh. The feeling seemed real as he awoke abruptly and tried to sit up, finding his legs constrained, his underpants around his knees, his singlet up over his chest. He looked down across his belly to the top of Meg's head moving rhythmically up and down as his cock disappeared and reappeared between her hand and her stretched lips in the faint light of the bedside lamp. Mesmerized, he was silent. Never, never had he felt such a thing, not even using the cake of soap to lather himself up in the bath when he had that rare time alone. Meg worked her way up his tummy and kissed his chest, bit at his nipples. His desire to come was almost overwhelmed by the smell of her, and the softness of her skin. Her mouth covered his with a slightly salty taste...

At this moment she was another girl, so much more than he could have imagined in any book he'd ever read. Meg rolled onto her back and pulled him on to her, removing his singlet over the top of his head as he turned. Her skin was sublime, her small hard breasts pushing almost painfully against him. He kissed her wildly, his tongue exploring her neck, her mouth, her breasts as Meg, suffocated by his kiss, pushed at his shoulders and chest, forcing him back down to her breasts.

Her skin was almost translucent, with spider veins mapping out over her hard tummy into the small patch of dark hair between her legs. Down she pushed, nails digging into shoulders. Billy resisted slightly at the pain, but obliged. This was new to him. The lads in the yard had joked at going down on dirty girls behind playground sheds, dirty girls with stinky knickers who demanded pleasure first before they wanked you off with a hand job for a packet of cigarettes or a bag of crisps—so he'd been told.

He looked up briefly as she rolled her eyes back and grabbed at the headboard with white fists. Her hands came down instantly when he stopped, extended fingers grasping at the top of his head, pushing down, urgently, demanding.

"Eat me," she hissed, and he scoured his mind for some reference as to what he should do next, frantic for knowledge beyond his experience. The words and laughter of the lads from the yards echoed around him, mixed with the scent of the room, and sweat, and Meg's juices.

"It's just like supping a cockle, lad, push your tongue in and feel for the man in the boat, you'll know it when you find it, or she'll tell you all right."

With Meg's hands now demanding, and the recklessness of too many beers, he slid his tongue into her, drawing in her scent. What would God say of this wanton lust—this fantastic lust. Love—was this love?

Meg's hands stilled as his breath moved hot upon her. He sensed the tingling spreading heat in her belly as she screamed at him, incoherent, she drove his face into her. He was perceptive enough to feel her respond as his tongue found a nodule of flesh, he assumed was the man in the boat by her reaction. Her climax was intense, and she screamed out almost in pain at the pleasure of it.

He sat up abruptly, shock and concern on his face as she twisted on the bed, curling into a fetal position, panting heavily.

"Sorry, did I hurt you?" He asked, shaken at her response. She said nothing, reveling in her cocoon of pleasure as he knelt there, slack-jawed, wondering what to do next.

"Come here and be inside me," she said breathlessly.

"Did I hurt the baby?" he whispered.

"No, silly boy."

He placed his hands on each side of her thin hips and lowered himself between her thighs. Meg took him in hand and guided him into her. He shuddered and was spent almost instantly—it was all too much for him. Meg shifted and quickly extracted him from her body as she rolled off the bed, crossing to the small bathroom. Billy remained still, hunched on his knees. Turning his head, he followed her lithe body to the bathroom and watched through the bathroom door, slightly ajar, framing Meg as she douched herself in the small sink and flushed the toilet after wiping herself dry.

"Sleep now my man, my husband," Meg said as she crawled back into the bed. She pushed the hair from his sweaty brow. "You have work in the morning, and we don't want to hurt the baby, do we?"

Chapter 12

Zillionaire

B illy felt the coolness of Meg's breath on his neck as she stood behind him, helping him slide into the crisp white shirt. She moved around him and tied his thin black tie in a neat knot then he pulled on his gray waistcoat. This was the Monday after their wedding. He regretted having no time for a honeymoon, but he needed to immediately start work in the clerk's office. Meg had agreed she wasn't going to let a little holiday get in the way of them getting on in the world, even if it meant living with Mam for a while, though she sullenly moped around when he favored Mam in some way. She made it known he was hers now and things would be changing sooner than later.

"I'll see you downstairs for breakfast," Meg said and kissed him on the forehead as he slipped on his fine leather brogues.

Billy was proud that his new position, and the wage that came with it, would qualify them for a little bungalow, eventually a car of their own, and perhaps a romantic holiday to Europe soon enough—and then, America. He was still introducing small amounts of laundered money into their daily life, but with DCI Williams sniffing around every time he made a small improvement to their circumstances, it was still too early to splurge on a trip to the U.S. That would take some finagling.

Billy made his way down the stairs to the kitchen and, as he came through the door, Mam handed him a cup of tea and a plate of toast, buttered and heavy with homemade marmalade. Meg saw him out to the hallway, where he pulled on his jacket, and gave him his wax paper-wrapped lunch. He noticed a little note stuck in between the semitransparent wrapping. She picked a speck of lint from his lapel and kissed him on the cheek. It would be the highlight of his day, weather permitting, to sit under the tree in the station entry and read the message from his wife. He kissed Meg on the forehead and patted her tummy.

"Good day to you both," he said, and kissed Mam as well. "Keep an eye on this lot for me, will you?" He looked back at Meg and Mam as he left the house, smiling.

He walked down toward the station with all the world before him, shouting out and receiving greetings from the town folks. Most of them loved to see one of their own get on a little, yet some still resented any progress—their attitude was the working-class way. He thought to stop in and thank Harry for the leg up he'd given him. It seemed like a lifetime ago that he first walked through those gates with his dad, then as an apprentice, now a clerk. He passed a small group of boys standing by the fence near the entrance to the yard. The older boys were looking for work, picking up coal for sixpence a pound or trying to bum a smoke from the workmen on their way into the yard.

He noticed a smaller, disheveled boy at the edge of the group, probably a little brother to one of the older boys, tagging along when he should have been at school. One snot-encrusted sleeve of his threadbare jumper looked wet and recently used. It had a veneer of grime that gave the rest of the rough, hand-knitted jumper a sheen on the remaining threadbare surfaces still intact around the holes and drags of what was once a dull grey school jersey. The yellow and black V-neck was ratted and stretched almost to an oval. The boy pulled the sleeve instinctively across his runny nose as he stared at Billy.

"Are you a zillionaire, mister?" Billy looked at the boy, a reflection of himself just a few years ago, although Mam would never have let him wipe his nose on his clothing or skip school for that matter. "That suit looks like magic."

"I dreamed it, and you can too if you want." Billy replied as he pulled a clean white hanky out of his breast pocket and offered it to the boy. "Here you go, wipe yer nose and here's sixpence if you keep using that hanky instead of your sleeve." The boy took the hanky in grubby hands and admired its cleanliness.

"Can I keep it, mister?" he asked cautiously before using it.

"Course you can." He felt deep compassion for the scruffy boy. "Forever. It's magic as well. Make a wish, but you have to believe it, and with a bit of luck along with hard work, you're on your way. In fact, I know where there's a paper route to get yourself started, just like me, if I can trust you at your word."

The boy's face lit up and Billy saw belief, a glimmer of realization that you didn't have to be what you were born into.

It was a Northern way, staying in your place, a vestige of the aristocracy, daily life as a culture of servitude. The war had broken that system of thinking and men returning from worldly experiences of war could no longer imagine going down coal mines or standing as footmen at parlor doors for men and women who dallied through privileged lives while their tenants farmed sodden land and had their children die in damp crofts. The world was changing. Billy knew he stood on the shoulders of people like his Mam or Harry and even his Dad, and he needed to push that forward somehow, not only for his own children, but within his own community.

He walked into the yard wondering how he could help change things. Perhaps his secret money needed to be shared somehow beyond just his own needs, Mam, Meg's and the new baby's? He would need to make that money grow—he needed to make enough to make magic happen.

As he crossed the yard, careful to avoid the mud puddles with his newly polished lace-up brogues, he reminisced about his own start in life. He was always the wee man enduring some shit, figuratively and literally, from schoolroom bullies to grown people who looked despairingly at his diminutive size as an encumbrance rather than a benefit. How they might laugh on the other side of their faces at the little hands that squirreled away a small fortune from a Royal Bank of England's railway car. Today was a new adventure indeed.

He entered the shed to thank Harry, who gave him a parting fart as the lads in the tea room cheered three hoorays and clapped him on the back. "You'll always be a tapper, son," Harry said tearfully. "You'll always have a hammer hanging here, but I'll kick your arse if you ever find the need to come back and use it. It's onward for you. Now get the fuck out of here, you're stinking the place up with all that hair cream and clean clothes."

Arriving at the clerk's office was entirely different to arriving at the yard, as he'd done for the past several years. For one, the smells and sounds were different. At the clerk's office, the smell of paper, wood paneling, and ink replaced the metallic greasiness of the workshop. The scent of pomade on cropped, brushed hair and of pressed shirts replaced the heavy smell of sweat and dirty overalls smeared and matted with axle grease and coal dust. He found the cleanliness almost more offensive in its ability to mask men and their true nature behind self-important faces. In the yard, you knew who could do their job by the exertion of their bodies and in the camaraderie of honest labor. In the sterility of the clerk's office, there was near silence, and a fastidious commitment to an environment of professional decorum as pens scratched monotonously in bulky leather ledgers. No shared cups of tea or the banter of nicknames that defined a man for life, no farting or pranks to break the drudge of dirty work and low wages.

He conceded willingly to the flow of paper, the in-and out-boxes that consumed and spewed the commerce of the railway relentlessly—bills of lading, schedules and timetables, wages and ticket prices—and, over time, he looked out the window toward the yard less and less. The formality of the office appealed to his aspiration as a businessman, but the physicality of his body yearned for the fatigue a solid day of work gave, rather than the aching, rounded shoulders of a pencil pusher. Payday, however, quickly eroded any longing to return to his work as a tapper.

Over time, Billy infused his own personality into the clerk's office. The head clerk liked him and soon realized his work ethic and understanding how the yard worked outside of the bubble of the office was valuable, mainly when they ran into a dispute of some sort—wages, timecards, holiday pay. The head clerk knew Billy would talk to the lads on his behalf and they trusted him as having their back, one of their own. The head clerk even allowed him to lead an introduction of the clerks to the yard workers, so they better understood the impact and realities of their work orders, schedules, and timetables that manifested into real work.

Billy relished the fact that he'd had a hand in the way communications improved so operations ran smoother with fewer delays, and that less frequently bills of laden disappeared along with consignments of goods. Success was due primarily to the head clerk arranging with the board of the railway for wage increases based on performance rather than the brutal practice of keeping workers down and in their place, as was the pre-war way of indentured workers. The head clerk promoted Billy to salaried clerk after just six months in the office, which gave Billy a perfect opportunity to launder some of the train notes into wage packets of stations further afield, while keeping the newer currency for himself.

"You'll be after my job next, young man," the head clerk said as he gestured for Billy to take a seat in his small glass-lined office. The office windows looked out over the station platform, from where he could also observe the clerks next door at their desks.

"I'll not say no to that seat in time, but I have a lot of learning to do before we get to that, sir." He knew better than to get ahead of himself. "I would like to ask for expanded training, if I may, sir. I believe there are regional seminars, and a formal University of Manchester qualification as a chartered accountant available for the right candidates under the railway education program."

The head clerk looked at him. "Is there now? I think I heard about it. Let me see." He nodded before he continued. "I admired your vim. I see myself in you, although after twenty years in the same position I'm not sure I ever had the initiative to ask for such opportunities, even if they existed."

"I believe I can prove myself worthy, even if I didn't do that well at my Eleven Plus exams, or school leavers certificate for that matter. My wife tells me the proof is in the pudding of my daily work. I know I may have to go the long way around, but I know I can do it if given a chance."

The head clerk smiled. Billy was to be his protégé, his legacy, the grand recipient of this corner office looking out on a grey world of trains, people, and goods that ventured into the world while he sat and watched, hands pressed to the glass in captivity. But the head clerk was wrong. He couldn't have imagined Billy's aspiration to travel, to walk barefoot on white beaches, to fly in jet airplanes high above the earth.

As Billy left the office one evening, he joked with the boys that still hung around the main gate begging coppers and cigarettes. In the months that had passed, the waif with the snotty jersey had gone back to school, and Billy periodically bumped into him in Meg's parent's shop as he returned from his paper route. Billy sometimes heard his paper being shoved through the letterbox at five AM with a shout of, "Wake up, Mr. Zillionaire, me old cobber."

Time had sped by since he had entered the clerk's office. Among various modes of laundering of the money, Billy was now in a position to explore the implementation of a plan to push his good fortune forward. It occurred to him that the law, business, travel, and charity were necessary siblings to wealth—to his stash of cash if he were to succeed.

He stopped in at St Mary's church where he'd attended his whole life, home to the order of the Sisters of Perpetual Penance. He asked Mother Superior how he might help and support them beyond his normal tithing, some small way now that he was coming up in the world. He promised her that he would pop in for an extended chat and a cup of tea after church on Sunday if she agreed to have some of her delicious home-baked biscuits on hand.

When he got home, Meg offered him his dinner and, after the meal, the newspaper with a cup of tea near the fire in the back of the house where Mam sat in the adjacent chair and snored deeply. She was still cleaning house—hard work for a woman with arthritic hands—and he loved to watch her at rest instead of running around washing or cooking. He noted a story on the front page of his paper—BOAC's had purchased fifteen Boeing 707's as part of their Trans-Atlantic fleet. America now seemed closer than ever in half the time. Nowhere in the world looked out of reach.

"You had a call from DCI Williams," Meg told him, "an invitation to pop down for a visit to the Manchester Metropolitan Police Headquarters tomorrow morning. He seemed quite insistent."

Billy acknowledged the message and swore under his breath, wondering what the fucker wanted now. One promotion and the DCI was back up his arse again.

Walking into the entrance of the impressive stone façade of the police headquarters the next morning, Billy knew the display of grandeur was meant to intimidate. The building's size was immense on the scale of Diggle, but every bully used these tactics. This wasn't his first rodeo he thought as he hitched his thumbs into his lapels and squared his shoulders.

He and DCI Williams exchanged polite hellos and stiff handshakes, and Billy took a seat in his office. Billy noted the smell of leather furniture that filled the mahogany paneled room. He watched DCI Williams as he sat behind the desk, which was clean of anything useful except a tray of yellow pencils and a notepad which lay within arm's reach of the DCI. He watched as the DCI leaned forward, picked up the pencil with clean white hands protruding from crisp linen cuffs secured by golden Masonic cufflinks. His fingers were fleshy and pink, with perfect white nails and unbroken cuticles, nimble and deliberate in their manipulation of the pencil. Billy looked at his own hands that held his cap in his lap. Even after working in the office for the past six months, the years of calluses were not washed away quite so quickly.

"Billy boy," DCI Williams said in his educated accent, another division beyond nails, "you may wonder why I've asked you in for a cup of tea today." DCI Williams paused almost defensively as a young policewoman entered the room carrying a silver tray with two teacups, sugar cubes, silver tongs and a delicate milk jug with the emblem of Special Branch imprinted in deep blue ceramic on the side. Billy thought of the tea stained mugs back in the shed, spoonsful of sugar shoveled into them with tarnished spoons.

"So, you're a married man now and still with the railroad," the DCI began as the policewoman poured their tea. "You never came to see me as requested after your stag night. I thought I might chase you up and jog your memory. Your young wife sounded quite lovely when I called your home. I look forward to getting to know her."

Billy saw the cat and felt himself the mouse as he accepted the tea. *This mouse will not hide in the shadows today*, he thought, and he asked for another cube of sugar from the smiling policewoman.

DCI Williams sat back in his chair only far enough to still reach his teacup and teaspoon, which he stirred monotonously in a series of small chinks and chimes as he waited for the policewoman to leave. The silence lay heavy between the two of them. Billy picked up a shortbread biscuit from the plate on the tray and bit into it.

"Nice biscuits Her Majesty provides for her lads. We don't get this quality down the office," said Billy, breaking the silence, ready for the questions.

"You seem to be a smart lad, Billy, doing well for yourself with a new wife and baby on the way, even a promotion into the clerk's office. You're going up in the world, young man." He paused and continued to stir his tea, then slowly placed the teaspoon in the saucer as he took his teacup up in both hands as he sat back in his chair. "I don't know what it is about you, lad, but I get a funny feeling you're living beyond your means and breeding." He supped silently at his tea and smiled at Billy, perfect white teeth between thin lips. "I heard you were abandoned, after all, and I'm curious about your father. Do you happen to know his whereabouts?"

"I don't, but there's nowt like hard work and the press of someone's boot on your neck to make you try a little harder, not to mention a good woman by your side who has some class and ambition. You know how it is, Mr. Williams, sir, with the common folk always trying to be what they're not supposed to be."

"I'm not sure I'm familiar with the compromise you infer." DCI grimaced and stood up abruptly. "I just wanted to see how you're doing Billy, old chum. Your success intrigues me, as does the location of your wayward father. Do drop in again sometime. Best regards to your family—and keep an eye open for me should you hear from your dad."

With that, DCI Williams picked up a small bunch of keys before offering Billy his hand to shake, forcing Billy to relinquish his teacup before even taking a sip. The two men stood facing each other, shaking hands. "Let me walk you out," DCI Williams said, twirling the keys on his finger. As they entered the hall, the keys slipped from his hand and fell into an air grill on the floor. Without thinking, Billy reached down, slid his hand in between the slats on the grill, and retrieved the keys.

"Fortunate, your stature, such small hands," DCI Williams said as Billy handed him back the keys. "Tell me, how is the hand you cut when you opened the wagon?" Billy's eyes held his unwavering gaze.

"Funny thing all that money we found, thanks to you, Not that you would've seen too many of those lovely five pound notes in your wage packet, but it seems some of the lads have ended up with them in their wage packets in various regions around the districts." He stared intently at Billy. "And what a coincidence, you now being the wages clerk, I thought."

Stone-faced, Billy pulled out his wallet. He removed and unfolded a large white five-pound note. "Do you mean like this one?" he asked. He noted the DCI's startled expression at the appearance of the disheveled note. "I got this one from my dad, whom you seem so keen to know about. It was part of his farewell gift when he dumped my mam and me. Too shagged out to use I thought, but this one is more of a keepsake anyway. My dad was part of the team that chased the Operation Bernhart Nazi's printers during the war. He told me about it."

He waved the note. "It's my pride and joy that I carry everywhere with me." Billy folded the note meticulously and slowly placed it back in his wallet. "I'll keep an eye out now that I know what you're looking for, sir," he said, and thanked DCI Williams for his time and the tea.

Billy paused as he made his way to the stairs and turned. "If we could meet at the weekend next time, for a beer perhaps with the other lads from the railroad. It's hard for me to get time off during the week. I have my reputation to think of, after all."

DCI William scowled. "I have an eye on you, Billy, just in case you get too far ahead of yourself. You are your father's son, of that I'm sure. Appearances do not deceive me."

Billy stood square to the DCI. "I get your message loud and clear, although I'm still not sure you know what you're looking for. I did spill my fair share of blood finding your wagon though, and the reward was well spent, thank you."

Billy realized as he left the building that he needed to be a little more cautious. This man was dangerous. He'd sped up the exchange of cash—not only had he been replacing the money in the wage's packets for the district railroad, but he also started to substitute cash in the daily takings at the ticket depot. *Sloppy*, he thought. *Bloody stupid*. And his training trips to Manchester, and sometimes Leeds, allowed him the opportunity to gamble with laundered money and make up more than he lost as he became proficient at blackjack and roulette in the underground gambling establishments where he masqueraded as Levi Sparkle. They didn't care what color your money was or where it came from. He needed to be more cautious. Although much of the money was well on its way to being clean—he now had a sizable amount of legal money in his tins.

To add to the discomfort of the visit with the DCI, as he found his seat on the train home to Diggle, he thought of the concern Mam mentioned to him before leaving the house earlier that morning. Meg had gone off to the doctor early for a checkup and, as Mam laid out his breakfast, she inquired as to the lack of growth in Meg. Her tiny frame showed little or nothing of a second-trimester pregnancy. He allowed she'd gained a bit of weight, and ate for two at dinnertime, and that she'd bought enough oversized maternity dresses to clothe an army of mothers, but they made it hard to see the true shape of her. She even, he noted, had cravings for Christmas meat pies and spicy Indian food. Mam wasn't deterred. She was concerned that Meg's trips to the doctor were private—that neither she nor Billy nor even her own parents could convince the spirited Meg to let of them to accompany her.

Billy disembarked from the train and walked toward home. He'd told Meg he planned to take the afternoon off from work so they could go for a long walk up on the moors and she could tell him how the visit to the doctor had gone.

To his surprise he found Meg sitting at the bottom of the stairs with a bloody towel and a small bundle of new baby clothes they'd bought together. Meg cried uncontrollably, and as he tried to understand what was going on and she blubbered something about the long drop toilet out back and said that the baby was gone. She'd expected him to come home sooner and wasn't sure what to do.

Heartbroken at the thought of the baby being gone, he had no stomach to press Meg for details. He ushered her up to bed and called the doctor. When Mam arrived home from work, she looked at him doubtfully, knowingly holding her tongue. The local doctor came and seemed confused at the talk of a pregnancy. He'd seen Meg on several occasions, but Meg always refused to let him properly examine her. He wasn't her doctor, he said, and he advised them to follow up with an obstetrician or gynecologist in the morning. The doctor was somewhat new to the village, and sensitive in his dealings with the locals as he built his new practice. He bade the

McTaggart's well and left, seeming happy to avoid any conflict with the distressed father and bereaved mother.

Meg was inconsolable for weeks and cheered up a little only when Billy came home and told her the head clerk had approved his training as a chartered accountant. His accountancy training and testing for his exams would be carried out in London and Manchester. This was a welcome distraction from the awkward feeling that filled the house as Meg convalesced. She was unwilling to talk about the loss of the baby and dismissed his request to meet with her doctor to discuss the miscarriage. Billy brought her presents daily and promised a trip away as soon as she was well, if she could wait for a break in his training.

Mam cared for Meg, but she was skeptical and sought opportunities to discuss the situation with Billy. He avoided any discussion as much as Meg did. The less said, the brighter Meg seemed to be, and Billy was willing to wait until Meg decided to bring the subject up herself. His mother's doubts about the pregnancy left him uncomfortable, but he couldn't even consider that she might have mislead him. Why would she?

In the following months, during the trips away for his accountancy training, Billy invested in several more reversible jackets for Levi Indigo, custom made on Seville row in London where no one asked questions as to a gentleman's fashion preferences and quality was guaranteed, at a price. In his crisp shirts and tailored clothing, he no longer suffered discrimination for his size. His money afforded him acceptance. He needed to keep up his guard and stay out of the reach of DCI Williams. London was a perfect place to do that. Within the year as Levi Indigo he'd gained proficiency and some notoriety as a gambler and was soon invited into high stake poker games where the well dressed and well-heeled sat in smoky rooms in private clubs. Levi, the young American, was entertaining and debonair, he was quick-witted and posed no threat to the bold athletic sportsmen whose families boasted Oxford and Cambridge. Levi used the excuse of having to return to the States between visits as a cover for his reluctance to take up invitations to visit the country estates of fellow gamblers on weekends. He played the loving husband with a wife back in California who was hoping to land a part in the movie business, hence her unavailability to travel.

To his real wife, Meg, Billy had spoken of trying for another baby, but the conversation always caused her distress, and the subject was pushed aside awkwardly. He found it easy enough to find other things that needed his attention. Billy threw himself into his studies and this pursuit gave them a common cause that replaced physical intimacy. She moved into the spare room with the excuse that her body was still healing, and she shouldn't tempt him. He thought of talking to his Mam about it, but Mam made it clear that she could have no opinion of the young couple's relationship without taking sides, and that would only make things worse.

As his money grew, he realized he needed more ways to invest it—more ways to make sure there was always enough for Meg's dresses—but for him it was the intrigue of the chase that spurred him on, bamboozling DCI Williams with a legal reason for his success, defying the inevitability of his birthright. The money was a byproduct of his endeavors.

When Meg's parents wanted to retire, he bought their shop and added a hairdressing salon to the back of it where Meg could be the center of the social goings-on. They hired two young hairdressers from Manchester who were up on the most recent hairstyles of Ann Margaret and Pricilla Presley. Meg never checked the books. The business was all cash and easy to push funds through without anyone asking questions.

"I want to buy a bus," Billy said one afternoon. He hadn't been this excited in a long time.

"A bus!" snorted Meg, almost choking on the tea she was drinking.

"Yes, the type we went on holiday in when we went to Redcar, or the one I went on when I was raspberry picking in Scotland as a boy with my dad's family."

Meg snorted again. "You mean a Chara… a Charabanc?" She rolled her eyes.

"Exactly!" Billy laughed and started to jump around the room holding Meg's hands. "I want to buy five!" he shouted. "I want to stand in the front of the bus and tell people about all the sights they'll see on the way to their final destination, Blackpool, Redcar, Whitley Bay—" He went on, now consumed by the idea for his next venture.

"Where will that sort of money come from?" she asked. "One Chara is expensive enough, never mind five."

"No, no, it's the perfect holiday for us working class folks," he answered. "People like us, we save up for an annual outing with a work or social club, an outing to the beach or fair. Then, on Sunday mornings, crowds of merrymakers will pile into our buses with brown paper packages wrapped in twine and filled with egg sandwiches on thick slices of homemade bread, cold sausages, wedges of cheese and a flask of hot tea between their knees. 'Off to the beach', I will shout, 'tally ho!'"

Billy came to life as he impersonated a tour guide, then dropped to his knees in front of Meg and looked at her. With all their time apart, his training trips away and the physical distance Meg kept from him, he had sometimes wondered if they would manage to last. Perhaps this was something new they could do together, something he could share with her. He wanted a baby, but she indicated that it was out of the question, for now—she was scared and needed more time to grow into herself rather than have something growing inside of her, she said—and she agreed this bus could be the thing that brought them back together.

That night he sat in the cellar and counted out five hundred pounds, the other five hundred he would borrow from the bank with the shop as security. The loan term would be short, but he would have a loan anyone could see if they wondered where the money for the first bus came from. There was always the question of DCI Williams and the nagging suspicion that Billy would be getting another visit from him again soon, so Billy kept solid books and the law on his side.

The next summer the busses they bought did well. Billy employed the now-retired Harry Two Bellies to run them, along with several other lads he could trust, also recently retired from the yard. Meg lost interest in the shop and hairdressing salon, so he hired a manager who moved into Meg's childhood home above the shop. He bought a house for Meg's mother and father out on a small farm where he kept a workshop and a large shed for the busses. Meg's father oversaw cleaning and maintenance of the busses, and Meg's mam managed the bookings.

Keep it in the family, all ship shape and legal, Billy thought. *Keep it in the family.*

He was still working as a senior clerk while building his businesses, and had almost doubled his money by this point, his tins in the cellar nearly inadequate now to contain it all and the official bank accounts healthy. He supported a small scholarship fund and a weekly trip on his busses during the summers, for children of lesser means who did well in school and attended Sunday school with the Sisters of Perpetual Penance. He had more than he ever dreamed of, and Elvis still held second place on his list. Perhaps it was time to go see him in person.

Chapter 13

Hawaii

Billy and Meg stepped off the aircraft onto the tarmac and paused to breathe deeply. The humid Hawaiian air filled his lungs, clung to his white oily skin and wrapped around him like a wet blanket. His English tweed jacket with leather elbow patches sucked up the wet heat. The year was 1961—and what a way to start his twenty-first birthday celebration, Billy thought.

"Fantastic. Fucking fantastic, Levi, my old boy," he whispered to himself. Hawaii, and the King was in town. They had front row seats for the show.

Meg tugged at his sleeve as she navigated the gangway with two hat boxes and a matching makeup case. A bead of sweat ran down her shiny forehead, into her heavily mascaraed eyes. "It's too hot, love, and the heat is killing me."

Billy broke from her grip and strode toward the terminal building, Meg in pursuit.

"Billy!" her shrill voice followed him. "Wait for me, and don't you remember, a gentleman always carries a lady's bags?"

Still, he walked ahead of Meg, in his own world, savoring the success of having organized the Great Hawaiian Breakaway—a raffle for the St, Mary's Sisters of Perpetual Penance and the Children's Charity Fundraiser, of which he was the founder, with a grand prize of this magnificent trip.

He'd done it all without being discovered as the instigator of such a grand prize. The whole process had been a work of art, he assured himself as he entered the terminal building. The prize consisted of a flight for two and front row seats to see the King in concert at the Bloch Arena Honolulu Hawaii on March twenty-fifth. Also included was one hundred pounds spending money, a stay in the posh Sheraton Hotel, and pick up at the airport in a limousine.

The concert was held to raise funds for a USS Arizona War Memorial. Tickets for a limited group of three hundred people were sold for a hundred dollars each—a fortune, more than a year's salary for most of the rail workers in Diggle. Just the idea of it was almost more than anyone in Diggle could bear.

Billy's plan worked like a charm, even with DCI Williams sniffing around. The poor bugger even bought a ticket, thinking he might win.

The ruse was simple. Fred Two Fingers Watson had been the ideal candidate for the donation. No one had heard from him in years, and Billy remembered the great sendoff he witnessed when Fred, minus his thumb and two adjacent fingers, set off for America after receiving his payout for the accident that took his digits. Odds were, Fred was probably lying in a gutter in New York, full of the beer, never having made it past the first pub and whore he found upon arriving in the U.S. Yet, as far as everyone in Diggle now believed, Fred was the lad who remembered his home when he'd made it big—a donation to his favorite church, St. Mary's, was a grand thing to do.

With the raffle in place, run and supported by Aunt Lil, the hardest part was making sure he won first prize. This was a thing he had to do—his best shot at breaking out. How else could an ex-tapper and current clerk from Diggle afford to go all the way to Hawaii to see the King, God bless and protect him? Even with his local success, a trip like that would raise all the red flags for DCI Williams.

Key aspects to his plan required perfect timing. Billy offered to pick up the raffle tickets for Aunt Lil on his next trip to Manchester. He reminded her that Dean's Stationary Emporium was only half a mile from the rail HQ where he'd be working for a couple of weeks on an audit of cattle shipping costs.

Aunt Lil gave him a five-pound note from the small stack of notes that made up a hundred pounds for incidental costs Fred had sent in an envelope all the way from Hawaii. They'd all taken turns with the envelope—touching it, holding it, looking at the stamp of the great mystical civilization across the seas. As part of his plan, he included the letter for the convent, along with a receipt for full cash payment to the hotel manager at the Sheraton Hotel in Honolulu. The amount added a generous little something extra for the manager if he would be so kind as to write out a letter and sign it as Fred.

With two hundred tickets to a roll, and the stipulation from Fred that each ticket was worth a five-pound donation, the nuns of St. Mary's were overwhelmed with the thought of raising one thousand pounds for the children's school fund. The sisters would be able to afford a new security alarm to keep thieves out and away from the holy relic they coveted, a replica of the Girdle of Thomas. Sacra Cintola. A Christian relic that according to medieval legend dropped from the sky as proof of her assentation for doubting Thomas as the virgin Mary rose to heaven as he returned from a pilgrimage to India.

At the stationery shop, Billy purchased the full box of two hundred rolls of tickets, each roll with matching numbers. He constructed a ticket box for Aunt Lil that would hold the tickets for the patrons in one half but flipping of a secret panel would reveal the other half of the box. Therein would be two hundred little red tickets for Mayor Althorp to rummage through with her long, slender, manicured hands, all tickets bearing the same number. His number. It was risky, but the Levi in him loved risk. Fred had also offered to match the funds raised and throw a great party at the grand draw. In this way, Billy could give more to the children's fund than he could ever donate in his everyday life. With a little help from the better heeled in the community, everyone would be a winner, with more than enough ice cream, buns, pork pies, and pints of bitter to go around, and a nice big bottle of gin for Sister Louise, God bless her.

Sister Louise even agreed, reluctantly but with the promise of all that cash, to get up on one of those contraptions that would drop her into a tank of water if a reveler hit the bulls-eye target. The crowd watching this event was almost as big as the line across the playground waiting for their chance to throw three balls for a sixpence, small revenge on the holy woman for years of upheld hands beaten with a ruler, twisted ears, and pinched underarms.

There were murmurs of disappointment when the winning ticket was drawn and called out. "Susan McTaggart and partner," Mayor Althorp announced over the tannoy loudspeaker system Harry had set up. "Susan McTaggart are you here?" she called out in her high nasal whine as Mam stood transfixed.

"Mum, it's you." Billy shook his mother gently by the arm. "It's you, you won." He caught Mam as she fainted, and he and Meg carried her to the St. Johns ambulance that was on hand for such events.

Making his mother the winner of the trip was his most significant and calculated risk. He knew she'd never go, and although it felt manipulative, he relied on the fact that he and Meg would be the ultimate recipients of the prize. He'd made sure there was a transfer clause in the conditions sent by Fred that allowed direct family members to transfer the prize to another family member, but not sell it.

After several cups of tea much later that afternoon, he finally agreed to accept the fantastic prize from his mother. Meg sat on the edge of her seat squeezing his hand and staring holes into him every time he refused to accept the tickets. "It would make me happy, son," Mam insisted. "Think of it as the honeymoon you never really had. My nerves couldn't handle the trip, airplanes and all. Bring me back something special."

As flustered as Meg had been for weeks before the trip—everything had to be perfect, dresses bought, and matching bags and shoes—the flights were uneventful other than Meg's reluctance to let go of his hand for the duration of them, including a trip to the bathroom mid-flight from LA. The air hostess was most understanding in her bright, upper-class British way as she ushered these two petite Northerners into the confined space of the bathroom.

During dinner service, Meg marveled at the embossed crockery and champagne the hostess liberally poured for them. "Dead posh, Billy, dead posh," she said, trying to cut her meat with one hand. He held her steak with his fork and then fed her one cube of overdone beef at a time. Meg suffered much as the plane landed and said she was relieved to still be alive as they taxied to a stop amid flowing coconut trees that lined the edge of the terminal building.

A stout man sporting a thick ponytail and dressed in a black suit stood at the door as they entered the Honolulu Airport VIP arrivals lounge. *Mr. William McTaggart* was printed neatly on his small, white, cardboard sign. Billy had never seen his name displayed other than on the school blackboard for detention, so he walked right past the driver until Meg noticed the sign and pulled him back.

"That's us," she told the driver as he proceeded to drape the two of them with orchid leis whose fragrance intoxicated Meg. Billy noticed her miniskirt ride up as she wiggled into the seat of the limo and complained that her thighs were sticking to the leather seat.

"Ohoooo, Billy will you look at this, I feel special, do you think the driver can see my knickers?" She tried to pull her dress down and cross her legs. Her red vinyl boots stood out bright in the dark interior of the car.

"I heard the King has ten of these, all in different colors," Billy said, looking out of the smoked glass windows as the lush countryside swept past.

They were welcomed into the hotel and guided to a lovely room. The bellhop stood expectantly with his hand out after unloading their bags into the room. Billy shook it vigorously and thanked him for his help. The whole trip fatigued Meg and, after going through the complimentary fruit basket and the various miniature toiletries, she decided to have a rest and listen to the ocean roaring several floors below the open balcony doors of their suite.

"If you're going to sleep, then I'm going for a walk," Billy told Meg. "Remember the show is later tonight, and there's another car coming to get us. We need to be ready."

He watched as Meg curled up like a child on the bed and said softly, "Okay, love, but don't wander too far. You know I don't like it when I don't know where you are—you might get yourself into trouble without me to keep an eye on you."

Billy found the diner a couple of blocks from the hotel—the fresh-faced lad at the front desk in the hotel had been helpful and extended his hand, palm up, after giving him directions. Billy shook it heartily. The diner was where he intended to have his first real American lunch. The outside was all red and white with aluminum and big glass windows; inside, salt and pepper and catsup at every booth just like in the films. The smell of fried food and coffee reminded him of the summer before he joined the tappers yard, when he'd worked in the local hotel kitchen.

Billy took a seat at the counter. A man next to him sat slumped over his coffee, looking disheveled in a light raincoat, a baseball cap, and bold sunglasses. The man ordered a fried peanut butter and bacon sandwich with extra banana, and another coffee. He kept his voice low and seemed to want to be left alone. Billy was impressed. God bless America—assuming Hawaii was an American state, though he wasn't sure about that. He felt sure no one in Diggle would think of frying peanut butter, bacon, and banana, though God knew they loved to fry food back home. Nothing so stodgy as pie and gravy, black, rag, or Yorkshire pudding could compete with a bloody fried peanut butter, bacon and banana sandwich.

"I'll have one of those as well please, and a cup of tea, miss, and put his order on my tab, dear"—he gestured at the slumped man— "he looks a little out of luck."

The man grunted a thank you. His thick, greasy hair pushed out over his oversized glasses, which themselves peeked out below a ratty Caesar's Palace baseball cap. The man's food arrived, and he eagerly stuffed half of the sandwich into his face, almost ravenous, grease running to his cuffs.

Curious, thought Billy. *I love America.*

"I'm from England, a tourist here." He extended his hand, but the man was too busy with his sandwich to free up a hand to shake. "My name is Billy… Billy McTaggart."

"Uh, huh, a tourist?" the stranger grunted between bites of his sandwich.

"Aye, I am, what about you, big man?" The man didn't answer, but stood up, reeling around, heaving, his hands clenched at his throat, and passed out, face down on the greasy diner linoleum floor.

Billy jumped up and rolled the man over. His skin was a shade of blue through his dark, day-old facial hair. Standard safety training was required for all employees at British Midland Rail, including emergency medical training, and Billy moved through the motions of clearing the air passage and was just about to consider mouth to mouth resuscitation when the man coughed and took a deep breath. A moment later a dazed, rasping man sat on the floor looking at him through bloodshot eyes. Billy stared at him, shocked, and was about to inquire if he might be the King when the ambulance arrived. In a flash, Billy watched him disappear into the ambulance. Only a lump of half-chewed sandwich lay on the floor.

"This one's on us," said the waitress, tearing up Billy's tab. "Saved us from another lawsuit. Bloody king lookalikes, fucking town's full of them, especially now, with his first live appearance in almost nine years." She wiped the countertop down and filled his teacup. "You move pretty well for a little guy."

Billy finished his peanut butter, bacon, and banana lunch and thanked the waitress, leaving a generous tip before he headed back to the hotel, the tropical afternoon hot and vibrant around him. He laughed as he walked—silly to think the greatest performer in the world would be in a greasy diner on the street in Honolulu. He decided best not to make a fool of himself by telling Meg what happened.

That evening Billy escorted Meg to the arena for the show. She wore one of her new frocks and the freshwater pearl necklace Billy had given her before they left for the Hawaiian adventure. At the concert, Billy followed Meg to their front row seats, where some of the most famous showbusiness personalities in the world—Dean Martin and Liza Minelli were seated directly in front of them; Frank Sinatra and Sammy Davis, Jr. stood up so they could pass to their seats. The show was set to start at 8:30 PM, with the pianist Floyd Cramer, the Jordanaires, jazz saxophonist Boots Randolph, and comedienne Minnie Pearl as opening acts. At intermission, a waitress refreshed their drinks and Billy took Meg's hand in anticipation as Rear Admiral Robert L. Campbell introduced Elvis.

Billy was awestruck from the start. The King looked resplendent in his signature gold lame jacket with silver sequin lapels. Billy jumped up from his seat as the King let out a brief yell of his own in response to the ecstatic audience before launching into "Heartbreak Hotel," then "All Shook Up," "Don't Be Cruel," "Are You Lonesome Tonight," and "It's Now or Never."

Elvis was in peak form, and Billy and Meg, along with the crowd, restrained themselves from jumping up to dance to every song. This was a dinner concert, and formal in that respect. Diggle, a tiny village on the moors seemed a million miles away—Billy was swept up in the brilliance of it all. His dream had come true.

"You're hurting my hand," Meg whispered in Billy's ear as the King finished the show with a rollicking version of "Hound Dog", during which he slid across the stage on his knees. The King apologized for being a little hoarse, expressed his gratitude for all the support that raised over sixty thousand dollars for the new USS Arizona Memorial Fund, and left the stage to the roar of the crowd.

Billy was still sitting, awed, as the rest of the audience began shuffling out of the arena. Meg was trying to get Billy's attention, asking him to help with her coat, when a large man dressed in a black suit and a turtleneck sweater appeared in front of them and asked them to follow him. They exchanged worried glances, but trailed obediently behind the hulk of a man, down through the guts of the building, passing what seemed like hundreds of people rushing around them. They stopped at a door with a prominent gold star on it.

"Wait here, sir." The man s knocked and slid into the room.

"What have you done, Billy?" Meg asked, clinging to his arm.

"What did *I* do?"

Meg confessed, "I only took four of those shampoo bottles, I thought my Mother would like them, and the shower cap for Gracie down at the salon, you know how she likes to keep her hair clips in all day. The chocolates on the pillows were for us, weren't they?"

He put his finger to her lips and whispered nervously, "Hush, pet, I don't know what's going on. It may be a tourist thing, you know these Yanks don't understand us Brits."

Before he could speculate further, the large man reappeared at the door and asked them to please come in. The room was well lit, full of cigarette smoke and people—all sorts of people, beautiful women, more big men in black, an old man in a white suit smoking a cigar while seated on a white leather couch.

"My man!" An unmistakable voice, unique and resonant, boomed. "Get over here!" The sea of bodies parted, and the King came into view, the lights around the mirror on the far wall surrounding him in a halo of God light, like one of those stained-glass windows where Jesus and his disciples glowed with open outstretched hands of welcome. He was beautiful thought Billy, a man in his prime, and clean shaven. It *had* been Elvis he saved in the diner after all.

Billy swallowed deeply before he could speak. "Sir, Mr.... King," he stuttered as he extended one hand and dragged Meg, slacked-jawed, forward with the other.

"Folks, this is the guy, the Limey I was telling you about, the best little guy around. Saved my life and even bought the lunch that almost killed me when I snuck off earlier today." The King lurched forward and wrapped his arms around Billy, bumping Meg accidentally on the chin as he enveloped Billy. "I love the fact that you thought you were just helping a guy down on his luck. You're one of a kind and thank you! I couldn't believe it tonight when I looked out there and saw you in the audience. I never thought I'd see you again. I sent one of my men to the diner to ask after you, with no luck. This is fantastic, God bless you, man," the King said, almost weeping. "Everyone out, get out of here. My man, Billy, and I are going to hang."

The room began to clear as he felt a tug on his arm and Meg pushed forward sheepishly.

"Oh, sir, this is my wife, Meg."

"Sure is, lucky fellow. I'll have someone take her shopping."

Billy shrugged helplessly at Meg as he watched her reluctantly escorted out of the room by a tall, dark-haired woman in a red jumpsuit with a particularly lovely bottom.

"Ever done blow?" the King asked as a slinky redhead entered the room. She wore nothing more than a bright pink feather boa and a sparkling G-string. She had the longest legs Billy had ever seen and carried a small tray.

"Blow?" Billy asked.

The King enveloped Billy with one arm and directed him to sit on the couch vacated by the man in the white suit. He could still feel warmth in the leather seat as he sat down behind the chrome and glass coffee table.

"This is Lola. She's here to please us." Billy extended his hand and Lola smiled as she took it, pleased to be acknowledged.

"Hello, Lola, nice to meet you, miss."

Lola set the tray down on the table and proceeded to scoop white powder from a crystal bowl onto the glass top of the coffee table. Deftly she used a razor blade to sort it into thin, neat, equally spaced lines about four inches long each. She rolled up a one-hundred-dollar bill and handed it to the King who proceeded to snort two of the lines, into each nostril. Billy followed suit without even thinking—if blow was good for the King, then it was good for him.

In an instant, he felt the drug coursing through his body, pulsing into his extremities, his fingers, toes and the top of his head tingling like little starbursts. He felt Lola's bright pink feathers brushing against his face, her perfume overpowering him, everything seeming to be twice as much, ten times as much. His nose consumed the air veraciously and he could taste it flowing down the back of his throat into his lungs. The perfume again, a heady smell, a little floral, but so, so much more vibrant, catching in the back of his throat and making his belly tighten. He felt aroused and tried to find a pillow to put over his lap as he sat transfixed, watching Lola dance before him. The lights from the dressing room mirror danced on her sequined G-string, a diamond triangle that hypnotized him as she moved around the dressing room. Small firm breasts peeped in and out of view as the feather boa swirled in the air. He felt as alive as he'd ever hoped to be. The King, on the other hand, sat slumped on the other end of the leather sofa, his white, monogrammed bathrobe blending him into the white wall behind, a small silver string of drool running to his chest. The King looked fucked, Billy thought through his own euphoria. He'd given the audience his all and had nothing left in him.

"What's your name, honey?" Lola's voice sounded high and grating, but she was beautiful beyond belief. She snorted a line and licked some of the powder off her fingers, rubbing it into her gums. "This stuff makes you go up, and then I go down, whatcha gonna do?" He suddenly wondered where Meg was and stood up.

"I need to go."

The dancer pushed him back down and straddled him.

"You're the first man who ever said hello to me," she said, slowly grinding her hips into his lap. "My, my, what do you have there, Mr. Englishman?"

My hard on, he thought, fighting the high and wrestling his conscious to the ground. "Stop!" he shouted.

Lola stopped grinding and tilted her head like a curious pet at a strange noise in a familiar setting.

"You want me to stop?" she asked, almost laughing. "Why would you want me to stop, don't you find me attractive?" Her own buzz soured as she sat back sullenly on top of the coffee table.

"It's not that—it's just that I've never done anything like this before..." He trailed off, straightened his shirt, and looked at his watch. It had been midnight when he'd come back to meet the King and now it was five AM. He didn't know where the time had gone, and had no idea where Meg was.

"Jesus," he pleaded, making the King stir even as the clean-up crew knocked at the door to the dressing room and minders flooded in, ignoring Billy and Lola as they picked up the King and swept him away. Still buzzed and with Lola sitting in front of him, he asked her if the King would be all right.

"Oh, yeah," she said. This is normal. They'll take a day or so to resuscitate him before filming starts on his next Hawaiian movie.

One of the maids pulled back the curtains and the room filled with brilliant, early morning light, an orange glow peeking over a turquoise sea through the window. Lola got up abruptly from the table and stood awkwardly in front of him. She was just a head taller than him in her stocking feet. He eased himself from the couch to straighten his tie and rebutton his shirt. He excused himself politely from Lola, again taking her hand and shaking it.

"You have blow all over your rather perfect bottom, miss."

He kissed her on the cheek and then found his way out of the building. He flagged a taxi and made his way back to the hotel through a light, warm rain. In the elevator up to the room he caught a glimpse of himself in a large and unforgiving mirror that covered the whole wall of the car. He saw a stranger looking back at him, a face he didn't recognize with tousled hair and baggy eyes.

Meg woke as he entered the room, she was still fully dressed, and all around her on the bed were bags and bags, the relics of her Elvis-sponsored shopping spree in 24 hour casino shops.

"I tried to wait up for you, wondering if the King would ever let you go. I've never not known where you were, even when you went to London. This is a strange country, and we've only been here one day," Meg cried.

Billy said nothing but fell into the bed, exhausted. Meg started to sob and curled up next to him. He could feel her body heaving as he drifted into a dreamless sleep.

They both awoke sweaty in the heat and agreed to freshen up and go for a light lunch down near the pool. Neither spoke as they ordered salad and water, no thought to ordering something exotic from the menu; everything seemed out of place to their simple tastes. As they sat poolside, a bellboy approached them and held out a small tray with a note on it.

Meg took the note and handed it to Billy as the bellboy extended his hand. Meg shook it happily. "You people are so nice," she said, glancing at Billy expectantly as he read the note. "Who's it from, and what does it say?"

"The King wants to see me again before I leave," he said, and frowned.

"When?" Meg asked.

"Now, I suppose. Maybe he wants to take me with him for lunch, in case he chokes again. Do you mind, my love? I won't be gone all that long, and he is the King."

Meg scowled. "We were about to have lunch together." She sighed. "I suppose I'll go down to the beach in my new pink bathing costume and order a fruity drink with an umbrella in it to match my outfit. Please don't make me wait too long this time. This is our holiday together, you know, and we only have a few more days."

Billy hid behind his sunglasses and kissed her on the forehead as he excused himself. "I'll pop up to the room and put on the new, lightweight linen suit I brought along. It'll be cooler, and make a good impression, I'm sure."

He changed quickly and took a cab from his hotel to the address on the hand-written note. Walking into the grand foyer of the Hilton Hawaiian Village Hotel felt overwhelming. He stood a moment and took in the opulence, dwarfed by the massive chandelier that hung over a table covered with more flowers than Reggie Green's fingers could grow on his allotment in five years back home in Diggle. The whole lobby lay under a glass dome of sparkling light, a magnifying glass for the sun and blue sky outside, pushing and penetrating the lobby in dazzling splendor. He blinked, swallowed, and walked up to the front desk.

"Good afternoon, sir," a lean, impeccably dressed young man offered.

"Yes, terrific," Billy replied nervously. "I'm on my holidays, came to see the King!" There was an awkward silence between them.

"Of course, you are, sir. I believe they're about to start filming any day now, and everyone is excited. How may I help you?"

"Room 1218," Billy said as the note had instructed him to inform the concierge upon his arrival.

"Oh! Of course, sir," the young man said, startled, as if Billy had given a secret password. "Take the elevator to the first floor and turn left as you step out," he said, extending his hand. Billy shook it vigorously with his sweaty palm and turned and walked away.

"Fucking Brits," the concierge mumbled, giving Billy a smile and a wave as he walked across the grand lobby toward the gilded elevator doors.

He checked his tie in the elevator mirror and pushed down a stray hair. The stranger in the mirror stared back at him, anxious, giddy, guilty at leaving Meg alone so he could go to see the King again. Panic didn't set about him until the door opened and he walked down the corridor to the room 1218 and knocked, his fist feeling small against the massive door. The door opened slowly, and a shapely leg curled around it to welcome him, and there she stood.

"I've been waiting for you. What took so long? Meow, come to Mamma."

Lola enveloped him with her long slender arms, her deliciously slim fingers tipped with vibrant red nails the same color as her lipstick. She ran her hands over his shoulders, her perfume embraced him, seeming to carry him as they walked a few steps into her room. She guided Billy past the couch as he tried to sit down and had him sit at the foot of an opulent bed bejeweled with a bedspread of a million tiny glass beads reflecting light into the revolving mirrors above. He took the glass of champagne she shoved into his hand, grateful for the opportunity to quench his parched throat. He tried to speak, his legs weak and his mind giddy.

"I think... I mean, it's nice to smell you... I mean see you again, Miss Lola."

"Where's the King?"

Lola held his gaze and slid onto the bed. Kicking off her pink, fur-lined slippers, she curled her impossibly long legs up under her and sat staring at him.

"The King isn't the one who invited you. I wanted you to myself. I believe I misled you." She grinned. "Naughty me."

He felt her every movement run through the beaded bed cover and up his body. Hypnotized, he watched as she stretched out, arching her back, taking in her firm tummy, her bronzed, perfect, breasts pushing against a fur-edged bra. Her neck, soft feminine, long, elegant, her hair gathered up into a thick fiery red ponytail high on her head. Fumbling with his glass, Billy slurped, and the bubbles exploded in his nose and in his throat, rendering him speechless.

"You said you liked me, Billy." Lola's words slid over him like molasses, thick, slowly encapsulating him, waist deep at first then deeper still he sank into the elixir she poured on him with every word that followed. "I've never met a gentleman, never met a man who cared enough to want to talk to me, someone who asked me my name without trying to fuck me first." He sank under her words, not sure what it all meant. He was feeling the effects of the champagne along with her heady perfume, which had him quite intoxicated.

"I was trying to be polite, pet," he stammered. "I... was, you were, are, so beautiful... and the king told me to be nice to you, I, I..." He trailed off.

"Hush, Billy, I want to show you my gratitude. I like you too, my first Limey, a real gentleman. I know what you're hiding in that well-pressed suit of yours."

Lithely, Lola slid across the bed and in one deft movement pulled him toward her. She removed his jacket, his protests hidden beneath her full red mouth. He felt her tongue wrapping around any words he might have tried to voice. She laughed as she worked her way down his shirt buttons with her gleaming teeth.

Hours later, Billy walked back up the beach near his hotel. He tried to recount the entirety of what had just happened and how it happened, but only came up with flashes in his mind's eye: tastes, smells, touches, eyes, hands, mouths, mirrors spinning above him with images of twisted bodies. He'd seen his pale white, almost blue, skin against her golden-brown arms and legs distorted to appear even longer in the kaleidoscope of mirror segments that radiated out from the center of the ceiling above the bed. Her blazing hair held fast in his hands as he stared up at the stranger he now was, the tightness of her back running in deep grooves of flesh down each side of her spine to a perfect bottom.

Billy stood facing the ocean, searching for remorse out on the glimmering sea. Bright, sparkling diamonds of light blinded him in the late afternoon as the sun slid slowly toward the ocean.

"I have never done anything like this before. I don't know what to say, what to do next," he had said to Lola in his guilt.

"You do nothing, darling," Lola purred, "This is my gift to you, our secret. No one need know, you can feed me and take me dancing one day in England, perhaps. But, for now, I work for Colonel Tom Parker, just as the King works for him, and until he sets us all free"—she shrugged. "He has big friends who keep us all on the merry-go-round, like his old carnival days." Lola looked a little sad for an instant, then she paused, wiped smudged lipstick with the back of her hand, and she teased at her unruly mop of disheveled hair.

"You are quite the most beautiful creature in the world, Miss Lola," Billy said, extending his hand formally.

She laughed, pushed his hand aside, and sprung from the bed, cat-like, "Clean yourself up, show yourself out, and remember I love you and you love me."

He watched her flee to the bathroom, perfect rounded bottom jiggling ever so slightly as she loped across the room.

He tapped on the bathroom door as he left, after recovering various pieces of his clothing from around the room and reluctantly washing the makeup and scent of her from his body in the bar sink. He checked himself for marks, bites or scratches in the large mirror behind the bar, and miraculously there were none. *There should be after all that*, he thought. But it was the stranger who looked back at him, a man with hidden marks of betrayal. He dressed as the sound of running water and the steamy smell of bath salts emanated from behind the bathroom door, Lola's singing light and delicate. He touched the door gently. "Bye, bye," he said.

He'd entirely forgotten Meg for the second time in as many days, and he now walked reluctantly back into their hotel room feeling like a different man, confused in his remorse, ecstatic in his discovery.

Meg sat at a small table out on the balcony of their room several frosted glasses with discarded fruit rinds and pink, blue, and yellow umbrellas beside her. Her mascara ran in streaks from dark eyes. He stood uneasily with whiskey on his breath from the brief stop at the lobby bar on the way upstairs and surveyed the carnage. She had ordered French onion soup from the room service, and the odor of onion and Parmesan cheese permeated the room. The stale smell mingled with the fruity tropical bouquet of the flowers delivered on behalf of the King. His tummy turned in his anxiety and guilt. He'd never been this far out of control, caught between paradise and purgatory at the same time.

Meg stared at him, raccoon-eyed, red-nosed, and exhausted. She asked through broken sobs. "Why would the King send flowers when you were with him?" She asked. "Why is it that here I am, just Billy's wife, relegated to my room by a rock and roll star who invited you to lunch and whom you worshipped more than me...your wife?"

He couldn't think of an answer in the moment. Back home he was hers willingly. He loved, honored and obeyed her, fulfilled her every desire and direction she gave for their future together. Now, two days here and he'd had slipped from her grasp. He knew it as he walked uneasily around the room, embarrassed and remorseful.

"I want to go home, Billy."

He moved toward her and tried to take her in his arms.

"I'm sorry," Meg mumbled as she pushed him away and burst into fresh tears. "I want to go home where I know what's what, where food is food, and I don't have to swim in a bikini or say aloha to everyone I meet. I want to go back to where my man is my man."

"I'll have the tickets changed for a return tomorrow afternoon, love, and perhaps we can have a farewell dinner together, something romantic near the beach, just the two of us with no fruity drinks."

The desire to see Lola consumed Billy the next day. As they packed to leave, he wondered how he could he manage a quick goodbye. He thought better of it, choosing to send a brief note and flowers instead. The ride to the airport was stifling, and he felt counterfeit in his tropical suit, a wolf in lambs clothing. When buying the suit, Meg had told him it made him look as if he was trying too hard, and that there would be little or no use for it when they were back home, so why couldn't he just be himself? Lola had liked the suit when he wore it yesterday; today it looked lived in and creased, a new skin that had a specific comfort about it here in Hawaii but would be only a costume in Diggle.

Meg's silence was shattering on the drive to the airport. They'd always had something to say to each other, he and Meg. She always had something she needed doing, but Meg hadn't recovered well from his neglect and continued to break into small fits of sobbing. Billy reached into his jacket pocket for a hanky to give her. Unexpectedly, he pulled out a pair of lace panties entwined with his hanky and panicked, scrunching them all together and shoving the combination into his face, faking a sneeze of epic proportions.

"It must be the tropical pollen," he said. He closed his eyes in disbelief at the close call, breathed deep, and drew in the essence of Lola as he rolled down the window and let the panties flutter into the wind just before the cab pulled into the airport. The minx he thought, I will kill her… if I ever see her again. Meg took her own hanky from her handbag and dabbed at the corners of her eyes.

Billy sat back, looking out of the window as the plane slid into the air circling higher over the luminescent blue sea and picturesque volcanic islands, a postcard picture from above. For every mile they flew away he felt longing, an abstract moment of desire for another way of living. How to put all this back in a box so he could go on? What would the lads back home make of such stuff? He would have liked to keep his lacy treasure in the place beneath the stairs and perhaps one day tell his son of how he'd been to paradise. Instead, all he could think was that Levi Indigo, friend of the King, had left the building.

Chapter 14

Fantastic

In time, fewer and fewer people wanted to hear stories of meeting the King, and Billy returned to the life of a husband and a boss. He accepted the promotion to head clerk and oversaw a dozen young lads who handled general day-to-day administration of the rail yard.

Even as head clerk, he was still Billy Tapper, looked up to by the lads as an honorary member of the Tapper and Shunters Social Club. This also gave him the ability to borrow money from a small syndicate of workers that invested in his ventures, for which he offered a nice return to supplement their wages.

The hairdressing shop, tour buses, and apartments in which he'd invested were all making money, which would eventually allow him to give up his job at the rail office in order to look after his growing enterprise. He focused on his existence with Meg and Mam, allowing memories of Lola to ebb as he hoped for a family of his own, his high adventure behind him. All things American still consumed him, however, and, although he and Meg stopped briefly in New York and Los Angeles on their way to Hawaii, he knew he had to go back—and next time he'd do it on his own terms.

Meg took her own time to come around after the strain of the trip, so Billy waited to broach the subject of another baby until they took a weekend down in the south of England to a picturesque village in Cornwall where they encountered a vicious jug of scrumpy. The rough apple cider bit into the cheeks of their mouths and kicked like a mule the next morning. Smocked locals laughed and cooed, "Ow, Ar, Miss," as Meg danced around the bar, almost bumping her head on the shallow ceiling strung with brass pots and farm implements. Billy had carried her up to bed after a rowdy evening of merrymaking. In the morning they had breakfast brought to the room, but Meg had it sent away as the smell of it sickened her in her hangover.

"How are you, my love?" Billy asked, rubbing the back of Meg's neck with a wet cloth. "You were on fine form last night on the dance floor, and in the room." She scowled at him like a small caged animal baring its teeth in defense. "I've not seen you like that for a fair while."

"Well don't get your hopes up. I can't remember too much, and you'll not be getting a leg over with my head in this state." She curled up and moaned into the pillow.

"I suppose I'm not that worried after the romp you gave me anyway, grand it was. I was wondering if you might be thinking of our family plans now that the businesses are going well, and you don't need to work." Billy held his breath.

"Get me when I'm at my weakest, did you? I suppose it was a fair shot. I know I haven't been the best of wives in the last while. I'm not sure I'd make the best of mothers, too selfish in some ways, but I do love you, and if it happens, then we shall make the best of it, shan't we?"

Billy smiled at her. "I'll take that my love. The new house would make a fine home for an expanded family. Whatever makes you happy—my Mam would make a great babysitter, and a doting Grandma."

Billy and Meg had asked Mam to move into an old gate-keeper's lodge they had recently bought. The lodge was the last remnant of an estate that used to take up most of the county in the heyday of the mills. Billy had Mam retire from daily cleaning for others and asked her if she'd be a sort of unofficial housekeeper, with her own help. They rented out her terrace house to a young man called Emanuel McGregor, Manny for short, who worked part-time for Billy doing his bookkeeping.

The Lodge overlooked the canal and Billy dreamed of turning it into a bed-and-breakfast in a couple of years, after they eventually had their family and needed something more substantial. He was determined to remain optimistic. They'd even spoken about adoption and other ideas for beginning a family. Meg dismissed the thought of anything other than their own children, but she lacked enthusiasm, reminding him of her concerns.

"Billy love, it's not just a baby, its everything else that goes with it. I'm trying, but I told you it's scary after losing the first one."

"I understand, pet, and perhaps we can see a specialist in London. Next time I go down there, you can come too. It would be a grand trip and might ease your fears a wee bit."

Billy relished life at their new home in the lodge. They kept up a busy routine, and the three of them found a comfortable rhythm. The house was spacious and bright compared to the cramped terrace house with memories in every corner, and Mam had left it reluctantly. She decided that her home was with Billy, but Dad still held a presence in the terrace house for Mam as she had packed up his yellowing shirts and tortoiseshell hairbrushes for the last time. The shirts would go to the church, and it was time to give Billy the brushes, although he now used a comb to slick back his hair into a prominent cowlick like the King. The brushes were quietly put away in his tin box as keepsakes. He now kept his treasure tin between stacked books on a high shelf beside his desk in the new office.

The move proved to be a welcome, just before Mam's thirty-seventh birthday. The growing relationship between Mam and Meg—Mam claiming Meg as the daughter she never had—was a joy for Billy. He loved the quiet mornings when the two would sit in the garden under the wisteria that hung heavy, the lilacs in full bloom above their heads. Meg told him reluctantly that Mam had shared in confidence with her that she wanted to go and visit a gynecologist rather than old Dr. Styles who treated ailments large and small, for almost everyone in the village, including local livestock when the vet was out of town. Meg thought Billy should know, because he would need to pay for the visit to a specialist. Discretion was obviously required.

Billy had Meg arrange the visit with a doctor in Manchester and neither of them ever asked Mam about the results of the consultation, assuming no news was good news. Billy did inquire vaguely if everything was okay, and she made light of the visit, saying her little news could wait. In her opinion he didn't need to have any distractions so soon after the move, especially now that he was launching so many new ventures. After Christmas they could all get a fresh start in the new year.

Billy and Mam shared a mutual joy of long walks on Saturday afternoons, arm-in-arm together, a ritual that built over the next year at the lodge. With everyone out of the house most weekdays Mam had become more reclusive, and Billy thought the company of a dog would be just the thing. Mam eventually gave in and allowed him to buy her a small Yorkshire terrier she called Woody, after one viewing of the Woody Woodpecker show on the new television. Billy loved the way everyone laughed as the little dog ran around and barked at almost anything that moved in the grass, reminding them of the manic little bird in the cartoon.

During their walks, Mam gently but persistently chipped away with question after question about the daily goings on of Billy's growing business interests—and the question of a baby was always hanging over them. This topic was a preoccupation of Mam's, her hope to give the enterprise a sense of urgency, knowing she might not be around forever.

"As long as Meg prefers dresses and social engagements to raising a family, my hopes of a grandchild are futile," Mam complained.

Respectfully, Billy asked her to be patient. "You're still young, and there will be plenty of time for nappies and babysitting."

The truth was that babies never came. None of them ever came. There was always a reason. First would be the reward of falling pregnant, then the fall that would end it, and a gift to make Meg feel better. A holiday somewhere sunny, a new car or curtains for the front room. Then there was The Pill, available in late December of '61 thanks to health minister Enoch Powell. Meg said it would help regulate her period until they were ready for the baby, and Billy acquiesced with a heavy heart. The pill seemed to allow Meg a renewed interest in intimacy without the risk of pregnancy.

At the lodge, Mam would sit for hours listening to the record player and the records Billy bought for her weekly in Oldham, after she had heard them on the radio. On Saturdays, after their ritual walk, Billy would sit with tea in hand as Mam played the favorites from among her latest acquisitions and tell a story to go with the song—something she'd heard or read about the singer or the lyricist. Her own passion for poetry—or ramblings, as she called them—was rarely shared, even on these leisurely Saturdays, but Billy knew the leather binder she kept in her top drawer held poetry, letters, and sonnets of love from her own pen. His own ramblings he jotted in the margins of old school notebooks or ledgers after a night with a bottle of whiskey.

"I'll put the kettle on, Mam," Billy said one Saturday afternoon after hanging his jacket in the mud room at the back door. He pushed his Wellingtons off at the heel and padded to the kitchen in his heavy woolen socks. On their walk, Mam said there was a story she wanted to share, a story that had its time in telling now that he was of an age when the realities of life were upon him, and she needed the weight of it lifted from her own shoulders. He took it as being much ado about nothing, as Mam worried about everything. She hurried on ahead of him, needing a nervous pee before they would sit down to listen to a record or two and she worked up the courage to tell the story.

As he finished making the tea, Billy heard the first record spin to life in the parlor—Billie Holiday singing "Summertime," always Mam's first choice. That was also the song she sang when she needed to coax him to sleep as a young boy.

"Billie Holliday and I had a lot in common you know," Mam started the conversation.

He noticed, as he brought in the hefty tea tray, that her voice shook a little as she spoke. He'd piled the tray high with cheese, tomato, and lettuce sandwiches on thick wedges of homemade bread, the bread fringed in the buttercup yellow of local butter and topped with a generous dollop of Branson pickle. He'd cut the sandwiches into quarters so the soft edges could fit into their mouths while they held firmly to the darkly marbled crust at the end of the wedge.

"Billie Holiday's mother Sadie had to leave her, you know, leave her with her own half-sister to be raised while she worked as a cleaner. That was the only way Billie would be safe," Mam said. "I understand how hard it is to give up your baby."

Billy looked up from the Supremes album cover he was holding. Mam had been intrigued by the dynamic presence of the lead singer, Diana Ross. Billy himself thought Diana was exotic and beautiful, not that he'd ever tell anyone—prejudice was rampant among the working class in England without even bringing race into the equation. "Who gave up a baby, Mam? What are you talking about?"

Mam fumbled to change the record. "I love Patsy Cline," she blurted, needle scratching vinyl under shaking hands, skipping over the opening chords of "I Fall to Pieces". "You know she was hospitalized after a nasty car crash just as this song became her first big crossover hit." Mam sat back in her chair and held her teacup close to her chest.

"What's that one I love, Mam?" Billy asked.

"'Nature Boy," Mam placed it on the turntable. "By Nat King Cole."

"...the strange and enchanted boy who traveled far over land and sea," Billy sang, a little off tune. "You know I believed in the words, that the greatest thing you'll ever learn is just to love and be loved in return." Billy and Meg had danced to "When I Fall in Love" on their wedding day, and he asked for this song to be next in Mam's rotation. "You know, Mam, it's just like Nat said—it would be forever."

Mam laughed. "Even in a restless world like this is."

For the next hour they listened to Mable Mercer, Ethel Waters, the Ink Spots, and newcomers Johnny Mathis and Barbara Streisand, but ended back where they had begun, with Billie Holiday, "I'm A Fool to Want You."

Mam's tears broke as the music filled the room.

"What's wrong, Mam?" Billy asked. "Is it about Dad?"

"No, Billy," she sobbed, "it's not. He has a part in it sure enough, but it wasn't his fault. He never knew until it was all said and done. He did the best he could, but the hard years were mine to suffer alone."

Billy sat up straight and moved forward in his seat. "What are you talking about, Mam?"

"All these songs Billy, or anyway, the old ones, I used to hear them play around town from the local pubs and dance halls, the music weaving through the alleyways into the dormitory in the workhouse where they put me when they found out I was pregnant with you. That's the story I've been trying to get the courage up to tell you—all these songs! They always make me cry and I don't know why I torture myself so. I suppose it's the only way to know I'm still alive, other than seeing you grow and succeed."

Billy knew better than to stop his mother now that she'd started talking. He would sit there for as long as it took for her to tell her story. The click of the record player resonated in the room as Billie Holiday's voice faded and the arm moved back to rest on its cradle. The static buzz of the speakers provided a neutral background upon which Mam spoke in fits and starts between sobs, drying of her eyes with the embroidered kerchief she kept up her cardigan sleeve.

"The pain of giving you up was eased only slightly by knowing my dad's sister would be raising you, rather than having you absorbed into the illicit Catholic adoption program that may have gotten you to America sooner than later," She tried to joke and even gave out a little-broken laugh. "I was a young pregnant girl out of wedlock."

This was a thing he'd never considered, believing they were off to war being heroes as he'd been almost five in the year his parents were married. His Mam and Dad had always made, for him, the perfect love story—up until the day Dad left and shattered the illusion.

He listened as Mam spoke of washhouses filled with young girls and the clandestine trade of babies to wealthy Americans, of the abuse she'd suffered at the place where sickly babies disappeared in the night only to be discovered years later in mass graves under old buildings. "This happened all across England, Scotland, and, notably, Ireland where my own family came from a hundred years ago to seek work in the ports and mills of England. I wasn't alone in my suffering, but I want you to understand my history as your stature in the town grows. So that it won't work against you."

Billy rose from his chair and knelt down in front of his mam. He took the teacup to which she clung from her hands and held each hand gently. "You are everything to me, my mam, my hero, my best friend. That is that, and nothing—nothing— will ever get in the way of it. If you have urgency, as it seems, to tell me these stories, then so be it, but I don't need any reasons to love you more. Tell me stories if you wish—good, bad, happy, sad, scary, funny, all of them are a time stamp to the days of our life, and when I hear them, I think of you and how much I love and admire you. That's all I need, and I hope it's enough for you too."

Mam nodded as he wiped the tears from her eyes. As he watched his mother slowly regain a fragile composure, he realized now for the first time that at fourteen her first and only love was burdened by his father's absence. In her youth and innocence, time held little perspective to the duration of her unjust persecution. She had endured it regardless, for her son, for him, at all cost to herself.

For two years Billy had followed the career of the King, always watching the newsreels with some slight hope he might see Lola for a moment as the King's entourage moved between movie sets or concerts. Only once did he think he glimpsed her in the wings of a rare TV appearance as the camera panned around to the audience. He'd received a card from Lola not long after returning from Hawaii; a simple thank you note written on hotel stationery. She had no fixed home, living in the entourage of the King, but she sent him her parents' address and phone number should he ever find himself in Wyoming with nothing to do. He buried the note at the bottom of his treasure tin and forgot about it as best he could.

There were new distractions, to be sure. The Beatles were an emerging band and Billy and Meg went to see them whenever they could—once in Hamburg in June of '61, taking a ferry across the English Channel for their first visit to Europe, and once at the Cavern in Liverpool later that year. This was a vibrant time for music—if the King broke the dam from

America, the Beatles were about to lead the British invasion as a counterattack.

Their trip to Hamburg was frustrated by a wait of several hours and a thoroughly intrusive search in the customs office at Dover, until a smiling DCI Williams wandered in casually, completely out of place.

"Billy, my boy, it seems there was a little misunderstanding between you and your dad. I had a passport check put out there just in case he wandered back into the country. Unfortunately, I told them if he popped up, they should check for any contraband he may have hidden up his kilt. Sorry you and your delightful wife had to endure the humiliation of a pat down or two."

The DCI had taken to randomly creating inconveniences for Billy, and Billy had always managed to contain himself. But he finally lost his composure when Mam was arrested for shoplifting when she absentmindedly left a grocery shop without paying. DCI Williams arrived at the police station at just the same time as Billy.

"Billy, Billy," he'd intoned as Billy had grabbed him by the collar of his tailored, double-breasted Prince Charles jacket, "is this any way for a fine upcoming lad to behave in front of his mother?" To infuriate Billy further, the DCI had peeled Billy's hands from his lapels and slid his arm around Mam's shoulders, promising her that, luckily, he wouldn't press charges—because of his friendship with her elusive husband. He added that he considered himself a father figure to Billy. Mam had looked confused and Billy shook his head, begging her with his eyes not to ask the DCI what in heaven's name he was talking about.

Billy and Mam left the police station, walking hand-in-hand up the road to the lodge, and considered what they might want to do about DCI Williams. Mam knew well about their ongoing interactions from the day Billy found the train full of money and the coincidence of the Bernhard money Dad had mentioned years before, but little more.

"We need to rise above the meddling sod," Mam said, giving Billy a wink.

"I know Mam. I do try, but it feels like he's closing in on our lives, always pushing me for no good reason. It's like that everywhere, Diggle feels so small, I'm feeling claustrophobic here."

A little further down the road Mam presented Billy with her idea of how they might rise above DCI Williams, and even Diggle. "Let's go to America. Let's go to the place on your postcard, get out of our history, make a fresh start. God knows we need one."

Billy was thinking about quitting the railroad as his other businesses grew too much to be considered sidelines. He thought about hiring a couple of new managers to look after the enterprises that already existed and getting into some new ventures—and adventures. Now he looked at Mam, excited and perplexed that she'd consider having an adventure with him. Florida would be warm for her arthritis, and she could sun herself all day long, if she liked—no heavy coats or winter chills biting at her. Perhaps he'd buy her a floral, spring dress and one of those big brimmed hats he'd seen at the flicks. He was in full flight now, ideas of how to make such a momentous move animating him. He could afford it, Harry and the lads could look after business while he was gone—he trusted Harry to have his back now that they'd managed to sort out his whoring and drinking and got him settled down with a new bride.

Billy could expand, set up an American office, and explore some new investments. All he knew was Diggle, and the thought of flying by jet to live in America was overwhelming, and Mam had said she'd go with him. For Meg it would be a fresh start—she too would flourish in the sun and have those grandchildren Mam needed to grow old with. He could buy them all a big house near the beach, just like the postcard.

He picked Mam up and spun her around, feeling the possibilities unfold. The only obstacle he foresaw was how to bring Meg on board with the plan.

"There's only one question. Who will tell Meg?"

"That will take a bit of putting together, so perhaps we need a little plan Billy," Mam said. "I think you need to set the stage for our Meg, since she wasn't that happy with your trip to Hawaii. You might want to make it worth her while, and no King this time. I suggest she be the only love in your life-- other than me that is." Mam grabbed his arm and laughed a little in her shy way. He loved to see that smile on her beautiful face, and he felt inspired to begin planning. He would surprise both of them, and it would be perfect. A few years away in the US would give him a chance to try out some of the new ventures he'd imagined after hearing stories of his great, great, great Uncle Abe who'd been a cattle rancher in the Chetopa Territory on the plains of south eastern Kansas in the late 1800's. Everything would be perfect; how could Meg not love it?

He needn't have worried. Meg was on board the minute she saw a photograph of the house he planned to buy for them—on a waterway leading out to the ocean. Each home in the development had its own jetty and was carefully placed around three sprawling golf courses and a lavish clubhouse. Mam was still amazed by the idea of having three inside bathrooms, air conditioning, and double-glazed windows. And there was a country club application the Florida realtor had included in the package he mailed to them. All trace of resistance vanished. The country club had been Mam's idea, knowing Meg would bite at this bait of upward mobility. Meg took the package into the salon and let her customers ogle over the pictures of smiling faces on a green golf course and lithe bodies draped at the edge of a swimming pool. The women all exclaimed about the comparison to their dreary, damp row houses and the tired faces surrounding them in Diggle.

Eight more months sped by at the gamekeeper's lodge as the family planned their great move. John Lennon married Cynthia Powell in an unpublicized, registry-office ceremony in Mount Pleasant, Liverpool. The Glasgow Corporation Tramway ran its last car in regular service, leaving Blackpool as the final tramway left in Britain—the beginning of the end that few could see coming for the rail and transportation industry in the decade ahead. Billy splashed out on a new Ford Cortina—he wanted something American, rather than a Vauxhall Victor or a Hillman Minx, though the lads in the pub gave him a hard time about not buying British. Harry Two Bellies purchased a Morris Oxford Farina when he found out his new thirty-six-year-old wife was expecting twins, giving him competition in the belly department.

A few months before their departure, Billy read in the local paper about what was being called The Great Train Robbery. On August 8, 1963, a band of East End London thugs stopped and boarded a royal mail train traveling between Glasgow and London. The robbers tampered with signals and managed to get the train to stop on Bridego Bridge at Ledburn near Mentmore in Buckinghamshire. Their haul was over two and a half million pounds, predominantly in one- and five-pound notes. One thousand, five hundred and seventy-nine of the notes had traceable serial numbers, and the rest did not. The money was quickly laundered through friends and associates of the crooks, or seized by predatory gangsters, relatives, or lawyers. The police discovered the robbers' identities thanks to incriminating evidence found at a place called Leatherslade Farm where the thugs hid for several days after the robbery. Within a few months of the heist, ten of the seventeen robbers were locked up.

Billy grinned when he heard the news. He'd be leaving Diggle with his own haul intact and growing by the day—and in America he'd be able to spend it freely; no one would care that he was a tapper from Diggle. Unlike Ronny Biggs, he would have nothing to run from; not even DCI Williams.

Chapter 15

Sunshine and Rain

In the end, Mam wouldn't fly, regardless of how safe Billy promised her the airplane would be, so Billy, Meg, and Mam boarded a ship at Liverpool, bound for Fort Lauderdale, looking grander than they genuinely felt. He'd agreed to the gentle transition of a couple of weeks at sea to ease Mam's separation anxiety, this being her first trip out of Great Britain. She was, after all, placing an ocean between herself and the vaguest hope that her husband would turn up at home one day. Her secret relief was that she thought the adventure would last a year or two at most, then she'd be back to the lodge and her walks with Woody, who was in the hold with other animals that would require quarantine once they arrived in America.

Billy sat on the first-class deck with the *New York Times*, reading about an agreement between Britain and France to develop the Concord, a supersonic airliner that would fly from London to New York in three and a half hours. The article said it would be 1976 before the new jet would be passenger-ready, but Billy daydreamed about putting down a deposit for the inaugural flight more than ten years in the future.

Meg spent her time being pampered, a new nail color every day, a massage, and shopping at a little lingerie store. She surprised Billy with a fashion show of sorts after dinner with the captain and several glasses of champagne.

Upon arrival at the new house in Florida, Billy watched Meg as she took in her new home—the large open rooms, the many windows, and the crisp vista sandwiched between blue ocean and white sands. The whole house was a slight shade of pink and off-white, inside and out, furnished with wicker furniture and shag rugs, a kitchen with counters that ran seamlessly into each other and terminated at the built-in cocktail bar next to sliding glass doors leading to a patio and pool. The house stood in stark contrast to their terrace house back in Diggle. There was no sense of the warmth the lodge had held, or the smell that fires had etched into the woodwork over a hundred years. Billy wanted to be optimistic, but his little family seemed like dirty marks in this pinkish space. God help Woody when he escaped quarantine and shit all over the floors.

They settled down with TV dinners on TV trays in front of their new color TV on their first evening in Florida. They might not have remembered the exact date of their first meal in their new home except, it was November 22nd, 1963, the infamous day when an American president Robert Kennedy was assassinated in Texas. Mam and Meg spent the night in tears. Billy sat in disbelief, hoping this horror wasn't an omen of things to come.

In the wake of the Kennedy funeral, Billy planned a distraction—a road trip to the Grand Canyon, New Orleans, Houston, and Oklahoma City, which, according to Nat King Cole, was mighty pretty. They would drive as much as possible on Route 66, stopping at every diner they could find to try all the greasy food America had to offer, and arrive, at last, in the splendor of their red Cadillac convertible, in Los Angeles for a tour of Hollywood. Mam was ecstatic with the plan; Meg, less so.

"It'll be the trip of a lifetime." Billy begged Meg to reconsider, kneeling at her side while she reclined on their brand-new, king-sized bed. "It'll be a time for us together, no work to distract me, and maybe, if you're ready, we could try for another baby—"

Meg cut him off with a kiss to his neck. "I was going to tell you— I think some magic happened on the boat over here. I think you're going to be a daddy..." Billy gasped, but Meg continued as if she hadn't noticed. "This's why I need my rest. A road trip is a little too much right now, do you understand?"

Billy was nodding furiously, trying to find words and, still, Meg didn't allow him to speak. "But you go. You and your Mam. It's early days and I'll be fine here by myself—happy even to have the quiet."

When Billy spoke it was to say, "Mam and I will buy an outfit for the baby in every state we cross, a cowboy outfit, an Indian outfit, a film star outfit in Hollywood...", words he knew were inadequate even as he uttered them.

Meg snuggled into him. "It's early days, as I said. Let's not tell your mam just yet."

A little more than a month later Billy set off with Mam. They had sandwiches and a flask of tea for the first leg of the journey, out through the Florida panhandle toward New Orleans. It was a glorious day and he'd put the roof down on the car, so the blue silk headscarf Meg gave Mam fluttered in the breeze as they drove.

"Postcards!" Meg shouted as they pulled away from the house. "Postcards from everywhere so I can follow your progress. And remember to call as well, call when you're headed home so I'll have everything perfect for your triumphant return!"

Billy and Mam made their way cross country with the top down more than up—they found the freedom they'd both been seeking as the wind rushed past them on the open highway. They marveled at the vast expanse of open space before them. After the confines of Diggle, the sheer size of the sky seemed overwhelming. They skipped all the big cities and towns along the way, looking instead for the small, simple roadside motels with diners attached; another small-town Deloris or Madge who would gush over their charming accents and bring them stacks of pancakes and endless cups of coffee. A chubby Madge with a magnificent beehive hairdo provided them with directions and, for an extra dime, a tourist pamphlet to the Grand Canyon on their first morning in Arizona. The site of the seemingly endless gorges cleaved into the dark red rock and earth left them breathless.

"You see that silver river? It runs all the way down at the bottom, Mam." Billy said as he read from the pamphlet. "It says here that, according to the Havasupai Indians who live in its depths, the Grand Canyon originated because of a disagreement among the gods. Before there were any people on earth, there were two gods. Tochapa of goodness and Hokomata of evil. Tochapa had a daughter named Pu-keh-eh, whom he hoped would become the mother of all living things. Hokomata the evil was determined no such thing should take place, so he covered the world with a great flood. Tochopa the good felled a great tree and hollowed out the trunk. He placed Pu-keh-eh in the hollowed log and, when the water rose and flooded the earth, she was secure in her improvised boat and could survive.

"Sounds like Noah's Ark, if you ask me, without the animals." Mam said as she leaned against the rail and stared down into the valley. "What else do they say in there?"

Billy read on. "When the flood waters fell, and mountain peaks emerged, torrential rivers forged themselves between the rocks into a gushing fissure becoming the Grand Canyon. Pu-keh-eh in her log came to rest on the new earth. She stepped forth and beheld an empty world. When the land became dry, a magnificent golden sun rose in the east and warmed the earth and caused her to conceive. In time, she gave birth to a male child. Later, a waterfall caused her to conceive, and she gave birth to a girl. From the union of these two mortal children came all the people on the earth. First, there was the Havasupai, and the voice of Tochopa spoke to them and told them to live forever in peace in their canyon of good earth and pure water where there would always be plenty for all."

Mam huffed. "Sounds like incest to me," she said, and then considered, "but I wish it had worked and the world did live in peace forever as one. Perhaps we should move here and live with the Havasupai Tribe."

"Mam, are you okay?" Billy asked. He'd never before heard such cynicism from her mouth. Or seen her looking so sad.

"I'm done, pet. Can you understand that I need to be back in my own bed? I'm even willing to fly if it would take us home more quickly."

"Whatever you want, Mam," Billy said.

It took nearly six hours to reach the airport in Las Vegas, where Billy spent a few minutes mourning that he would get to spend no real time in the legendary city. He dutifully booked two tickets to Florida and left Mam at the airport while he drove to the nearest used car lot and sold the red Cadillac—at a loss—then returned to wait with Mam in the airport lounge in time to place a call to Meg and tell her they were on their way home. He'd just bought Mam another cup of tea when the ticket agent, noticing how unsettled and anxious Mam seemed, offered to try to find them an earlier flight.

"I would like that, Billy," Mam replied softly.

They arrived home very early in the morning, four hours earlier than he'd told Meg to expect them. Billy closed the cab door quietly, so as not to disturb Meg, likely asleep inside the house at this hour, and let himself and Mam into the house using the key under the front door mat. He piled their luggage inside the front door—any unpacking could wait until later in the day. He settled Mam in her room and made his way quietly to the bedroom he shared with his wife.

He was surprised to find Meg wasn't in bed, but he noticed the bathroom light shining behind the door that stood slightly ajar. He tapped on it and, as he pushed it more fully open, saw Meg standing over the sink daubing a large rump roast against one of their pristine white terry cloth bath towels.

"What are you doing, love?" he asked, truly perplexed until he saw her eyes darting around the bright bathroom trying to find a place to hide from him, and her own image in the well-lit mirror.

"My mother never recovered from my birth," she said erratically. Simply. "She never wanted my father or me, we were an encumbrance. My father had no affection for either of us, and my mother resented the damage done to the life she'd expected." She had, by this point, dropped the towel and the meat and crossed her hands over her chest, trying to contain and hold herself together by the thinnest thread. "It worked before. It seemed easier than anything else I could think up," she said, her eyes now on the bloody towel on the bathroom floor. "The falls hurt and brought doctors. I never meant to hurt you...or Mam."

"I have no answer for this," Billy stood before the staged tragedy. He thought, for a moment, to take her into his arms and comfort her, but he turned and walked out of the bathroom, his limbs feeling detached from his body as he walked into the den where he locked the door, put on Billie Holiday and dialed the volume up to full, no longer concerned about disturbing anyone, only comforting himself.

He sat down in the plush white leather chair at the big glass and stainless-steel desk Meg had chosen for him. He kicked off his shoes and pushed his toes into the thick, deep carpet that filled the room, trying to get some purchase in the moment, something to ground his reeling thoughts. He reached under the desk and pulled out his old tin treasure box, pried the lid off and rummaged to the bottom where he found the small envelope on hotel stationery. He held it to his lips and breathed the slightest fragrance that lingered on the pages inside. "Where the real me lives," Lola had written just above the address and phone number of her parents in Wyoming. He hadn't not responded to the note all those years ago, not while there was a story to be written with Meg. But what legacy could he and Meg hope to build now that could survive such deception? He wrote the number on a notepad and stuffed it in the back of his wallet. He placed the note back in his treasure tin and slid it back under the desk robotically. He gazed across the desk with angry, vacant eyes. How could he hope to face Mam with the truth that he'd been such a fool?

He picked up the phone and called the number on the card. Perhaps this was still the correct phone number for Lola's parents, and perhaps they would know where she was. Maybe she would want to see him, maybe not. It was an entirely random, unreasonable thing to do but in his hurt and anger it seemed like a viable option. An older man with a sleepy voice picked up.

"Hello?"

"I'm an old friend of Lola's," Billy offered.

Considering the hour, the old man answered with good cheer. "She's not here, of course, but I can get a message to her."

He decided not to leave one. He wouldn't be home to receive a return call.

Billy watched a fine mist of rain settle on a web that had been spun in his absence in a wheel hub of Meg's baby blue Cadillac. The car had white leather upholstery and lashings of chrome detail that ran to spaceship-like wings, and red, rocket-fire tipped brake lights. The car had been Meg's fantasy, the ultimate sign of living large in America. Billy stared at it now as a sign of his utter failure. He had locked the door to the den and left Billie Holiday blaring insider before he called a cab to take him back to the airport and climbed out the office window. He felt sick that he was leaving Mam with the liar Meg, but Meg had a way of talking herself back into his good graces—she always had that knack—and he needed to get away from her before she had the chance to do it again. With the den door locked and the music on repeat, he knew she'd leave him be, assuming him asleep on the couch, and he would have a head start for his heavy heart.

Chapter 16

Frisco

It was late afternoon when the plane landed in San Francisco and Billy was happy to catch a cab to his hotel. He felt revived after a shower and sliding into a new Ralph Lauren jacket he picked up in the hotel lobby shop. Nobody knew Billy McTaggart in San Francisco; there would be no secrets here—he could be Levi Indigo without turning his jacket around from grey to gilded.

He resisted the urge to call home as he headed down to the hotel bar; time had yet to make any headway in healing his hurt and confusion. And he had no idea how to explain his abrupt absence to Mam.

His spirits lifted as he thought about the smooth single malt whiskey he was about to order, the way it would burn all the way down into his hungry tummy. He hadn't eaten in over fifteen hours and was enjoying the raw, angry feeling of emptiness. He slid onto a dark leather bar stool and looked into the back-bar mirror, a sea of amber nectar and golden labels for the taking.

"Glenmorangie, please, large with a block of ice and a slight dash of water," he told the barman, and was served quickly. He closed his eyes and let the light gold liquid run over his tongue confirming his appreciation for the pure spirit. He sighed as he swallowed and opened his eyes to see an attractive, slender, well-dressed young woman with an improbably familiar face sitting at the bar two seats to his right, eating a bowl of the hotel's famous seafood bisque.

"Hello," he said without thinking.

"Hello," she replied from the rim of her wine glass and, when he kept frowning at her, obviously trying to place her, added, "I was sitting in front of you on the plane from Houston."

Billy nodded, suddenly unsure of who he was, Billy or Levi. "Join me for dinner?" he blurted before he'd figured it out.

"Okay," she said simply, smiling as she slid long legs out around the bar stool and straightened her dress. "I'm Sophie."

"Billy," he answered, motioning to the barman that they would be taking a table.

He pulled the chair out for her as they were seated, and the hostess brought over their unfinished drinks and smoothed a wrinkle in the crisp white tablecloth. She placed napkins on their respective laps and poured fresh ice water into long-stemmed water glasses, the ice chinked, and glinted brightly in the reflection of the silverware. Sophie reached a manicured hand toward her glass of wine and smiled across the table at him. Billy shifted in his seat and wondered what the hell he was doing.

"So, Billy. What brings you to San Francisco?" Sophie asked.

"No real reason, I suppose. I'm looking for something I seem to have lost, and this was the first flight out of the Jacksonville

Airport." He took another sip of his Glenmorangie to give his mouth something to do other than talk and tell Sophie things even he didn't yet know about himself. "And you?"

Sophie leaned forward, resting her chin on an elegant hand. "Have you heard of flower power?" she asked. When Billy shook his head she explained, dropping her tone. "I'm a reporter for a magazine called *Time*. You may have seen our recent cover with Lee Harvey Oswald on the front. I'm going undercover tomorrow, exploring the Hippies and the Flower Power movement here in Haight-Ashbury." Billy nodded, and Sophie made one more attempt to engage him. "I'm leaving at eleven AM sharp. You can tag along if you're up for an adventure."

"Where's the sun?" Billy asked when he met Sophie in the lobby the next morning. She looked much different this morning than when he first met her. Last night she'd been a classic-looking career gal. This morning she was clad in white vinyl boots and a short floral mini skirt that showed off well-defined tanned thighs. "Really, I thought this was California. Isn't it always sunny out here?"

Sophie laughed. "It's the Bay, wet and wild with sprinkles of sunshine," she told him as their cab pulled up to the curb. "Haight Street," she said to the driver and handed him a ten.

When they were on their way, tucked too close together in the back of the cab for Billy's absolute comfort, she turned to him and ran a hand over his short-cropped hair. "We'll need to do something about that buzz cut of yours. Everyone you're going to meet is sensitive to the military, the war in Vietnam. And those clothes"—she laughed at him. "This is the 60's, not the 1950s." She leaned in even closer, to whisper. "This isn't my first time undercover, Billy. I have friends here, lots of them.

They run a yoga studio a few days a week, the rest of the time they're too stoned or busy fucking to worry about the rest of the world." She leaned back again and smiled at Billy. "Sounds like a fun life, yes?"

Billy sat back and watched the wet, gray streets rush by. He let himself wonder what it would feel like to move through life like that, with no sense of responsibility. He liked the sensation.

At Sophie's instruction, the driver pulled over on Haight to let them out. Sophie tipped him and led Billy into a small grungy bar on the corner.

Sophie made her way through the crowd and a cloud of cigarette and pot smoke that filled the room. Billy's eyes adjusted to the light as they cut a path through the patrons. He noticed a phone on the wall surrounded by all sorts of brightly covered flyers for musical events and meditation practices, dirty handprints, and scribbled phone numbers etched into the scarred plaster. He felt the urge to phone home, knowing by now that Meg and Mam would be worrying about him, but Sophie reappeared with a drink in each hand.

"Let's get some booze into these traveler bodies," she said, and then laughed aloud as the sound of Jimi Hendrix's "Hey Joe" filled the bar. She downed her drink in three quick gulps, ditched the glass on a nearby table, and began to dance, blending into the gyrating crowd. He heard a cheer, and quickly spotted the reason—Sophie shedding her blouse, revealing perfect breasts. Another lamb to the slaughter, or a wolf in lamb's clothing, he thought, God bless America.

"Buy me a drink!" she called to him.

"Same again, and one for the bar," Billy shouted back just as a pretty young girl dressed in bright scarves danced toward him and asked him to stick out his tongue. She placed a small square—stamp—on it like a priest giving communion. That was the last he remembered.

Fleas were the least of it, Billy realized as he awoke a day later on the cushion-strewn floor of the apartment over the yoga studio. He was almost suffocating under the weight of naked bodies. Every shape, size, and color were entwined like a cosmic pretzel, undulating as a singular living beast, a Celtic Knot of skin, cigarette papers, and matted hair that stank of patchouli oil. Billy saw Sophie wriggle free from between two large black men as one of them made a lethargic and unsuccessful attempt to grab her and pull her back into the pile. She coughed and gave a hacking laugh, sounding like one of the old Diggle women Billy remembered from his childhood, women with the life drawn out of them by hard work in the mills and child rearing without birth control or enough food to guarantee survival, each breath fought for and resented at the same time. It wasn't an attractive laugh and he closed his eyes against it, which only made him more aware of the fleas biting him back to reality: The reality that he'd just abandoned his wife and his mother.

Sophie picked him out of the dazed maze of bodies. "Billy, darling, there you are, do you have a joint? I need a little pick me up, sweetie."

Billy untangled himself and made his way over to her as she picked through an overflowing ashtray and found a damp roach. She lit it and took a long hit, then held what was left of it out to Billy between two long fingernails.

"Let's get some food," he said, refusing her offer and picking through the eclectic array of discarded clothing around the apartment to find as many of his own items as he could, including his leather jacket and wallet.

Billy wanted out of San Francisco, yet he stayed—in Sophie's guest room in the apartment she'd arranged to rent two stories above the yoga studio. It was located inside one of the weather-beaten Queen Anne row houses stacked throughout the city like gingerbread cakes in an array of gaudy colors that trumpeted the residents' resistance to convention. Sophie's apartment had one saving grace—a substantial roof garden, of sorts. The building backed onto the workshop of the former owners; a printing company run for years by a Greek family. They had prospered in San Francisco as an immigrant family, building first their printing shop and then their home, which they connected across the first two stories of adjoining buildings, one decorative and iced to perfection with various decorative architectural details that would put a wedding cake to shame.

The other was just a sponge, a plain beige building with a two-foot red stripe around the middle that looked like a jam filling. Within that red stripe a passerby could squint and still read the name of the original Greek family's business in washed out gold letters. At the top of the sponge, however, was a large flat roof that had been, at one point, painted white. With one step off the balcony of his bedroom, Billy could transport himself onto that rooftop and into a Bohemian wilderness of ferns and pot plants as tall as a man. Old furniture and carpets rotted gloriously in the fluctuating weather. It was a sanctuary where the tenants held rooftop parties lit by candles that cast shadows of delicious proportions.

The following few weeks played out in psychedelic melodramas of music, free love, too much cheap wine, too many easily-available street drugs, far too little food, and poetry. Sophie and Billy and a revolving group of friends and lovers would start their evenings listening to pontificating beatniks and enjoying arguments over the curse of war, man's inhumanity to man, and the futility of killing the Vietcong as a symbol of Democracy. Then the evenings would drift, inevitably, into the small hours of the morning where the world needed love, not war, and peace, of course, bodies sinking slowly under the weight of booze and copious drugs toward the universal matrix of desire and connectivity and the elusive compassion they all sought to prove as tangible and sustainable in the Age of Aquarius. Billy relished the distraction and was content to drift in the sea of humanity and free love around him.

Then, one bright morning while Billy was making coffee and coughing until he could light a cigarette to sooth his throat, Sophie announced she had enough material for her article and was returning to L.A. Three weeks had passed, but he still wasn't ready to go home. The sun would shine on his skinny body as he bared himself on the rooftop, stretching out like a vampire on cushions warm in the daylight emerging from a hundred years below ground. He still resisted the urge to call home as it had become easier to ignore the issue. As Mam would say of a bad situation, "Don't knit a blanket out of it." He made his way to the greasy bar where Sophie first introduced him to flower power, took a seat at the bar with the few other early morning barflies, ordered a beer and drank half of it before he made his way to the pay phone at the back of the bar. He rummaged in the pocket of the jeans for his wallet and pulled out the paper upon which he'd transcribed Lola's number. He dialed her parents' phone number.

Much to his surprise, Lola answered.

Chapter 17

Lola

Lola watched the plane land and taxi to a halt on the tarmac. She felt apprehensive as the first passengers disembarked. She wore a simple outfit—slacks and a knit top, sandals, her hair pulled back in a ponytail, light foundation and mascara her only makeup. Not the way Billy was used to seeing her. She wasn't sure he'd even recognize her without the stilettos and sequins, but then she saw him coming down the stairs, and he saw her. He smiled and waved and quickened his pace.

In the small terminal building, they stood facing each other. "My real name's Anna," Lola said. "Everyone around here calls me Red." She shrugged as she pointed to her naturally red and curly mane. "I thought we'd best get that out of the way."

Billy stepped up to her and extended his hand. "Nice to meet you, Miss Red, I'm Billy. Now, is there a place to get some breakfast around here? I'm starving."

At the local diner, she marveled at Billy's enthusiasm for consuming two servings of pancakes doused in thick maple syrup and surrounded by a yellow sea of egg yolk.

"Now," Billy said, through a mouthful of breakfast, "tell me what happened."

And, so, Red did.

"It was quick, the officer said. A big rig and a tired driver. Mamma and Pa had little protection with the top down. It all happened just about sunset, on Highway 15 not far outside of Mesquite on the Arizona/Nevada border.

"When I first got back to my parents' place," she continued, "I kept looking around the empty house expecting to hear my mother call out dinner was ready, or to hear my father's laughter coming from the den while he was watching a rerun of, *I Love Lucy*. Ever since it first came on the air, that show could make him laugh so hard…

"Everything in the house was just filled with memories—photos, furniture, my sixth-grade track trophies, Mamma's cookbooks, Pa's war novels and farmer's almanacs and his *National Geographic* magazines. It still smelled like Mamma's cooking when I first got back. I could still see Pa's shape in his chair. Smell his pipe tobacco…

"They never got in the way of my need to go out and explore the world—to find something beyond horses and cows and endless prairie. I'm sure they didn't actually approve of me being a showgirl, hanging around with the King and his entourage, but as long as I came back to visit every few months they didn't complain.

"Last summer, Elvis bought me a Cadillac.

"Pa loved that car. It was a palace on wheels compared to his 49 Chevy truck which he had bought brand new—I mean, the Cadillac had more amenities than their house. The back seat was the size of a sofa, made out of enough leather to make a small herd. He loved riding around town with me with the top down when I drove it home to visit them. He had long, gray hair and it would flap around in the wind, unlike Mamma who would wrap one of my Chanel scarves around her head, to keep her hair in place when I took them joy riding. She looked like Grace Kelly there in the back seat.

"They enjoyed the car so much that, when my visit was over, I gave it to them. Pa didn't want to take it. Not at first, but I insisted. I mean, we were about to go on tour, and I wasn't going to use it anyway, and, you know... It was the least I could do for them after all they did for me all my life. The last night of my vacation we all drove down through Carlisle Junction and into town for milkshakes at Betty's Diner in Sundance. And the next day Pa drove me to the airport in Rapid City for my flight back to Las Vegas."

"After we got back from our tour, Mamma and Pa decided to drive the nine hundred miles to visit me. It was the first time they'd ever thought to do that, a lifetime trip Mamma called it, something they could never do with all the responsibilities of the ranch... and no real desire to leave their homestead, I think. When I was a kid and asked why we never went on vacations like my classmates, Mamma would ask me why I thought I needed a vacation. 'We have everything right here,' she'd say, 'the biggest, bluest sky you can get, all the seasons in the world, and our own five-star porch to sit on and watch the world go by as we drink our coffee at sunrise.'

"All that's left of them is the ranch and the collection of teaspoons I sent them from around the world. Mamma really liked those spoons, I don't know why. She didn't even drink tea." Lola let out a small laugh as Billy wiped maple syrup from his plate with his last bite of pancake. "I roamed around the ranch for days, wondering what I was going to do without them and then, one day, the phone rang, and it was you."

Devil's Tower loomed over Oshoto, Wyoming. Billy watched Red walk ahead of him on the thin gravel path that wound through the trees at the base of the Tower, her small hips tilting in a sweet rhythm as she loped effortlessly forward in determined strides. Here she was natural, no longer Lola, but Red, with no glitter, no makeup, no mask of the sort she wore every night when she took the stage or decorated a lap.

"Red," he mouthed as he watched her, baggy white T-shirt, frayed and misshapen at the neck and sleeves, casually elegant, hanging off one shoulder, taunting to reveal the shape of her slight delicious breasts. Raising her arms in salute to the glorious sun that sparkled through the trees exposed ever so briefly a slim brown tummy and fluted waistline that he fixed in his mind along with the smile on her face.

He watched the dancer's flowing limbs as she relaxed into her own skin. The pine-scented air wrapped around him, a light breeze tossed her hair around her shoulders. He smiled, realizing she'd forgotten him in her freedom. He picked up his pace to catch up with her.

"Kiss me," she turned and asked, the words breaking the silence of the woods.

"I shall," he said, surprised by his own voice in the stillness, his accent harsher in all this softness than he would have expected. "I shall, indeed," he said, and her mouth was soft, and tasted sweet. He didn't know this new girl who stood before him. But he wanted to.

"I don't know you," he said, reluctantly withdrawing from the kiss.

"Boots! You'll need cowboy boots if you're going to stay a while." Red said in reply.

A general store with creaking, graying floorboards, sold everything from ammunition to ant traps, with a large selection of cowboy gear at the front of the store—Western-style shirts, blue jeans, hats, belts and big, broad buckles, plus an entire wall of men's, women's, and children's boots.

"These, I think," Billy said, holding out a pair of tooled brown leather boots with Cuban heels for Lola to inspect. They would be practical on the ranch—and they'd give him at least three more inches of height so he wouldn't have to stand on tiptoes when he next kissed her.

Red approved, he paid for his purchase, and they took seats at a table in the small restaurant attached to the store and ordered beers.

"So, Billy, what brings you to Wyoming?" Red asked. "I'm sure it wasn't just because you found my number after all this time."

"Cattle," he said, leaning back in his chair, tipping back the black Stetson he'd bought along with the boots, deflecting. "I aspire to own cows like my great, great, great uncle, known around our parts as the Mossley Cowboy." Red tilted her head with curiosity, and he continued. "It was my mother's family, the Barbour family of Mossley. My Mam had a great, great uncle Abraham who was born on the sixteenth day of July,1834, the son of Aaron and Sarah Barbour." Billy tried on his best cowboy accent. "Mr. Barbour was probably one of the best-known men in cattle circles in Southeast Kansas and the North of the Indian Territory. He possessed a striking personality and when once seen was never forgotten." He shook his head and smiled and took her hand over the table. "The truth is rather different. I'm a little lost."

"This is what my parents did every evening at sunset," Lola said as they sat on the wide front porch of the house her parents had built with their own hands.

"Thank you for letting me come here," he replied, feeling his eyelids begin to droop.

"Come," Lola told him.

He followed her into the house to her old bedroom and into her single, girlhood bed with its heavy woolen covers. Their tryst in Hawaii couldn't have been more different as now she was tender and less possessed or demanding, there was no showmanship or facade. They made love slowly, cautiously, with an intimacy for which both seemed desperate.

The intimacy did not end with their lovemaking. They lay together and talked into the night, listening intently, voices raised to barely whispers.

"My Mamma and Pa never spoke of my real parents, other than the one time when I asked my Mamma why I had red hair and pale skin. Mamma and Pa's roots were Italian., and I looked so different than either of them. Mamma told me that my birth mother was a local girl, and that I was half Irish, half Cheyenne Indian. I was the product of an Irish farmer seeking his fortune on the way to the fertile Central Valley of California."

Billy pushed himself up on one elbow and turned to face Red in the dim lamplight; he wanted to see her face as she spoke.

"My daddy was a war veteran, battle weary, with nothing to live for in post-war Europe. He was a wild man, so I've been told, and he thought the West would suit him. He made his way across America as a farm hand. His tenure on Pa's ranch was only one summer, though he spent another couple of years in Sundance, Wyoming, seduced by whiskey and his new bride. He caught the eye of my birth mother, a young native Indian girl who worked cleaning house and stealing from Mamma. Their union was volatile from the start and resulted in my father deserting us when I was just four."

Billy pulled her close, and she turned, spooning her back into him as he slid his hand on to her tummy where he could feel her catch each breath.

"I only have a few memories of my real mother—no one knows what became of her. Mamma shared what little she knew. What she did tell me is that all mothers were once daughters, they become the grandmothers that complete the circle, the natural cycle of things. An evolution of the feminine handed from generation to generation as a rite of passage." She let out a sob and Billy tried to hold her tighter, but she needed to breathe and pushed away, full of the outpouring of her story. "I understand now that a fragile teenage daughter can become a mother too soon, bloom too fast. My pregnancy had not come as a surprise. Mamma offered me kind words and stroked my hair as she washed my skin and bandaged my wounds.

"What happened?" Billy whispered.

"Mamma found me staring at my own face in the mirror, crusty mouthed, morning sick, tears running, my hand still on Pa's straight razor. The kick of a tiny foot in my gut, and the pain of the first cut brought me back around. But I conceded and told myself, 'Not today.' I knew then I was strong beyond my own knowledge, but it took years to remember the rest, the pit from where Mamma and Pa pulled me."

Billy found it hot in the confines of the bed and the intensity of the story made it hard to find comfort, but he didn't want to let her go or have her stop talking.

"Mamma always said that with guiding hands a girl might travel the journey on the road to womanhood in splendor and grace. She told me I had simply paused, distracted and curious, by the wayside, like so many others with a desire to sniff the ditch and explore the road less traveled. She told me the pause didn't have to be my whole story." Red lay silent for a time then, with a crack in her voice, continued.

"At ten years old, I watched my mother take pleasure from strange men as I hid behind bedroom curtains, a voyeur to the unexplained. The muffled voices intrigued me, the twisting bodies evoked an intrigue, a tingling in my belly I didn't understand. That was after my parents' war of whiskey and jealousy between their Irish and Cheyenne blood became too much. My mother had barked at the moon until he left forever.

Thankfully, Mamma and Pa never looked too hard for my parents when things fell apart, and Sheriff Crow put the adoption paperwork through for the good folks he knew they were. Mamma and Pa saved me best they could. Even so, at fourteen, even with all the love they gave me, I found refuge in a ditch of hard brown liquor. That's when they found me in a pool of my own piss and puke, unsure who the father of my baby might be."

The sun was starting to rise on to the vast open plains around them. Lola gave out a wail of pain that cracked the still air as the sun broke over the horizon and seeped in through the crack in the curtains at the window.

"I never had the baby. My body gave it up all on its own, but it left a hole in me I've tried to fill ever since."

Billy pulled her to him and asked no questions. He knew the dull sound of the hole of which she spoke. He knew its shape and depth. He had never shared his true story like this with anyone—not with Meg, though she was such a part of it. The expansiveness of the ranch seemed to allow for expansiveness of emotion in a way the confines of the village of Diggle could never do. He pushed thoughts of Meg and Mam away hard even as he realized he needed to tell Red his truth as she had told him hers.

But not today; not yet.

In the weeks that followed in the isolation of the cabin, they consumed each other, breathing each other in one breath at a time. Neither was in a rush to exhaust time for fear it would end. On most days they would wake, make coffee, cook eggs. The sun would shine on their bodies as they went about the labor of chores on the farm and the pleasure of each other, stretching out like prairie dogs emerging from below ground to live warmed in the sunlight.

With kisses they devoured each other. They made love for the sake of reckless vulnerability, exposed and raw, an emotional unraveling, floating away from the safety of convention into the unknown.

In these moments, he could barely hold on to a fragile thread of light to save himself from disappearing entirely into her as the moment rang true.

Billy awoke one morning to the sound of a guitar and singing. He stretched out on the bed and breathed deep the smell of coffee that she must have put on while he slept.

"Little town by the railroad track, lived a girl, she was doing fine, just marking time – watching the sun shine."

Her voice was soft melodic, yet the sadness was present deep in her song. Uneasily he thought of Meg and Mam back in Florida. He had forgotten them in the past weeks, a reality check of responsibility, his fate and the promise he had made. He'd run away, and they would be looking for him. Red's voice carried through the house as she lost herself in the song.

"At that local store that sells coffee and more…"

Red's singing tailed off with the ending of the song and Billy could hear her pad softly toward the room. He lay back under the blanket and pretended to be asleep when she entered the room and jumped on him, shouting for him to wake up.

Their time on the ranch seemed consumed in but a few short breaths. Everything has a beginning and an end. One evening after a light supper and a long walk they sat in the cozy lounge of the cabin. Billy poured them both a glass of wine, looked at Red, and started talking.

He began with the story he'd learned of his own birth and his mother's fall from grace, his father's return and departure, his marriage to Meg, and of course the babies that never came.

"I don't know who I am anymore. I was raised a Northern English working man by a mother who taught me tenderness and a wife I loved and admired without reserve, until I stumbled onto her deception. I'm not sure how to be in the world anymore, but we can't hide here forever, can we?" he asked, hoping she would say they might.

"I love you," he told her.

"And I love you," she answered. "That's why I need to send you back to your wife."

Almost on cue the phone rang and broke the spell.

"No one ever calls here except silly English boys," she said as she pulled a cushion over her head.

"Let me answer it." Billy said as he jumped up from the couch, I'll scare them off."

"Hello, hello!" Billy recognized the voice instantly and the hair on his neck shot up, Dumbfounded, he sat there, unable to move. The voice on the other end of the phone was small, desperate, and fluttered like a bird being tossed in the wind.

"Is Billy there? We've lost him, and we need him back."

"Hello, hello, Billy love, are you there, are you there? I need to talk to you if you are.

"Mam, it's me." he heard her start to cry, and he tried to soothe her,

"Oh Billy, love! Billy is it really you?"

Chapter 18

Alone

Mam coughed, a deep hacking cough she knew would bring blood and spit in contrasting dabs on to the crisp white tissues next to the bed. The pink blotches conveyed a reality she refused to address. Each tissue reminded her of the bright pink plastic flamingos that dotted the white pebble driveway to the house, a reality check of sorts each time she drove up the road to her loneliness. Billy had been gone now for months that seemed like forever.

In the time since they came to live in Florida, she'd never entirely settled in and was always talking of home and wondering how everyone was doing, what was the weather like, how much a pound of mincemeat would cost at the local butcher on the High Street. She always compared the American way with all things at home.

"It would be grand if we had the sunshine like here but without all the gadgets and plastic," she said as Meg ignored her. Mam tried to talk to Meg, but it seemed impossible, an inconvenience. Didn't family talk? She'd always spoken to her sisters, but perhaps with Meg being an only child she never had the time for small talk about big issues. Maybe it was that without Billy there to glue them all together, there was no reason to pretend.

Luckily, she had Mimi to talk with over cups of tea

Dr. Weinstein and his wife Mimi were neighbors in the development where they lived. The doctor was a gentle balding man with substantial dark eyebrows that looked ready to fall from his forehead where they hung above his sagging eyes like sleeping caterpillars. He had a kind face, and she befriended his wife, Mimi soon after their arrival. With Dr. Weinstein's busy practice, she and Mimi had plenty of time to get together for long walks along the beach. There was thirty years difference in age between them, but the two were of another era to which they clung ferociously in fear of falling into the fast-paced modern world. She converted Mimi to tea from coffee, and Mimi managed to get her to take on the custom of 4 pm "Bubbles" on the front veranda that encircled her southern style home.

"It is a veranda if it goes all the way round Suzie," Mimi would say, "a porch only sits on one side, my dear."

Mimi's traditional Sand Hill cottage stood in stark contrast to Billy and Meg's minimalistic home. Mam preferred the ornate yet comfortable furniture rather than the steel and leather furniture. When they first arrived, she convinced Billy to get her an overstuffed lounger for her room. These days she preferred to sleep in it, because the bed made her feel like she was lying down to die. She missed Billy dearly and still had no clear answer from Meg that could justify such a departure. He'd never just gone off, not without telling her, asking her advice, or wondering what surprise he could bring back for her. He'd never left for more than a week or two at most. She knew

Meg was stonewalling her and just kept promising an answer tomorrow or the next day.

Suzie knew Mimi noticed the moments when she tried to hide her discomfort, first small winching movements of a deep-lying pain that brought her hand to her tummy as she smiled. She would dismiss it as upset tummy or an old work injury tied to her days washing laundry that caused her arthritic hands, which she couldn't hide.

"What is it my dear, have you seen a doctor?" Mimi asked politely.

"I did in England, but I've not had time here yet." She changed the subject.

Suzie found peace in their long chats and one afternoon, after finishing over half a bottle of bubbles between them, she asked Mimi something that had been bothering her for quite some time. It was brought on by thinking she might never see Billy again, much like his father.

"Mimi, when do you know the last time something will happen? A conversation, a kiss, a visit with an old friend or someone you love, seeing my son? We don't know, and we can never know until we realize it's gone and will never happen again."

Mimi leaned forward in her seat and rested her hand affectionately on Suzie's knee. "I have no idea about your son, but he will be back I'm sure. Part of our lives always get lost to posterity. That's the nature of getting old and trying to be graceful in the process. It's beyond our control or desire."

Tears welled in Suzie's eyes. "I remember life briefly once like this champagne held in a crystal glass pressed against my lips and softly consumed. A promise, a temptation to a young girl." She paused and drank deeply from the glass she held and prompted Mimi to do the same. Both women drank. Suzi appreciated Mimi simply listening, as a good friend will do. She went on, slightly inebriated, pulling from every novel she'd ever read or poem she had ever written, an eloquence she never allowed herself to consider. Her education up until her pregnancy had been good. She had promise, people said.

"I know it sounds funny coming from me, but I think of this champagne as a metaphor of sorts." She felt a tear come to her eye as she looked at Mimi before continuing. "First taste almost burns with bubbles on your curious lips and tongue, then in a torrent, down your throat it rushes, cleaving a track through your chest into the pit of your tummy. Eagerly, your body consumes it. Now within, deep within you, it crouches, waiting, ready to spring as it feels your rising breath." She paused again to catch her own breath, trying to hide a cough from Mimi in a hanky. "Slowly in stealth, it ebbs out from your core, creeping through dilated veins, consuming you on a visceral level, becoming you. Tenderly it invigorates as it moves from tissue to nerve end, out through stiff shoulders and stretching arms like honey drizzled over tight hungry skin to fingertips that call out for a caress."

Mimi nodded in agreement, seeming a little consumed as the champagne had taken hold of her too, and years of her own repression threatened to reveal themselves under Suzie's description of an intoxication.

"I never thought of it like that," Mimi said as Suzie's voice rose and she continued.

"It fills every cell of your body, it no longer burns with the same vibrancy as it crosses your lips, but feels part of you, inevitable in its integration into your system as natural, and accepted. Quite normal now this feeling of euphoric light-headedness that sets you at ease."

Mimi agreed again, with a murmur.

"Down we sink together into the very base of the feeling, a deep need brews there, longing pushes for release, for recognition in the light of day."

Suzie was consumed now and started to weep freely as years of pent up feelings poured out, knowing she would never again have love as she'd had it on those Sunday mornings so long ago. As the two women sat together Mimi admitted to Suzie that, out of concern, she'd told her husband about Suzie's pains and early onset of coughing fits. He chastised her for not mentioning it to him sooner and demanded to take Suzie for proper tests. Mimi took Suzie's hand and begged her to see the doctor.

The tests were conclusive: a form of cervical cancer had spread throughout her body and now manifested in her lungs. It was only a matter of time, and the doctor suggested she get her affairs in order. It would probably be best if she found her son and let him know the situation.

Meg received the news with regret but admitted to knowing something had been wrong for a very long time. She told Suzie she'd been happy to ignore it as she dealt with the move to Florida. She'd been set on establishing them as a prominent family in the development, and then with the abrupt departure of Billy everything fell out of sorts.

When Susie demanded the truth, Meg finally showed her the note Billy left. It came as no surprise, as she expected no less of the girl to whom she'd given the benefit of the doubt for so long.

"I was sure Billy would return in a couple of days, if not weeks. He always came back no matter what I did. He always came back bearing gifts."

Sheepishly, Meg revealed the story of the blood-stained towel and the hunk of raw meat.

"I realize it must have been hard for Billy to fathom. Billy is smart," Meg said to Mam, "but a little ignorant to the real ways of the world. That's part of his appeal, and what sustains his youthful optimism and wondrous schemes that always seem to make money from fresh air. I know his desire to please me was his biggest motivation. I relied on that as a proof of his love. Where could he have been for these past three months?"

Mam found herself reeling in anger, feeling betrayed on all sides. How could Billy not have shared this with her? How could he leave? She struck out at Meg.

"I can't say I blame the boy after all the shenanigans you pulled over the years, but I never thought his heart could be broken enough to abandon us… me, his Mam," she said with tears falling from her eyes. "He's become his father's son, something I swore would never happen. I never could believe he'd be broken enough to abandon me," she repeated with a sob that fell untethered from her throat as she tried to stifle it with her twisted fingers that allowed too many gaps to contain her intense grief.

"He'll be back, Mam," Meg offered weakly.

Suzie realized a sudden awareness was heaping upon her that Billy was indeed gone and might never return, however unrealistic that seemed. She went to her room and didn't come out for a week, living only on cups of soup or tea Meg would leave at the door. Eventually, Mam conceded she needed to hold some hope for Billy's return. Meg said she would hire a private detective to find him, wherever he might be in the world. Suzie felt a pathetic sense of hope as she helped in the interview process with the private detective. Stan came recommended by the woman who did Meg's hair, but Suzie disliked him from the start and considered him a fool.

"I've thought of everywhere he might be— had he gone back to Diggle, but no one has seen hide nor hair of him there. Harry Two Bellies put the word out and heard nothing." She broke down into tears. "I even wondered if went to find his dad, that's how desperate I am, but being as we don't know where his dad is either, it seems futile."

Meg watched Mam and wanted to wrap her up in some big blanket until Billy came home, some form of suspended animation that would keep her safe until they found him. The life was ebbing out of her before her eyes, and she now knew the cough was brought on by more than Stans cologne.

"Is there anything Mr. Billy has that's personal and he left behind?" Stan said in a thick South American accent. "Anything he'd never leave behind should he not intend to return?"

Meg and Mam looked at one another. Billy had lots of things he loved, his suits, his car, and even the boat they'd bought last summer. But nothing he'd ever been possessive over, nothing he couldn't live without or give away if someone needed it. Everything he owned was still here other than a canvas hold-all, two pairs of jeans, a couple of tee shirts, and his leather biker jacket. Even his den was ship shape. Meg found his note with clear instructions for money and how to keep the house in order as he didn't know when he might be back. Mam was to be taken care of as a priority. He asked her to apologize for his departure, unable to face either of them in his devastation and embarrassment.

"His treasures," Mam said abruptly, she stood up and shuffled to Billy's den. "Where is his tin, his treasure tin? He'd never leave that, would he?" She went to his desk and rummaged in the drawer where she pulled out papers and files that were neatly stacked. "Nothing, I can't find it. If it's gone then so is he."

Her search became more frantic as a coughing fit overtook her. Meg rushed over to help her up as she curled up on the floor, hacking and trying to catch her breath. Meg tried to lift her head from the carpet just as Mam shouted and reached for the bottom of the desk where her hands grasped and found the edge of the tin.

"His treasures!" She gasped.

Meg helped her pull the tin out and place it on the desk. She'd never seen it before. How was that possible? She knew everything about Billy, everything, how was this tin then real? They crowded around the old tin and Meg took the responsibility of opening it. She pried the tight lid with her freshly manicured nails, breaking two in the effort as she smarted with the indignation of having to reveal the contents of her husband's Treasure Box in front of Mam and Stan the PI. The lid popped with a dull, sucking metallic release and they all looked down on an eclectic array of mismatched items that seemed to only be of sentimental value. Suzie noticed first his father's hairbrushes as the largest of the items, some old pen knives, several large tattered white five-pound notes pinned together in one corner, a lock of hair Meg said was hers from years past, her gift to him to remember her on one of his business trips.

The tin held several old bank books Meg was amazed to see the contents of, along with receipts for someone called Levi Indigo from tailors in Manchester and London. And last the small envelope from Hawaii. After Meg read it, she threw it at Stan and said she supposed this would be his first lead and best he get to it.

Stan copied the number and put the card back in the tin. Mam knew Billy had a few months' start on him and God knows where he might be by now.

Meg stormed from the room after knocking the tin from the desk and letting Billy's treasures crash to the floor. PI Stan ignored the spill in his own haste to get out of this madhouse, leaving Mam alone. She sat holding a blood-spattered hanky to her mouth and staring at the contents spread on the floor around her. Broken hearted in the reality of the situation, she wondered if she would ever see her boy again as she slowly began to repack the tin with its contents. Her twisted fingers cupped each treasure lovingly, knowing that it was also the last time she would see them as she placed the lid on the tin and slid it back under the desk. She made her way to the stark kitchen where even the kettle was voiceless, as no one but her drank tea anymore. There were no comfortable nights in front of the fire in big old chairs that carried the smell of home, no laughter, and banter over a game of dominos, no caresses or kisses on the top of her head from her boy.

"When was the last time someone held you?" She said into the dark empty kitchen. "When was the last time you had reason to live?"

She returned to her room, slumped back into her favorite chair, picked up the phone, and dialed the number she'd copied from the card. She had nothing to lose by hoping.

In the time Billy had been gone, seeing Mam's health deteriorate, Meg convinced her to forsake the Catholic church for the People's Tabernacle, a large charismatic evangelical church run by a self-proclaimed disciple to Jesus Christ, the everlasting savior. Graham Baker was a nom de plume adopted from both Billy Graham and Jim Bakker by a used car salesman turned evangelist. Meg read and believed that he had found the lord after a hunting accident in the swampy Florida Everglades where mysteriously he was the sole survivor of an attack that killed his business partners, their wives, and children. By God's grace, he would say from the pulpit on Sunday morning, he survived the attack when everyone else was killed and eaten by gators.

He believed that by divine grace the Lord spared him when he was only shot in the legs as the band of rogues who attacked them departed amid his last hail of bullets while trying to defend his friends and their families. He had crawled fifteen miles through the snake-infested swamps and was found on the side of the road almost dead. In his battered state, it was a week before he could remember where the camp was, by which time all the bodies were gone; mothers, fathers, and children. As the sole surviving partner with no heirs to claim the insurance or assets, he inherited everything.

Within a year he was walking again by the grace of God and launched The People's Tabernacle in the vast and newly converted building that had once been the car showroom. Mam and Meg watched his TV commercial telling everyone there was ample parking for newcomers, and buckets of free fried chicken in anticipation of the end of days. On Sundays, the crowd loved to watch him as he would hobble onto the stage using crutches and then throw them away while he fell to his knees and wept for salvation. Then pulling himself up the pulpit, he stood shaking as he preached redemption and contribution. He wore a wide-open shirt that showed his broad hairy chest and the alligator tooth he claimed was pulled from his thigh, although he didn't remember at what point he endured this agony. The Lord had seen fit to let him survive to bring the gospel to the visitors and patrons of his church.

Meg resented that Mam was always skeptical such a story could be true, but she conceded she loved the drama of it compared to the mundane ritual of Catholic Mass. She agreed that even if this lot were Protestants, they might be on to something where the Lord was a lot more accessible and less likely to chastise you with guilt. In their desire to bring Billy home they both hoped for healing to happen. The blind were made to see, the lame could walk, and the poor found hope in a new life after their own small contribution of whatever money they had. Meg also loved the glitz and glamor of it all, the flowing décor, cascading lights and music, the showbiz of it. It was God with glamor. And then there was Graham as he liked to be called, a simple man by his own declaration, on first name terms with the Lord and his parishioners alike. A hero, a man of substance and infinite compassion all wrapped in a well-groomed package, a real man. It didn't take Meg long, in her grief over Billy's departure, to find a way to share her story with Graham, who frequently offered to meet and console affluent wives or widows in direct need.

"Why, come in my dear," he expounded with sweeping gestures and Southern affection as Meg entered the room. "You are a picture of delight and so fine. I hear you are English and recently abandoned by your husband who was of some worth. Come to me my child and let me wrap my arms around you in the name of the spirit, our Lord, Jesus Christ."

Meg hesitated for a moment as she wondered how he knew about Billy leaving, but quickly dismissed it in her haste to be near this delightful man. She walked directly into his arms and allowed herself to be pulled to his chest as the alligator tooth pressed against her forehead and her face bedded in his chest hair. His voice reverberated boldly through her body. He held her so tight Meg could hardly breathe, and shortly fainted under the intensity of the experience. She awoke to Graham wiping her brow with a cold compress that smelt of mint.

"How long was I out?" Meg asked as she shot up into a seated position.

"Not long my dear girl, a few moments for the Lord to enter your soul and begin the healing. I did lay hands upon you and channeled the Lords will into your body. Forgive me, but I sensed it was what you needed most." His breath was sweet, and his blue eyes mesmerized her.

"I have to tend to my mother in law, she's waiting outside. She's the one who's sick and needs the most help." She straightened her clothing and made to leave.

"Be still sugar. I'm here to help. Tell me what you truly need." He probed her for details, and she responded in a silky voice.

"My mother-in-law is sick. She won't tell me the details, but I'm sure you could help revive her spirits or heal her melancholy. My husband is missing as you know, and I may have been the cause of it." She drew out the words as much as one could, trying to hold on to her time with him.

"I can see your burden," Graham offered. "Perhaps we need a little more time than these few moments together. A $100 donation for the Lord doesn't go as far as one would believe these days."

Mam was waiting outside and asked why Meg had taken so long, and why she looked so flushed. Was she okay? Meg brushed off the question and suggested they come back the following week when the pastor would have more time. Meg looped her arm with Mam and left the building. Halfway across the parking lot a young usher ran up to Meg and offered her an envelope.

"Graham requests that I deliver this to you Miss and that you best read it when you're in a place of privacy, comfortable and relaxed." Meg tipped him a dollar when he walked with them to their car at the far end of the parking lot.

"Thank you, Miss. Graham wants you to have the Lord's guidance home," said the young good-looking boy, who opened her car door and politely waited until they drove away before running back to the temple.

Upon arriving home and in the privacy of her room, Meg read the note, which was a request for dinner the following evening at 7pm. A car would be sent.

Much time had passed since she had dressed for a man, so Meg took her time. She bathed and selected the best of her lingerie, relishing the fact that her body still looked good, with firm thighs and flat tummy. She pushed up her small firm breasts to fill the low-cut dress of velvet and accentuated them with a pearl necklace she tied in a knot just above the line of her cleavage. She dusted herself with fine glitter and sprayed all the essential spots: behind her knees, and each ear, her wrists and at the base of her spine where her dress swooped decadently. Her stomach fluttered in anticipation of dinner with Graham.

She decided not to check in on Mam before she left. Questions would be awkward as to her dress, or destination for that matter. The incident with the P.I had been enough, and she didn't want to spoil this evening in any way. With any luck she'd be home before Mam woke up as usual for her soft-boiled egg and toast.

The car arrived promptly at seven and the driver instructed her Graham was anticipating her arrival. The car drove out of town and after half an hour turned into a large ornate gate preceding a water lined driveway. The house at the end was grander than anything she'd ever seen, other than Buckingham Palace on a summer school outing to London. She was ushered into the lobby and asked to wait on a small couch in the foyer. Irritated, she gave the first and second point to Graham as he emerged from a wood-paneled room off the lobby. His smoking jacket was lustrous, his hair groomed. She admired his white linen shirt which lay open at the neck framing a mat of coarse blond hair that sprung up around the alligator tooth. His perfectly manicured fingers felt soft in her hand as he reached out to welcome her.

Meg felt almost diminished by comparison to this handsome man. He launched into conversation without preamble or recognition of the effort she'd put into her own appearance. At dinner, the table was set intimately for two on the terrace. The scent of honeysuckle and jasmine hung heavy in the air and overpowered her well-placed perfume. The table held an array of glasses and cutlery that threatened her sensibilities, but Graham instructed her to start from the outside and work in as each course came to the table.

"Do the same with the wine glasses, which should be easier as the staff will fill the right glass with each course." He said as he launched into the conversation over chilled peach soup decorated with fresh goat cheese.

"I asked myself today, why I'm so intrigued to engage with this girl. And I guess it's simple. I've always lived my life as fully as I could, and some moments stand out. These are memories of intensity that make living worthwhile, stories we remember and share as defining. I have few regrets, but I do hope we'll be spending more time together. I have no reasoning for that, I just wish it."

Meg realized this was a man who not only got what he needed but also took what he wanted, politely.

"As an aspiring man of God, it's like living in the story, pushing each word out through scripture that took years to travel to the faithful across the seas and mountains," Graham said excitedly as he buttered a bread roll, "The word is how I imagine life. It's as if we were dancing together, very, very slowly between scripture, and then twirling and leaping when the Lord arrives amid loud fanfare." He paused and regained his composure, no longer caught up in the fervor of his own ecclesiastic beliefs, and it would seem, Meg thought, the need for justifying his actions and God's approval of his intent. She realized he was justifying going where he wished to go, regardless of the Lord's will.

An amusing thing happened this morning. My wife was getting dressed and whistling a tune. Yes, she does whistle," he added as Meg was about to ask. "I asked her if that was 'God Save the Queen? Yes, she said wondering why the heck she had it stuck in her head. My dear wife lived there with her English lover for a while years ago. She suggested we should visit it someday together with you and your husband. I laughed and thought of the four of us, me, her, you and your wayward husband having dinner. What would we talk about?"

"Your wife whistles," Meg said cotton-mouthed as she reached for her wine glass. *Was this the best retort she could manage?* In her desire for him she neglected any thought of an inconvenient wife, and now she felt embarrassed.

"I am sorry, I didn't consider… when accepting this dinner, I was selfish."

"Of course, I considered your husband. I'm happy and content in my marriage if you wish to know. That's a natural question for a femme fatale like yourself. I have no reason to complain, having all I need and more. I am by nature passionate and I shall struggle eternally to live in a world of mortal reason. My wife Mary is amazing and allows me to crucify myself almost daily, it is our arrangement."

Meg found the comparison trite.

"We have an understanding of our needs." Almost reading her thoughts, he reached across the table and took Meg's hand, "Tell me about your needs?" He rose from his chair abruptly, rounded the table, and slid his hand into the small of Meg's back as he guided her out of her chair.

"My needs?" Meg said.

"Let us walk." He directed her to the stairs that led down to a well-lit path through the garden.

Her body began to hum with anticipation as he tugged gently on her hand after a short distance, leading her away from the well-lit path to a more secluded area. She desperately gulped at the fresh air, unsure of the rapidly shifting evening.

"Trust me to guide you through the darkness." His fine leather loafers crunched lightly on the gravel as he took her to the base of an ancient oak tree with great branches that spread out like tentacles draped in Spanish moss, defying gravity in their span. "I believe you yearned to test yourself, to explore desires that sit heavy in your heart." Graham said boldly. "Do you not? You've held your aspirations for so long, and the sweat running down your back feels so good against the night air, does it not?"

He asked her directly, and she could only agree with a nod that was barely distinguishable in the moonlight. She thought his audacity knew no bounds, but like his sermons, he spoke truths to the ordinary soul, and she followed.

The humid air thickened around Meg; her romantic notions overwhelmed by his direct pomp. Still, she wanted there to be more, a kiss, a taste of him. Abruptly she rose on tiptoes and skimmed her lips over his mouth, attempting to regain some control, playing with him, teasing him with a touch of her tongue. He claimed her mouth with a firm kiss.

"You want me to surprise you with my sweetness and the little romantic gestures you'd never expected from a man like me." He said.

"I do," she conceded.

"Then let me lay my jacket on the grass and summon Eve."

He guided her down to the ground. His fingers threaded through her loose hair as he pressed her back against the jacket. His mouth tasted of sugary sweet iced tea and blueberries, of which she could not get enough. She shivered as his hands slid along the curve of her bare thigh beneath her dress. He nuzzled her neck and nipped lightly at a sensitive spot there. She moaned softly and pressed against his searching hand as it moved deftly between her thighs. She fluttered with anticipation.

"Are you sure this is what you want?" he teased as she twisted against him, mindless of her compromise, desperate for the attention and physicality of the man. When he touched her plumb colored panties a cry escaped her lips, and she lifted her small hips to aid their removal as he tossed them aside into the nearest pool of light. Feeling her thighs tighten she trembled with excitement at his request as she glanced around, suddenly aware of how any staff member might see them.

"What if we're discovered this way?" She asked, though the thought of it added to her arousal.

"No matter. I'm lord of my domain, and you can't deny me now." He clasped her hips and slid his shoulders down between her thighs. She felt incredibly open and vulnerable lying out under the stars, yet gloriously free and liberated beyond all expectations; dominant, the heroine of her own novel at last. She gripped her thighs and held her breath in anticipation of that first wondrous touch of his tongue. She inhaled sharply. It was all she could do not to cry out. She was conflicted between wanting to come right then and wanting to draw out the experience for as long as possible, to enjoy every second of pleasure. It was her moment, her *Lady Chatterley, Gone With the Wind, Wuthering Heights* rolled into one.

The orgasm built in her lower belly, waves rippled through her thighs and into her chest, her stiff nipples stabbed against the fabric of her dress as she tilted her head back and fought to breathe. Eyes closed, she concentrated on the incessant flickering of his tongue and the sparking light behind her eyes until she exploded with a tremendous rush of ecstasy she had never experienced. She thought she might pass out from the sheer perfection of it.

She'd barely come down from one peak when he drew her into another. Shattering into a thousand pieces, she melted into the cool grass that she held balled in her fingers beyond his jacket, biting her lip to keep from crying out. She pulled him up over her chest, and he tenderly caressed her face and kissed her mouth. The musk of her own passion clung to his mouth. She ran her tongue over his lips, gathering her own flavor. There was something so incredibly intimate about sharing this moment. She reached for his trousers and started to work at opening his belt. Abruptly he stopped and stood up, then walked over and picked up her panties. He asked her to stand as he knelt down and helped her into them. Her legs and belly quivered when he pressed a kiss to her sex through the cotton. She fanned her fingers through his short hair, wishing for more time to return the favor, but he made it clear the evening was now over. He thanked her and escorted her to the car and told her goodnight.

Meg knew he had his convert and she had found her savior. She sat breathless in the back of the car. She had been manipulative and abandoned by Billy for her sins, now she'd been unfaithful, but it felt like redemption for the number on that terrible card from Hawaii.

Upon arriving home, Meg let herself into the house where she discovered Mam in the lounge holding a cup of tea, sitting stone-faced on one of the white designer couches.

"Mam!" she said with a start, "I…I, got held up after dinner, it was nothing…serious."

Mam stood and walked out of the living room, turning as she reached the hallway.

"I found him, and he'll be coming home soon." Her words were dry, and she held nothing back. "I'm not sure what the two of you have done to each other, but two wrongs don't make a right and the sooner you figure that out, the better. It's time to go home to Diggle where we know who we are."

Chapter 19

Home

Billy sat in his kitchen looking over the ocean. Rain came in sheets against the large glass doors and the rhythmic sound lulled him into numbness. Elvis had just married Pricilla Beaulieu in Las Vegas and the Beatles had released *Sergeant Pepper's Lonely-Hearts Club Band*. There were protests against the Vietnam war and Muhammad Ali refused to carry out his military service, losing his Heavyweight Championship belt. In England, the first North Sea gas was being pumped ashore just one hundred miles from Diggle in Easington, East Riding in Yorkshire. The noise of change seemed overwhelming.

A simplicity of sorts overwhelmed him. He felt like John Glenn, one of NASA's new astronauts returning from the edge of space with proof that the world was indeed round and no matter how far you might travel you would inevitably return to that beginning place from which you ran. However, experiences along the way brought you back a different man. But the truth was, as his grandfather had said, "Wherever you are, there you are."

His return to Florida had been difficult as he and Meg tried their best to reconcile. Mam was instrumental in trying to mend the fences between them. She had an urgency about her, as Billy found out when she shared the status of her cancer.

"I've not got long Billy, a month or two at best," Mam told him. "Cervical cancer gone to my lungs, and I'm okay with it, now that you're back. I have my boy, and some hope you and Meg will work things out. You've both had to grow up a little, and I'm sorry for not seeing how you spent most of your life trying to be the man of the house. That sort of thing can keep a boy from truly growing up at all, and Meg is still a child too in her own way. She was never ready for the babies we two put on her, and she used that to get what she wanted."

"I'm sorry, Mam," he wept, wrapping his arms around her. "It all just became too much and I ran, but I have to tell you that I did discover you can love more than one person in your life and I wish you'd found another man to give you the love you deserved."

Mam sighed, "Pack me up and take me home where I can sit on the mantle and watch you and your family grow son, that's my only wish. The only love I needed was yours and that you'll promise to stay with me to the end."

Meg went home ahead of them in the hope of getting things ready at the lodge for Mam, should she rally, but Mam was unable to travel.

Billy sat with her as she slipped slowly into a deep sleep from which she never woke. He felt her body ease and his heart broke; his Mam was gone. His own health had suffered in the passing months, and he fell into a deep depression softened only by whiskey and eventually a stay in a rehabilitation clinic. It was a further six months before he wrapped up their life in Florida and boarded a plane with his mother's urn to go home. He gave Woody to Dr. Weinstein who had taken to walking the dog while Billy was in rehab.

Billy sat on the train from Manchester to Diggle and listened to the rhythmic click-clack of the train wheels on the track, the steady passing of moments and miles. It was a sound he knew so well as a railway tapper, simpler times when he would define good or broken with just the touch of his long-handled hammer to an iron wheel.

The pulsing of blood in his chest, tingling arms, and slight headache set up a conflict inside of him, not unlike a band of noisy children toying with instruments they didn't know how to play. Like a counting metronome that amplified his lack of synchronicity to the world he was returning to, and the world outside that was speeding up beyond comprehension across oceans and psychedelic minds. The cacophony grew louder as the train came closer to Diggle Station, and he found it hard to breathe.

He wiped condensation from the inside of the carriage window and watched the dull grey of the countryside fly past. Then, suddenly the Diggle station platform appeared like a flickering old film and froze into a frame outside the window.

He saw her through the window wedged into a portal in the wall of the station, huddled against the cold, her grey coat and headscarf muted against the quarry stone like a dead chameleon. The train stood dreamlike through the billowing steam as the large platform clock struck 6 AM and gave off a hollow chime that would start the day for most in the town. He saw his own reflection in the window, eyes sunken and dark as he held a fixed stare. He felt as if he might not move, not get off the train now that he'd seen her. Meg stepped toward the train and he blinked, then stood and made his way to the door where she was waiting.

Their embrace was polite, a cautious coming together after so long; a tentative and passionless act.

"Hello, pet," he said with a tired voice, still using the endearment out of habit.

"Hello, Billy," Meg replied, keeping it formal, trying not to cry. Her voice broke as she added, "You look well." He knew she was lying, "I have the car and some breakfast ready at home, I mean the house, if you're hungry. Do you need a porter for your bags?"

"This is all I have, just my mam and me," he said as he brushed a stray strand of his greasy dark hair out of his eyes and hiked his bag up on his shoulder.

They walked out through the station arch and she slid her arm through his. He wondered if it was just to make sure he was actually there, or perhaps to make sure he didn't run away. His arm was thin beneath his heavy coat, and he wondered what she might think of him when only a cup of tea sat between them. He knew she would have many questions, and patience would be essential for both of them. He figured she might begrudge him that.

At home, Meg hung up their coats. He couldn't help but think how his paisley shirt and bell bottom jeans seemed out of place compared to the rows of suits he knew hung upstairs in the cupboard like cardboard cutouts of who he used to be. His reversible jackets were useless now, as it was he who felt turned inside out.

"I'll put the kettle on and pull the food together," Meg said as he made his way over to the new couch and armchairs, she'd bought in anticipation of him coming home to the lodge. "Make sure your jeans are clean before you sit down," she said with a tight lip and made her way out to the kitchen.

Billy sat on the armchair nearest the fireplace and relished the warmth of the hearth against his legs. A chill ran over him as he realized he would never again sit with Mam at the fire and chat. He slid off his shoes and noticed the holes in his socks. Putting his shoes back on quickly, he felt more a guest than a husband returned. He pulled his shoulder bag up to his knees, removed the hand-carved wooden box that contained Mam's ashes, and sat them by the side of the chair with the intent of placing them more ceremoniously on the fireplace mantle once he and Meg settled a little.

The day Meg left Florida she'd left him a letter propped up on the clean white kitchen counter. It took him until Mam died to find the courage—or maybe the interest—to open it. Now he shifted uneasily and rummaged in his bag again until he found the letter. He looked at the back where he'd attempted a response, an awkward effort to save face, barely legible chicken scratches from a drunkard. He had sat at the stark clean kitchen counter, a contrast to his dirty clothing, with the simple wooden box containing Mam's ashes as he consumed another bottle of whiskey and cried the last of himself out.

Her questions were simple—"Would I fight for you? Would you fight for me?"

He deciphered his own crude hand in hopes it would give him some anchor to the conversation that would come after the bacon was eaten and the last wipe of egg soaked up with fried bread.

Your request is about a promise I made to both of us, a pledge undertook without much doubt back then. I agree I did not fight hard enough, happy to hide behind clouds of dust and dreams. There was no more than just you and I, and that became too much, then not enough with the world unfolding in torrents before us in our rush to be adults. Too many times in my haste I missed the look upon your face, the melancholy at my bravado when stories of dreams I told were not yours.

Would you fight for me, you asked? I fear that you would not.

I would fight tooth and nail for you, and for Mam, and in that I failed. In my weakest moments, I left you both bare. My mam is gone, and that is the most profound pain I thought to know, but nothing is worse than knowing that you too are letting me go. Forgive me, please.

Billy folded the letter away as Meg entered the room with a tray of food and Mam's big brown teapot. His response had seemed a little flowery with rereading, but it was the truth, written at his lowest ebb, that he needed to share with her if they were to stand a chance.

"We'll eat off our knees rather than sit in the kitchen; it's not the same without Mam at the table just yet." Meg poured the hot tea and he sipped at the cup, glad of a reason to keep their mouths busy with eating and drinking rather than talking.

"I wrote a letter," he mumbled, as they finished eating. "I answered the letter you left."

Meg looked up with wide eyes as she held the teacup close to her chest to hide her shaking hands.

"I had to make the journey home from America, to a town where darting eyes and gossip betrayed me at every corner. And *where is Billy* I was asked again and again behind polite, smirking smiles. Read me your letter if you must."

When he had, Meg rose from the armchair opposite him and crossed the small space between them. She knelt down and looked him in the eye.

"I have always loved you. I made my fair share of mistakes, I'll admit, but I have always seen the man you could be." She sighed so heavily her chest heaved. "Yes, I will fight as I always promised to do, and so will you, harder than you ever fought for anything in your life. Because if you leave me again, the last thing you will lose will be your breath and I will be the one that takes it from you, so help me God."

He watched Meg clear away the dishes. She walked from the room with a straight back and a resonance that was palpable as he held his breath so that he knew it was still there.

From the kitchen, Meg called for him to go up and have a bath. "I laid out some clean clothes, your father's brushes are on the dresser next to your treasure tin, and Muriel Winslow will be around in an hour or so to give you a haircut." Billy smiled as he went up the stairs. It would be good to sleep in his own bed tonight.

"And you're in the spare room with the single bed," Meg shouted once more. "You need to earn your rights as man of the house. My man may be home, but he will need some fattening up before I take him apart, as is my right and my need when I'm ready."

Billy closed the bathroom door. He understood it would be months of trust building, thought the fattening up sounded good. He held the craving for a whiskey in check.

As Billy reacquainted himself with the daily running of the business, Meg took on responsibility that was put out to managers during their time away in Florida. Meg's Mam and Dad were still running the busses, and Harry Two Bellies had expanded the ownership of rental houses and shops to include a couple of pubs and a small tea room and bakery. At home, Billy moved cautiously around Meg in their day-to-day dealings as new routines and expectations were forged. He found solace in following Harry around the various holdings as he got his feet back under the table and gradually took hold of the reins again. They set up an unofficial office in the corner of the tearoom—a constant flow of cups of tea quenched the thirst for anything stronger. He laughed when Harry suggested that with all the comings and goings, he was more like a Mafioso boss in a little Italian restaurant in New York than a landlord and benefactor in Diggle.

"What a good idea," Billy said. "Let's turn the tea room into an Italian restaurant. A little pasta will fatten up both of us."

"I've lost so much weight now, drinking only tea instead of my usual pints of beer a day I'm close to losing my nickname and street credibility." Said Harry.

Almost six months after returning, Billy came home to find an invitation to a friend's wedding propped up on the kitchen table. It was a simple crisp white card with silver lettering in distinct Western font. Little horses and guns in holster belts adorned each corner.

"They've gone cowboy on us, Billy," Meg giggled. The two of them had started to find the beginning of an old rapport, and he appreciated that they still shared the same sense of humor, even in the worst of times.

"Yahoo, partner," Billy whooped as he galloped around the kitchen on an imaginary horse. Meg laughed until tears filled her eyes. It felt so good to laugh together—and the invitation itself felt good, being asked to be part of something romantic and new.

Shannon Weir, the bride, was a tiny girl who'd grown up several doors down from Meg's father's shop. Hers was a small family of slightly misshapen proportions, not entirely dwarfs, but unconventional and prone to ridicule and taunts that exceeded even the hardships Billy and Meg had endured, being small themselves. Billy knew all too well that school children were vicious. Any sign of difference or weakness was exploited and deflected on to diminished shoulders by bullies shrouding their own deficiencies onto lesser backs.

She was marrying Jeff Stoker, a similarly sized lad on the engine, a wiry strip of muscle who could shovel coal all day long in the heat of the big steamers that ran to Leeds and back. He'd met Shannon when she came around the yard looking for coal to keep her family warm the previous winter and it was love at first sight. Meg had been witness to their growing love affair as Jeff would frequently pick her up for their evenings out at the salon where Shannon shampooed heads and swept floors.

"Shannon will be a beautiful bride," Meg offered over Billy's hoots and hollers. "She's talked about being a bride someday ever since she started working at the salon. My bet is she's had her wedding planned in her head for years."

The return to Diggle had been an exercise in patience. Billy realized how much he admired Meg. She'd come to know the ins and outs of the town as a businesswoman, not just a source for gossip. She built a fine reputation with her staff and had earned their appreciation and respect. She approached each day with a purpose and determination he hadn't seen in her for a long, long time. And he could see she was trying to find her way back to him, though he couldn't miss the pangs of confusion that unexpectedly rose in her whenever she showed affection or attraction for him. His other women, his whiskey stupors, the despair she suffered when he'd abandoned her and Mam—she resented all of it. But love him she did, and that was her solace, for she knew she'd been far from the perfect wife.

"Let's get dressed up, pet, like the old days, best of the best with a little western flair for the wedding." Billy said. "It will be grand and, if you're up for it, I'll take you for a spin around the dance floor." He stepped toward her and took her in his arms but felt her stiffen.

"Sorry," she said, straightening her dress. "It's not you. I mean, it's me. I'm scared. Scared to fall in love again because it hurts so much."

"No, I'm the one who's sorry," he said in the quietest of voices. "I love you, and I've missed you."

"And I love you," Meg replied.

The silence that followed was thick.

"It's not like it was when I used to sneak you in while I was babysitting for Gloria Price's children. You would chase me around the couch," Meg laughed.

"And I would again a thousand times," Billy vowed. "But let's take just a wee start in the right direction." He held out his arms and she stepped tentatively toward him. When he embraced her, she relaxed into him for a moment before straightening up and hurrying away.

Shannon and Jeff's wedding reception was in the basement social room at the church. The music was provided by a group of four local boys who made up what they called a rock band, though they could only play four Beatles tunes and one Herman's Hermits cover; the décor was compliments of the bride's Mam's cutting garden; and the food was catered by the Mam and four of her friends. The cake tasted delicious, a vanilla cake with tart, thick lemon frosting. Billy and Meg sat at a small, round table at the end of the room as the band played "A Hard Day's Night" for the third time.

"It's all so beautiful, isn't it?" Meg whispered, moved not by their surroundings but the sight of the bride and groom in the middle of the dance floor, slow dancing to the rock 'n' roll.

Billy scooped a dollop of the lemon icing into his finger and held it out to Meg.

Meg looked at the offering and turned her face away, though he saw her smile.

"Taste the icing Meg," Billy whispered to her. "Taste the icing."

That night they walked home arm-in-arm, rain filling the street, and they stopped in a dark alleyway silhouetted by orange streetlights that muted the rosy flush on Meg's cheeks.

"I want a baby from you, Billy McTaggart," Meg whispered in Billy's ear as he pressed her to the wall.

"I can promise you, my love, if you'll see it through, I will do anything for us to make our family."

Meg sighed. "I'm almost twenty-seven-years-old. Getting on for becoming a mother."

"Hush, now. Let's start by getting you home and into our bed before you lose the notion. No child of mine is going to be conceived on a damp night up a street alley."

Chapter 20

Remorse

Only a week had passed into the new year of 1968. Billy and Meg had been back in Diggle for almost a year, with a baby on the way. They still lived in the lodge but were in the process of renovating an old farmhouse Billy had bought, overlooking the Saddleworth Moore and twice the size of the lodge. Billy promised Meg it would be ready for the birth. Possibly for the first time his life, Billy's world was at peace.

And then the letter arrived.

Airmail, postmarked Haifa, Israel, the words written in the smooth hand of a fountain pen, a distinctive S.W.A.L.K across the envelope's flap. *Sealed with A Loving Kiss*, Mam had told him. The envelope was stuffed to its limit with light blue ultra-thin airmail paper, each page hypnotically inscribed with flowing, diminutive script that covered both sides. Reading this letter would take as much effort as to write it, not only because of its density, but because he knew his father was a man of few words and here lay a volume of sharing that was unbecoming and, in truth, unwanted.

Billy's impulse was to cast it aside and refuse to open a chapter that was long over. He wanted no more pain in his fragile life, and he couldn't spare a break in the delicate truce he and Meg had established in the past while. He stuffed the envelope in his trouser pocket and went into the kitchen where Meg had the table set with tea and toast. She was busy chopping a soft-boiled egg into a cup with a slice of butter, salt, and pepper—his favorite boyhood breakfast. A memory of Mam came to him, and he touched at the letter, wanting to convey his loyalties.

"I've had a letter," he said as he buttered his toast and spread the soft-boiled egg onto the toast. "It's from Israel, from my Dad." He held his breath, waiting for a response.

"I know. Betty at the post office mentioned it when she was in the salon yesterday. She noticed the postmark herself, nosy cow, it's like the secret service of Diggle." Meg poured the tea stoically and heaped two spoons of sugar into each cup. "He's back from the dead then, I assume, a bit like yourself." She took off her apron and folded it precisely into a drawer of fresh tea towels next to the stove top, then smoothed her skirt over her tummy that was starting to show and sat down to breakfast, one hand brushing a stray hair from her face. "Let me know when you've read it and give me fair warning if you intend to go away again, to Israel or anywhere else for that matter. Like your mam, I won't be looking for you again after spending years wondering why I wasn't good enough."

"Meg..."

"I've done it once, and once was quite enough, and now you have two of us to let down." After breakfast he saw to the business of the day at the workshop and met with Harry Two Bellies and a couple of the other managers. It was early afternoon by the time he managed to retire to the office in a back room of his house where he wouldn't be disturbed. The office had been converted from Mam's old bedroom. He placed the letter on the burgundy leather desk pad, edged with a swirling gold motif atop the mahogany desk Meg found for him at a local auction house. He felt lost behind the oversized piece of furniture, overwhelmed in both body and spirit as he looked at the letter. He'd taken to a moderation of whiskey and he poured a healthy drink now from the decanter sitting on a small silver tray on the matching sideboard next to the desk. Slowly, he unfolded the delicate, ink-laden pages.

Then he forced himself to pick up the first sheet of paper and read.

Son, I heard through the grapevine that Mam had passed, and I am sure you have no mind to hear from me after all the destruction I have left in my wake. However, if you will indulge me one last time, I believe I owe you an explanation for my actions and at the very least a reason, not a justification.

Billy swallowed hard as the whiskey bit at his throat.

I can't redeem myself to your Mam, and you are the only one I can share my reckoning with now, the single living soul who will care to know of my folly.

He felt anger rise in his chest in contempt for this sheepish outpouring and almost crumpled the pages in a ball and threw them into the fireplace.

Where to start? An unexpected moment in time when I would meet one of the four great loves of my life. Four conflicting passions that have brought me to today and my sad state of affairs. There was your Mam first, then the unexpected revealing of the bookkeeper's sister, Rebecca, then you as I discovered when I found your Mam again after the war. But above all there was the opiate of my life—adventure. A destructive but fundamental need to test myself beyond the mediocrity of my beginning. In indulging this last love, I lost everything and everyone I have loved and cared for, those who loved and cared for me. I owe you this story, and I beg that it may clear the way to your forgiveness.

Billy huffed. *Forgiveness.* Unlikely that would happen, but he kept reading.

I honestly left my heart with your Mam when I shipped out, but we were young, and the world was exploding around us. I was a soldier first and last. It was my calling, a natural state that allowed me to indulge every instinct I had, a perfect vocation. I could not live a mundane existence when I knew that adventure lived out in the world. Adventure was my muse and a passion to which I was best suited.

Billy felt a strange conflict between contempt and pride as he read. Regardless of the disappointment of his abandonment, he'd always revered his father's bravery. He'd always longed to hear the stories now unfolding on the pages before him.

I was reassigned early in my military career when I volunteered for the Long-Range Desert Group in North Africa, an operational band of misfits who fought the Germans and Italians behind the Axis line in Libya. I told you some of those stories when you were a lad. Those were grand days, as me and Monty Banks would set out with our team over the cold desert using only the stars to navigate by, patrolling dusty roads and stumbling into various scraps that lit the night with bullets and flares. There were rowdy nights in Cairo and early morning climbing of the great pyramids of Egypt together.

You would have loved Monty. I always wanted him to meet you after the war when I was living with you and Mam, but he suffered in the same way I did. He never really pulled himself together before I left our home. When the Long-Range Desert Group was disbanded, the lads were the nucleus of the new Special Air Services Commandos. The Jerry's hated us and put a price on our heads. We did the dirty work and got into places no one else could. During this time, I was assigned to a Captain Williams who needed men to find money the Germans were forging, and a German Officer called Bernhard. I remember telling you a little bit about it that night by the fire when Mam came home after winning the bingo. I should have kissed her and laughed with her in her excitement, another regret. I was too far gone by then and already thinking about running away like a coward in the dark of night. I wish she had won a million pounds as it might have made it easier for the two of you. You would have had more than the few five-pound forgeries I left for you, though that money was still good to spend then.

Billy sat back in his chair and tried to string together his thoughts. If his Bernhart money—those five-pound notes—came from the train DCI Williams was sending to be destroyed, was he the same Captain Williams tasked to track down the money in war, and still mothering it in peacetime? Had his dad worked for DCI Williams in covert operations? The questions as to his dad's whereabouts made sense in that light and Billy suddenly felt vulnerable in a way he never imagined after so much caution.

He finished the last of the whiskey in his glass and picked up the next sheet of blue airmail paper, so light in his fingers, yet heavy on his heart.

Working with Captain Williams was intriguing, to say the least, what with the freedom of movement we had and the connectivity to power centers that would spare nothing to fulfill our request for anything we needed in the chaos in the last days of the war. Captain Williams was a bit of a stiff collar, among other things I could not understand or agree with, but he let me get things done that most thought impossible; things, and that needed doing for our mission to be successful. Some of our activities were illegal, or in contravention of the Geneva Convention, but we couldn't adhere to those restrictions. We needed answers, and my job was to get them.

Billy felt the effects of the revelations like whiskey, rising in a deep burning in his empty belly. He'd missed his usual lunch with Meg, and he guessed she hadn't complained about it because she thought it best to leave him alone with the letter.

So that is how I came to meet the bookkeeper and, ultimately, his sister, the catalyst for the biggest adventure of my life.

I know you and Mam should have been my biggest adventure, I am sorry that I could not fulfill that responsibility. Perhaps the balance of this letter will explain my choices. The night before we went to the bookkeeper, Oskar Stein's, house in Prague, I had a run-in of sorts with Captain Williams. It was that thing I mentioned, not something I can't even talk about except men should love women, it is that simple. I know war does things to a man, but I don't think it was the war in his case. He was soft in a way that real men aren't, or not the lads I served with anyway.

Homosexuality was a criminal offense, even if you worked for Special Branch. Billy poured himself another short snort of whiskey.

When we first got to the house in Prague, Captain Williams conducted the interview as always. I stood guard and watched and listened for anything out of the ordinary—a look, a movement, a phrase that seemed strained or a heightened voice of fear in a lie. I remember so distinctly when Rebecca first came into the room, her head down. I could sense her fear and the slight shaking of her hand as she passed out coffee and little sugar powder-covered biscuits. Sugar was a luxury and I thought they must have some money to get it on the black market. She had a dusting of powder on her cheek, and I wanted to wipe it off. Silly, really, in the moment. I noticed as she handed out each cup, she would pull at her sleeve which rose up revealing a crude, tattooed set of numbers. A visible reminder for the rest of her life of the years in the camp, a scar of survival she wanted no one to see. Rebecca was beautiful in a haunting way—her hair still short under her headscarf and her eyes deep-set and gaunt, perfect cheekbones. As she passed me my cup of coffee, we touched fingertips for an instant, and a jolt of electricity ran through my body. She felt it too and stepped back and looked at me full in the eye. No one in the room noticed as they spoke heatedly of a journal in which the bookkeeper said, he documented every forgery he had ever done. Rebecca walked past me toward the kitchen and gave me the slightest smile—I will never forget that smile.

I asked to be excused to the toilet and walked back out through the kitchen hoping to see her, but she wasn't there. When I came back into the house after using the toilet, she and I did meet for a moment—just a moment. Captain Williams saw me and Rebecca in the kitchen. I barely had the time to hand her my service number as we drove away with Captain William red-faced and screaming. I watched her for as long as I could in my rearview mirror—then she was gone.

I came back to your Mam after the war. Son, she was more than just a beautiful, bright-eyed, sassy girl to me. But everything had a sense of urgency in the days we met. She was just fifteen and I was barely eighteen myself, hungry to be off to war to become a man. I had left my heart with her best as I knew how to, but in our haste, our youth, and our ignorance we failed to make any plans beyond the moment. We lived in each other's eyes and bodies for a few brief days. You might be old enough to understand that now.

The apple doesn't fall far from the tree, Billy thought, and he hated the truth in the words.

When the war was over and I found your mam, I was outraged at the injustice done to her. I swept Suzie Barbour away from the sisters and the workhouse in grand fashion, kicking down the door to the local wash house when they denied me access. I carried her out amid whoops and cheers of the many other girls who would never be saved and die in disgrace amid piles of soiled linens and boiling water. We were reunited as mother, father, and son and were married within the week. Now I had a mission, a purpose, a reason for action—that was what I knew how to do.

Billy read the last few pages of the letter, now caught up in the story with so many new questions pushing out the old assumptions he'd made. His father needed something after a war that had stripped him of any belief in humanity or the possibility of normalcy in its aftermath. So many unfulfilled expectations that he understood, in hindsight. They had settled down, and Dad had taken a job as a Tapper on the railroad. He wrote of the initial contentment he found in getting to know his 5-year-old son, and of Sunday mornings with Suzie, tea, and crumpets, Billy bouncing between them singing soldier songs to impress his new Daddy. It was perfect, for a while. When the change came, he'd put up with Friday nights with the lads and achieved promotion to Yard Foreman as a natural progression for a leader of men. But it wasn't enough.

And then a letter from Rebecca found me, battered from travel and handling. Redirected so often that new labels had to be pasted on the front, the letter found its way to regimental barracks and government disbanding stations, and eventually the station where I was employed, according to the British home office. The letter, which was short of four years old, had been on its own journey and now found me against all probability. Prague was its origin, the postmark 1946, and I knew it was from Rebecca before even opening it. Her request within was simple; she needed me to help her. Her heart told her she could trust me because God had tied us together. On the day her camp had been liberated, she made a promise to her dying friends as she walked away, determined to return home— friends who were too weak or sick to walk to their own homes. They could only wait and suffer in boxcars that sat on the railroad for days as the Germans were escaping. There were hundreds of people in each boxcar and of the five thousand prisoners awaiting liberation, some three thousand were already dead upon the arrival of the allied army at her camp.

The bookkeeper and a few of the other prisoners transporting a shipment of counterfeited money between Sachsenhausen and Redl-Zipf had managed to overwhelm their captors and escape with the spoils of war, dressed as Germans. In the chaos, amazingly, they drove all the way to Prague without incident. If Captain Williams and I had searched the basement of the bookkeeper's house that day, Rebecca wrote, we would have left with more than a small leather journal. The journal was the red herring they used to distract us. They were committed to do good with the blood money they had been forced to produce for the Germans.

From Rebecca I learned that by the winter of 1946 there were about a quarter of a million displaced persons, or DP's, in Europe. Britain refused to allow displaced Jews into Palestine. Rebecca and her brother were part of a small group of Jews *who had formed an organization called Brichah—"flight" in English—in order to smuggle immigrants to Palestine. Ships and crew were procured for the passage across the Mediterranean to Palestine with the forged money they found in the truck. Some of the ships made it past a British naval blockade of Palestine, but most did not. The passengers of captured ships were forced to disembark into British operated DP camps on Cyprus, where Jews could apply for legal immigration to Palestine. Fifty-two thousand Jews were interned on Cyprus before the General Assembly voted to partition Palestine and create two independent states, one Jewish and the other Arab.*

Rebecca wrote asking me to join the struggle. She believed I could help move money and people. She wanted me to start a new life with her in her promised land, even if we could never marry. The traditional tenets of marriage and bearing children held no truth for her, and she would bring no children into the world.

It took me two years to find her after receiving her letter. Fighting had immediately broken out between Jews and Arabs in Palestine, as soon as the State of Israel was proclaimed. In 1951, Rebecca was at the forefront of the "Law of Return" movement recently approved by the Israeli parliament, which allowed any Jew to migrate to Israel and become a citizen. They needed men who could fight and train soldiers for the new Israeli army and I heeded the call for adventures anew with Rebecca at my side as a fighter and a lover.

She introduced me to a young and dynamic man called Ben Gurion who had united the various Jewish militias into the Israel Defense Force, and as the first Prime Minister of Israel formed a group of special forces he called the Mossad. I was under his leadership when in 1956, they invaded Egypt along with British and French forces after Egypt nationalized the Suez Canal during what became known as the Suez Crisis.

It was a grand time, I will tell you. Rebecca and I made a fine pair, and no one bothered us about our unusual union, based on their respect for her and all she had done for the state. We lived by the sea in Haifa. She died around the same time as your mother. Without her to hold me steady the money has run out, and no one wants an old gentile soldier, so the remorse has set in and my bones ache. My thick, black hair has turned silver, and the young girls dance out of reach. The bars stink of piss and the cheap gut rot Arak has taken its toll. I have enough borrowed money for a one-way ticket home to Diggle if you will have me. I need to beg forgiveness. I expect nothing.

Billy slowly folded each page of the letter and slid them back into their thin envelope. Reaching under his desk, he pulled out his battered tin box of treasures and placed the letter inside. He thought again of the apple and the tree. Of Mam and Meg. And Lola. Then he removed a large tortoiseshell fountain pen, tapped the nib gently, and drew out the ink in dark globes on the note card that held the letterhead of his business in fine gold lettering. He wrote simply in a flowing hand.

Welcome home.

God Speed, I am still here, waiting.

Billy.

He placed it in an envelope along with a hundred pounds and wrote across the seal S.W.A.L.K.

Chapter 21

Family

B illy held a memory of a simple time when all seemed right in the world, a time of boyhood freedoms. Summer days were spent guddling trout up on to the river banks and swimming in peat infused island streams that turned him blue as the snowpack waters ran over his skinny white body. He loved the solace and the freshness of the water. Sliding under the frigid rush he would lie on the pebble riverbed with a large rock held tightly to his chest, looking up through the rust colored water.

He would watch the orange orb of sunshine that diffused like a splintered diamond flecked between thousands of darting salmon and trout as they hurried to spawn upstream. Dashing dark brown digits ran overhead like some form of visual Morse code that he tried to decipher as the language of nature, dot, dot, dash, dash, dot, dot. He would blow out bubbles that rose in silver orbs punctuating through the dashing fish, and then frantically at the last moment, he'd push up to the surface, gasping for air. The icy water froze his head numb with physical proof that he was alive and all was right in the world he knew.

Meg, Harry, Billy and Dad sat around the breakfast table eating a hearty meal after a Thursday morning managers' meeting. Billy suddenly declared he needed a swim, something he felt inspired to do, even as the snow lay on the ground outside. A baptism of sorts he thought, a new start on February 1st, 1968.

"Are you mad, you silly fucker?" Harry Two Bellies looked up from his plate of eggs, fried bread and black pudding as Billy pulled off his shirt, "You'll catch your death and where will that leave Meg? You're almost ready to be delivered a baby, you wanker."

Billy walked out the door of his house, crossed the yard, and made his way down through the snow to the canal that ran by the Lodge. The morning was crisp and clear, with the delicate ice on the grass and frozen spider webs strung out like laundry lines. The crunch of snow underfoot broke the sound of birdsong as a red breasted robin sprang from hedgerows when he passed. He stripped to his underwear and jumped into the canal through the almost invisible beginnings of ice on the surface. He hung for a moment, eyes shut in the wet darkness, and savored the cleansing, a dropping away or casting off of all the years that now seemed impossible to have survive.

Meg was going to have a baby, and he needed to be ready. He burst from the water and scrambled up onto stone coping, then ran barefoot through the snow, leaving his boots where they sat, crashing through the front door of the house as he ran to the fire.

"Blimey, what a stupid idea that was!" He lunged for the mug of tea that his Dad was about to pick up and swallowed it down, then he held the warm mug to his forehead to relieve the pain.

"Ay, it's not the river at Burnt Island now laddie, it's time to be a man," Jim admonished. Billy smiled and slapped his sides; he was ready for it. Meg rushed over, frowning as Billy dripping water into a pool on the stone floor. She pulled a woolen travel blanket from the couch and wrapped it around him. She tutted at him, then suddenly grabbed him by the arm.

"What is it, Meg?"

"Nothing, pet, I'll be fine," she said, but Billy looked down and saw she stood in her own pool of water.

"Bloody hell!" Billy took the travel rug off himself and wrapped it around her,

"Get dressed, lad," Jim shouted, "while I get the car warmed up."

"My overnight bag is packed behind the bedroom door, where my coat is hanging."

"Get your pants on, Billy," Jim shouted, a man on the most crucial mission of his life. "God help anyone who would get in the way of my first grandchild."

Two respective babies arrived within the hour of each other. The King and Pricilla were the proud parents of Lisa Marie Presley, while and Billy and Meg welcomed little Susan Lisa-Marie McTaggart, worlds apart in many ways, connected in others.

Billy wished Mam was there to witness his one real success. He knew she would've been the best granny ever. He also knew his wee Suzie would never have to suffer the pains his Mam endured. Taking the small hands gently between his fingers, he counted to ten. He promised his daughter these hands would know only love and compassion, and never suffer the degradation of forced labor in a challenge to her innocence. He made this promise to the child, and as a prayer to Mam, whom he knew was there making baby noises and begging for a hold of the swaddled infant, her granddaughter.

Meg told Billy she would allow visitors, but not before she had two of the girls from the salon in to do her makeup and her hair that was now jet-black, just like Pricilla Presley. She'd packed her silk pajamas and a matching dressing gown, anticipating a gathering. Billy thought she looked like a movie star, and if she was now a mother, then she would be the best-looking mother in town. Billy filled the room with flowers and stuffed toys, chocolates and balloons.

"I don't want to regret motherhood," she whispered to her husband.

"It looks like a carnival in here," Meg's mother complained as she made her way toward the small bassinet next to Meg's bed. Everyone held the baby, and after an hour the noise became too much when Harry Two Bellies burst into the room singing "Ain't She Sweet," followed by "O'Danny Boy." He kissed Billy and started to cry when he found out he was to be the godfather. Meg finally pressed the buzzer to the nurses' station and had them ask everyone to leave.

A few days later Billy watched television as Pricilla Presley and the King were whisked away in a long dark limousine to Graceland. Billy felt the same sense of pride when he ushered Meg into the back seat of his new 1968 Ford Mustang and drove them home. Meg noticed Billy had had a new sign placed at the front of the renovated farm, Graceland Farm & Dairy.

Billy received a card of congratulations from DCI Williams who asked if he might visit with Billy. He wanted a look at Billy's tax returns as he was retiring soon and wanted to wrap up any loose ends he felt old cases deserved.

Billy called the Special Branch office in Manchester and made an appointment to visit with Williams. He still held all his secrets regarding the train, with not a single word ever leaving his lips about his original windfall. His successes were the result of luck followed by years of hard work, ingenuity, and risk, with lots of uncertainty and charity. He knew he'd given as much, if not more, than he'd taken. His books would hold water; he had nothing to hide. In truth, he now knew his finances had less to do with DCI Williams fascination with him than DCI Williams would have him believe, and it would be fun to do more cat and less mouse this time.

Tea with DCI Williams was brief, as Billy knew it would be. The policeman had little interest in his books, brushing aside Billy's attempts to walk him through accounting procedures. Williams got right to his point: "I understand your father, Jim McTaggart, recently arrived back in Diggle."

Billy had grinned, gathered up his paperwork, and packed it away in his briefcase. "I think, DCI Williams, that next time you demand to see me at your convenience, I'll bring a lawyer, not my books. As for my father, your interest in him may prove to be unprofessional, and perhaps a shade too personal." He chose his words carefully. "I have no opinion on the matter, but I don't believe that interest would look good on your record so close to the end of your career. Let's be gentlemen, shall we?"

DCI Williams rose from his desk visibly shaken. Billy stuck out his hand, bade him good day, and turned without permission to leave when the DCI refused to shake his hand.

As he entered the elevator, he imagined a Tom and Jerry cartoon, where Tom the cat had just been hit in the face by a hot iron and the imprint was perfect as Tom fell to the ground dumbfounded. Jerry squeaked and squealed from the top of the cupboard in victory. *Today the mouse won*, thought Billy.

Several months later Billy stopped at the Navigation Pub, his dad's favorite spot, partly thanks to a voluptuous bar maid with rosy cheeks and a boisterous laugh he'd taken a shine to, Lilly Potter, the farmer's daughter as she was known. She was indeed a farmer's daughter, although her father's farm, and her father were long gone. She was a few years younger and conveniently single. Dad would stay until the end of her shift and walk her home, for safety's sake he said, and it was on his way.

Billy found his father seated at the bar about to dig into a steaming plate of cottage pie, another convenience. He seldom cooked at home and food just tasted better with Lilly's smile and cheery disposition.

"Hello love," Lilly burst into a welcoming laugh, as was her wont, her ample breasts rising and falling in a low-cut dress. You could house a small nation of refugees in there Billy thought as he said hello and nodded to his father in such a way that he knew they had something to discuss privately.

"Put that in the oven for me pet, will you?" Jim asked Lilly as he ordered a whiskey for Billy and brought it to the table. "What's the matter lad? You have something on your mind?"

Billy took a sip of the whiskey and cleared his throat, "Do you know a DCI Williams from Special Branch? He was cautious not to sound as if this were an accusation. He'd just reached the point where he might tell his father the truth about his lucky break and the train when he was younger. "I don't," said Jim. He raised is eyes upward, thinking, and then closed them and scrunched up his face.

"But you knew a Captain Williams, back in the day. You said he was your commanding officer at the end of the war."

Jim opened his eyes widely and recalled that he'd written of it in his letter to Billy not that long ago.

"Well, he has it in for me for some reason. When and if the situation arises, I may need to call on you for some help with him."

Jim looked stoically at his son and raised one eyebrow. "I'm hoping you're only having a bit of trouble with the law, and not the other how's your father kinda stuff!" He gave Billy a stern look as a slight smile broke on his face. "Come on lad, I know it's the law. No son of mine would trade in a fine lass like our Meg for an old floppy arse like DCI Williams, would you?"

He paused again, and the two of them burst out laughing, setting Lilly off into a high-pitched holler, even if she had no idea what the hell they'd just been talking about.

"I have your back boy. Just let me know and I'll sort it out. Me and the Captain may well have some unfinished business to attend to.

Billy had two more whiskeys and sat with his father while he ate his dinner, "I can give you a lift up the road if you like," Billy offered, but Jim thanked him and said the young lass needed an escort of some stature and he was the man for the job.

The next evening Billy watched as a rowdy bunch filled the living room to witness the landing of the first men on the moon. Not everyone had a TV, so he decided to host the historic event. Meg and her parents, Jim and his lady, Harry Two

Bellies and his wife, the managers of Billy's various ventures, and the lads from the yard, sat glued to the television as the free world celebrated Neil Armstrong taking man's first steps on the moon.

"If they can send a man to the moon and he can walk on it and return to Earth, there isn't anything we can't do," Billy proclaimed and everyone in the room cheered in agreement.

As Neil Armstrong started down the ladder to the moon's surface, Billy felt overcome with emotion. It seemed incredible to look up at the moon and realize they were hearing the voice of someone who was actually there.

"That's one small step for man, one giant leap for mankind." Static filled the room.

Billy saw Meg take a photograph of the television screen as President Nixon was superimposed onto it to commemorate the momentous occasion, this incredible technological achievement. Billy had, for weeks, read everything he could get his hands on about the venture—speculation about what the surface of the moon would be like—an immense, deep sea of powder, into which the astronauts would instantly vanish or so hot that it burned them? Would they ever get home again? All these worries tempered the excitement of seeing the event, live, on the flickering television screen. Billy put wee Suzie in her cot in front of the TV so forever after she could say she'd been there when it all happened.

Later in the evening when everyone left, he pulled a day bed out into the garden and invited Meg to curl up with him under a big comforter, beneath that inscrutable moon. The sky was so clear it seemed they could see every pebble on the moon's surface. They held each other tight, in awe and trepidation, as they thought about the astronauts sleeping now on its surface.

"The future is here now; in the most blatant way we might imagine. It's real." Billy said.

"It's more than just that, pet," Meg said as she turned to him. "It's so much bigger for our child. Her future is so much greater than ours—she might live on the moon one day. You yourself have reached for it all your life, 'til now."

Billy believed he might have missed the big push into space—that it might all be done and over before he ever made it back to America. "If they can send a man to the moon and he can walk on it and return to Earth, there isn't anything we can't do," he repeated, and Meg snuggled into the side of him. She slid her hand around his waist and pulled at the string on his pajama bottoms. He responded by taking her hand gently.

"Are you sure, pet? Are you ready? I can wait."

"You've been a patient man, Billy McTaggart. If there were ever a night to make our son, this might be it." She laughed as she tugged at his pajamas and slid deftly out of her own knickers and pulled him on to her.

Chapter 22 ⊤

Déjà Vu

Billy walked into the kitchen, where a freshly baked cake sat under a glass dome in the middle of the cleanly scrubbed table. He had bought an old kettle that gave out a throaty pitch to remind the whole house it was teatime, and because it reminded him of Mam, who always had time to savor a good cup of tea. Meg had already set the table; Mam's brown teapot with its crocheted cover and an array of cups, saucers, and matching sugar pot and milk jug sat on a large tray with small side plates and cake forks with linen napkins. They agreed that if he were up and out early in the morning, then they would find time to do elevenses as a family.

He emptied his pockets onto the table, a menagerie of old and new coins—full currency conversion to the new pound and pence was just under six months away. He separated the money into two piles as he sat at the table and waited for Meg to come down from the bedroom with wee Suzie. He had a neat pile of shillings, pence, and an old halfpenny that was now useless as legal tender but worth a thousand memories of toffee dainties and chocolate mice. Billy picked up a half-crown worth two shilling and sixpence.

He flipped it, heads or tails, and watched her majesty Elizabeth II land face up on the table. She looked to the distance in stately profile, the epitome of feminine grace. Ay, she was a good lass, and he would wave a flag for her any day she chose to tour greater Manchester again, as she had after her coronation in 1953. She had done her old dad Bertie proud, and now she would usher in the new decade with decimalization, men on the moon, and the price of a season ticket for Manchester United a whopping eight pounds and fifty new pence—more than double what he used to make in a week when he first started as an apprentice tapper.

He swept the coins from the table and placed the old coins in a leather pouch he kept in his treasure tin, which still lived under his desk. The rest of the new money he slotted into a little pink piggy bank that sat on the mantle and belonged to wee Suzie. It reminded him of the jar Mam would keep coins in to feed the gas meter that sat ever hungry under the stairs. He ran his fingers over Mam's urn that still held pride of place in the room. It was a time of change—the money, the music, and most of all, himself as a father, a husband and a businessman.

He looked around the room and appreciated its comfort; Mam would have liked the brightness when the sun shone in on sunny days and the fine view over the Yorkshire Dales through the conservatory. The hills glistened multifaceted as he looked out over the farmyard toward The Obelisk on Alderman's Hill, which lay smocked in a dusting of snow below a rare crisp blue sky. He was pouring hot water into the teapot as Meg came into the room.

"I thought I heard you skulking about," she said with a smile as she leaned in to kiss him, slightly off balance with wee Suzie on her hip.

"Who is this monster stuck to the side of my beautiful bride?" he asked as he poked at Suzie, making her giggle. "I think I will have you for elevenses with cream and jam."

Meg put Suzie in her chair and found a knife to cut the cake, and Billy crossed to the back door where he had dropped his satchel onto a chair. "Let's see what Daddy has for his special girls," he teased, reaching into the satchel with his free hand to retrieve a thin paper bag that held a seven single from the local music store in Oldham.

Collecting and listening to records was one of the traditions he missed sharing, with Mam gone. He still added to their growing collection of vinyl records almost weekly as new hits came out.

"This one is for Mummy," he said, looking at Meg, "special order all the way from the United States of Elvis!" He handed the record to Meg and finished pouring tea. "'If I can dream,' by the King himself—it's the song we saw him perform on the TV special, his first top ten song in as many years. Our man is back on top and I know how that feels."

An envelope fell onto the kitchen table as Meg removed the black vinyl disc from its sleeve. She picked it up cautiously. "This is typical of you, Billy McTaggart. There's always a surprise in everything you do. Generous and reckless all in one breathe." She opened the envelope and pulled out two blue and gold tickets: Elvis and the Las Vegas International Hotel take the pleasure inviting you and your lady to our opening show, July 31st, 1969.

Billy stood, smiling and expectant, but and Meg seemed dismayed.

"It's his first stage appearance in eight years," Billy enthused. "I got us our own private table, and we'll go via New York on the new Pam Am 747." When Meg still didn't respond he added, "wee Suzie will go with us, of course. We can hire a nanny once we get to Las Vegas, and it will be grand."

Wee Suzie began to cry at the heightened voices and the rise in energy now thick in the room.

Someone knocked at the door before Meg could think of what she wanted to say, and Billy was grateful for the interruption. Jim stood solemnly at the door with his cap in his hand.

"It's the Tappers lad. They are to be no more. This is the passing of an age, and we're set for a meeting at the lodge. They want you there."

The return of Billy's dad had cast a wave of discontent thought the village. A second prodigal son returned the more pious had said, hiding behind the sanctity of their religion to atone for their own boring sins and resentment at the stories they elaborated on in ignorance regarding Billy and his father's wanderings. Over a relatively short time the whispering fell away under the charisma and natural rapport of Jim's social gravitas. He soon became the belle of the ball with stories and pints to share in The Navigation Pub. The one person he never allowed himself to be familiar with was Billy; they built a fragile relationship over time and slowly a trust formed. They became compatriots in the pursuit of opportunities and business ventures, with flashes of humor and camaraderie that sat deep in their common nature.

Jim, as Billy now called him, set his own rules of engagement and exaggerated respect. He knew a self-made man when he saw one and he recognized the leadership they both embodied. There was only one lead Tapper and he knew it was Billy.

Meg had watched the dance between the two with trepidation over the past months and felt proud seeing them work through a fragile acceptance. Jim had endeared himself to her; he was smart, funny, honest, and above all remorseful for his folly. There was not a day that he didn't do some form of penance with some kind gesture.

Billy invited him in. "Meg just made tea Jim. Will you have a cup?" Billy used the interruption of the visit to ease the tension of his invitation to Meg to go to Las Vegas and the Elvis show. He would need time to set Meg's trust in place and manage his own expectations.

"So, the Tappers are dead," Billy proclaimed, in confirmation of the news he'd already heard in whispers around town. He handed Jim a cup of tea and said simply," It's time. The world is becoming technological, man and machine will compete from here on out. We'll build machines and computers to replace our manual tasks, Barclays Bank had an automated Teller Machine, or ATM two years ago The Apollo Guidance Computer reduced the size of the Apollo spacecraft computer from the size of seven refrigerators to a compact unit weighing only seventy pounds and taking up less than one cubic foot."

Meg and Jim looked at each other and then back at Billy.

"Where the hell did you find that out? asked Meg.

"I read the paper and other journals. You have to know what's happening around you to take advantage of it."

"That's my boy, and if it means your children will never have to swing a hammer to a wheel, this is a welcome day. I only hope it includes not going to war; I wonder if we could get robots to do that too?" Jim asked.

Billy agreed and added, "I want to try and go to California to meet with a man called J.C.R Licklider—he has an idea there could be an electronic commons open to all, a medium of information for governments, institutions, corporations, and individuals. ARPANET, he calls it. The US Department of Defense has already made a huge investment, and there's a new opportunity called *venture capital* through the Draper and Johnson Investment Company, so working stiffs like us can get in on it too—"

"My boy, that's heady talk! I'll tell you this: You go off to California and meet with your mister ARPANET, and I'll stay and look after things here, work with Harry Two Bellies to keep things running smoothly for you."

"You'd do that for me?"

"I'm your man. When are you leaving for America?"

"We aren't sure we are," Meg said firmly.

"Billy, are you ready?" Jim asked, "I told the lads we'd be at the lodge at four o'clock. There are retirement watches and medals of service to hand out for many of our friends who have no idea what technology is, or what they'll be doing for British Rail now that there are no more steam locomotives and passengers rather than freight is our mission. I'm sure diesel engines and electrification will be followed by computerizing the switch houses and drivers one day."

At the lodge all the lads congregated for a final Tappers Social, a ritual that had endured for 120 Years from 1849 to 1969. It all seemed inevitable, and most of the lads knew that the age of steam, like the horse and cart they'd grown up with, was at an end. Some had the initiative to look for work outside the town with museums and private collectors that were fanatics about the age of steam and planned tourist rides on closed rail lines. Most resorted to apathy and took a severance that would only last as long as it bought pints. In general, the night was a somber occasion until enough of the brown stuff loosened up thirsty voices that needed venting. Old rebel songs for some and old war songs for the rest—a time when they knew who they were fighting for, and against. Billy and Jim saw the lads off and with the help of Harry Two Bellies and a couple of the younger lads they managed to get Tommy Tightrope and Eddy Shunter home to frightened families who knew that even the new decimalization of Pounds and Pence would not put any more in their pockets.

As Billy and Jim walked back to the lodge a figure stepped out from the darkness of a side street and approached them. They could smell his expensive cologne and see that his Macintosh was clean and well made. His collar was pulled up and his broad brimmed hat slung low over his face. When he lit a cigarette and said hello them, Billy recognized the voice of DCI Williams.

"I see you're still working the streets, Detective," Billy said withal much indignation as he could muster without being too insulting. He knew DCI Williams could still make his life difficult.

"You still think you have a smart mouth on you. Fortunately, I could care less. I thought I'd see your old chums for the last time, see if any of them have done better than expected. But it would seem it's only you. Yard rat, office boy, businessman, and now lord of the manor it would seem. I've always had a hunch about you, Billy. Something doesn't quite fit. Perhaps it was that old man of yours. They say the apple doesn't fall far from the tree."

Billy clenched his fist as he felt his father take hold of his arm.

"You'll be right in thinking that, seeing as the tree is here, Captain." Jim pulled off his cap and stepped into the street-light. DCI Williams sagged at the knees and fell back against the wall, knocking himself out.

"Bloody hell!" Said Billy "Was that some secret martial art you learned in the army?" Jim laughed under his breath and said,

"I always did make him go weak at the knees." Jim reached down and hoisted Williams to his feet, "Come on Billy, this one can come home with us. I can't wait to see his face when he wakes up as I'm putting a blanket over him on my couch. Deja Vu!"

Billy and Jim soldier-marched the groggy DCI Williams up to Mam's house at the end of the terrace. Billy and Meg still owned it and Jim was more than happy to stay there, partly in penance, and in part because he said he could speak to Mam there when the night was as its darkest. He believed he could hear her laughter from their first few happy years together after the war. It was the Sunday mornings he'd given up and never returned to that he missed the most.

They settled DCI Williams into a big comfy chair and gave him a double shot of whiskey for his pains. Billy had recently told Jim about the train, the money, and his pursuit by Williams. He'd held onto the story for all these years, with just a bundle of the more damaged notes left as souvenirs. Now there seemed little risk, and he had an ally. Jim had laughed at the absurdity of the coincidence. He chased forged money around the world, and it turned up on his doorstep of its own accord. Billy gave him the bundle of notes as a birthday gift, fifty pounds for turning fifty.

Jim pulled them from the dresser drawer and placed them on the table in front of DCI Williams who was finally coming to his senses, but still in shock.

"Your hair is silver," he said softly.

"Aye, it is that sir," Jim said, falling back more by force of habit than respect. "But that won't be a concern of yours now as it was back then." He filled both their glasses and sat down facing the Captain. "We have a few things to sort out, this money, and my son.

Billy took his leave of them, knowing there was talking to be done.

The next morning Jim walked up the hill to the farm with a spring in his step. Billy watched him proudly and wished Mam could see his swagger. She would understand, Billy believed, and he knew she loved Jim until the day she died, always holding some thread of belief he might appear at her door.

As neither of them had been arrested, Billy assumed Jim and the Captain resolved their differences. Jim walked up and knocked on the kitchen door, waiting to be asked in.

"You'll not be worried about that lad again," he said holding a smile in check lest he be seen gloating. "He has the last bundle of cash in England that we know of to close his case, and a solution to your good fortune a week before he retires. I took a little credit and mentioned some Egyptian gold I found."

Billy knew better than to ask for details.

"And one last thing, I would ask if we may have a job for a retired Special Branch detective who may come in handy where research is needed for some of those new ventures you mentioned.

Billy slapped Jim on the back and called him an old bugger,

"Less of the bugger, thank you very much, I get my intelligence the old-fashioned way, not in the back seat of a car or public toilet on Hampstead Heath."

Billy let out a loud laugh that brought Meg into the room.

"What are you two doing here? One night out at the Tapper Social Club and you're acting like a couple of schoolboys. I need to know you'll look after things responsibly when we go to see The King in Las Vegas."

Billy turned to Meg who had taken Suzie out of her chair and was bouncing her on her lap. Meg looked up to see all eyes were on her. "Yes, I'll go," she sighed. She laughed when Billy let out a whoop.

"When will that be asked Jim?"

"Sometime before July thirty-first, as long as Suzie comes along soundly. I want an old battle axe nursemaid, not some glamorous Swedish au pair with long legs and blond hair. And first class all the way. I'm not sure we need to meet the King again, but if we do, I want it to be over lunch in the middle of the day."

Billy acquiesced without reluctance, as his intent was indeed pure.

"You have my word Pet, again. I will treat you like the princess and mother you are. Luxury all the way," he promised.

Billy let out another yelp and picked Meg up and spun her round twice.

"The baby, the baby," she shrieked half-heartedly. "You don't want your son getting upset now, do you? Put me down, you beast, and pour the tea before it gets cold."

Billy burst out laughing and shouted, "How, what, so soon, it has only been a few weeks since. . .," he trailed off.

"I thought it best not to wait at my age. I'm not that far off turning thirty, at which time I shall need my body back to keep you hungry.

Jim gave her a huge hug and left them together. Billy sat down in front of Meg and his eyes glistened as he tried to get words of appreciation out of his chest.

The night before Elvis's show, Billy and Meg decided to go out for dinner. They walked the floor of the International Hotel casino Las Vegas arm-in-arm, amid the smoke, ringing bells, and flashing lights, dodging waitresses in tiny revealing outfits carrying drink-laden trays.

Meg wore a baby blue satin cocktail dress with a white mink collar she'd purchased that afternoon at one of the swankier dress shops in Las Vegas. The first bump of her belly just showing. Billy was in a dark dinner jacket with thin silk lapels and fishtail cuffs. The slight tummy he'd acquired over the past few years restricted him from fastening the button, but he cared less for style now as he might have in years past. As they passed the blackjack table, Meg stopped him and straightened his bright crimson bowtie, making sure it was perfectly straight.

Meg smiled indulgently when she saw him eyeing the dealer with longing. "One time only, Levi Indigo, now that you're finally in Las Vegas." She ordered Billy a Tom Collins while he changed a hundred-dollar bill to chips and started to play.

When the money was gone, they made their way to dinner in the casino's steakhouse restaurant. Their waitress brought them two large, fruity drinks while they studied the menu.

"The bow tie," Meg said.

"What about it?"

"I like it. It could grow on me. A bit like you I suppose, after all these years, all brave and daft at the same time." She stared him full in the eye, her blue eyes shining with unspilled tears.

"You are so pretty," he said as Meg held his gaze. He leaned in to kiss her, this woman who'd stolen his heart when they were both only children, a mother of a child now herself. His child. He reached over and gently cupped the back of her head in his palm, all the distractions in the whole, beeping, blinking casino falling away as he leaned in to earn her lips, all the distractions in the world falling silent—

Save one.

Lola with the King walking through the middle of the casino toward them.

The End

Acknowledgments

It is an arduous task to write, and all the more difficult without support and the guidance. If this book had not taken so long to write, I would not have so many people to thank or acknowledge for their role in its development.

First always is family: My wife Eva and daughters, McKaleigh and Camryn. One third of our marriage and their lives has had Billy Tapper in the sidelines. There are mentors and friends, Elizabeth Slater, Lynn Vannucci, Julie Colvin, and Lisa Fugard without whom Billy might have been less adventurous or a little naughtier. Professional education platforms and services are an essential tool in a writer's tool box, I have been lucky to work with Jericho Writers, Water Street Press, Quiet House editing, and Eric Maizel, among others. Of course there are the readers that labor alongside the writer, reading draft after draft. I thank John, Matt, Kim, Kathrin, Lotta, Karen, and all the readers kind enough to share a testimonial of their journey with Billy in the front of this book.

Last but not least, I extend a heartfelt thanks to Dee and Sammie Justesen of NorLite Press for taking time to create a platform where aspiring writers can get a break into publishing. The journey to publish usually includes finding an agent, but NorLite Press has helped circumnavigate that endeavor, I'm pleased to say, and offers welcome to authors.

About the Author

Born in Scotland and raised in Zimbabwe and South Africa, Gary Finnan splits his time between Sonoma Wine country in California and his farm in Aiken South Carolina, along with his wife Eva and two daughters. Gary is an award-winning inspirational author. Billy Tapper—Zillionaire is his first full novel.

Also by Gary Finnan

Hector: At Ground Level – A Very Simple Love Story

Visit us at www.GaryFinnan.com

Watch for Gary Finnan's next book:

Billy Tapper Extraordinaire

Cabbage

The smell of cabbage filled the room of the small Tijuana Hospital. A petite dark-skinned woman in soiled surgical greens shuffled into the room singing in Spanish and placed a tray on the side table next to Billy's bed. She moved the trolley up to his chest.

"La comida, la comida. You lunch, you eat..." Yellow pudding and green jelly jiggled on the tray just below his nose. A plate held grey meat in a broth of cabbage and carrots with two dried out tortillas rolled up on the edge of the plate.

"What's this?" Billy asked through his morphine haze. The woman smiled a toothless grin and pointed at the food then at her mouth, indicating he needed to eat. She put a spoon into his one free hand. The other hung in a sling suspended from a wire stand. He squinted at the black and blue welts running down his arm and the scabs of dried blood on his hands as he painfully grasped the spoon.

"What happened to me?" He realized his head was bandaged around his jaw, which slurred his speech all the more. The Hispanic woman just smiled at him and left the room.

The rustic starkness of the room was a contrast to the bright mottled green bedspread and a thin band of red and yellow tiles that ran around the walls. From the hallway Billy heard voices and footsteps approaching, then the door swung open. A small group of medical students entered, dressed in green scrubs, led by a tall, good-looking dark-haired man in a white coat. Billy assumed he was the doctor and hoped he might find out what the hell happened to him—and where was his dad?

A couple of months earlier on the eve of his 35th birthday, Billy sat at the large mahogany desk in his office and considered disappearing from his life. His thoughts had been of how he would be remembered in the days to come. Why wait for the inevitable disappointments he found in the daily drudge of life. Now was as good a time as any to reemerge where no one knew his name or expected anything of him. He drank a long pour of whiskey, thinking he now understood how his father felt. He sighed and dropped a new seven single onto the turntable beside him. He still bought the record of the week in remembrance of Mam, although he now had no one to discuss the lyrics with as they used to do. Wee Suzie was his muse for a while, but now she was consumed by the new pony Meg insisted they buy.

That week the lyrics affected him profoundly: *Bohemian Rhapsody* by Queen, featuring the mesmerizing voice of their flamboyant singer Freddy Mercury. The haunting lyrics swirled around the room as the whiskey warmed him from within.

Is this the real life?

Is this just fantasy?

Caught in a landslide,

No escape from reality.

Open your eyes

Look up to the sky and see...

Not another 20 years of this, he thought as he listened to the record. Were these his words, his own feelings, seeping out through pore and voice, stifled in their release from fear and bravery all at the same time? How many hours, days, and years had he wasted in pursuit of the American Dream?

Billy's head pounded and he felt nauseous with the smell of the cabbage. Then he remembered the woman waiting, crouched in her black leather corset tightened to breathless and the thick braid of red hair between her stiff shoulders.

I'm just a poor boy, I need no sympathy

Because I'm easy come, easy go

A little high, little low

Any way the wind blows doesn't really matter to me, to me...

Printed in Great Britain
by Amazon